THE CIRCULAR STAIRCASE

Mary Roberts Rinehart

NORTH BOOKS

2001

This book is printed on acid-free paper

ISBN 1-58287-165-5

NORTH BOOKS
P O Box 1277
Wickford RI 02852

This is the story of how a middle-aged spinster lost her mind, deserted her domestic gods in the city, took a furnished house for the summer out of town, and found herself involved in one of those mysterious crimes that keep our newspapers and detective agencies happy and prosperous. For twenty years I had been perfectly comfortable; for twenty years I had had the window boxes filled in the spring, the carpets lifted, the awnings put up, and the furniture covered with brown linen; for as many summers I had said good-bye to my friends, and, after watching their perspiring hegira, had settled down to a delicious quiet in town, where the mail comes three times a day and the water supply does not depend on a tank on the roof.

And then the madness seized me. When I look back over the months I spent at Sunnyside I wonder that I survived at all. As it is, I show the wear and tear of my harrowing experiences. I have turned very gray–Liddy reminded me of it only yesterday, by saying that a little bluing in the rinse water would make my hair silvery instead of a yellowish white. I hate to be reminded of unpleasant things and I snapped her off.

"No," I said sharply, "I'm not going to use bluing at my time of life, or starch either."

Liddy's nerves are gone, she said, since that awful summer, but she has enough left, goodness knows! And when she begins to go around with a lump in her throat all I have to do is to threaten to return to Sunnyside and she is frightened into a semblance of cheerfulness, from which you may judge that the summer there was anything but a success.

The newspaper accounts have been so garbled and incomplete–one of them mentioned me but once, and then only as the tenant at the time the thing happened–that I feel it my due to tell what I know. Jamieson, the detective, said himself he could never have done without me, although he gave me little enough credit in print.

I shall have to go back several years–thirteen, to be exact– to start my story. At that time my brother died, leaving me his two children. Halsey was eleven then, and Gertrude was seven. All the responsibilities of maternity were thrust upon me suddenly; to perfect the profession of mother- hood requires precisely as many years as the child has lived, like the man who started to carry the calf and ended by walking along with the bull on his shoulders. However, I did the best I could. When Gertrude got past the hair- ribbon age, and Halsey put on long trousers–and a wonder- ful help that was to the darning!–I sent them away to good schools. After that, my responsibility was chiefly postal, with three months every summer in which to replenish their wardrobes, look over their lists of acquaintances, and gen- erally to take my foster motherhood out of its nine months' retirement in camphor.

I missed the summers with them when, somewhat later, at boarding school and college, the children spent much of their vacations with friends. Gradually I found that my name signed to a check was even more welcome than when signed to a letter, though I wrote them at stated inter- vals. But when Halsey had finished his electrical course and Gertrude her boarding school, and both came home to stay, things were suddenly changed. The winter Gertrude came out was nothing but a succession of sitting up late at night to bring her home from things, taking her to the dressmak- ers between naps the next day, and discouraging ineligible youths with either more money than brains or more brains than money. Also, I acquired a great many things: to say lingerie for undergarments, "frocks" and "gowns" instead of dresses, and that beardless sophomores are not college boys but college men. Halsey required less personal super- vision, and as they both got their mother's fortune that win- ter my responsibility became purely moral. Halsey bought a car, of course, and I learned how to keep my eyes off the speedometer, and, after a time, never to stop to look at the dogs one has run down. People are apt to be unpleasant about their dogs.

The additions to my education made me a properly equipped maiden aunt, and by spring I was quite tractable. So when Halsey suggested camping in the Adirondacks and Gertrude wanted Bar Harbor we compromised on a good country house with a golf course near, and within motor distance of town and telephone distance of the doctor. That was how we went to Sunnyside.

We went out to inspect the property, and it seemed to deserve its name. Its cheerful appearance gave no indication whatever of anything out of the ordinary. Only one thing seemed unusual to me: the housekeeper, who had been left in charge, had moved from the house to the gardener's lodge a few days before. As the lodge was far enough away from the house, it seemed to me that either fire or thieves could have completed their work of destruction undisturbed. The property was an extensive one: the house on the top of a hill, which sloped away in great stretches of green lawn and clipped hedges to the road; and across the valley, perhaps a couple of miles away, the Greenwood Club House. Gertrude and Halsey were infatuated.

"Why, it's everything you want," Halsey said. "View, air, good water and good roads. As for the house, it's big enough for a hospital, if it has a Queen Anne front and a Mary Anne back." Which was ridiculous: it was pure Elizabethan.

Of course we took the place. It was not my idea of comfort, being much too large and sufficiently isolated to make the servant question serious. But I give myself credit for this: whatever has happened since I have never blamed Halsey and Gertrude for taking me there. And another thing. If the series of catastrophes there did nothing else it taught me one thing, that somehow, somewhere, from perhaps a half-civilized ancestor who wore a sheepskin garment and trailed his food or his prey, I have in me the instinct of the chase. Were I a man I should be a trapper of criminals, trailing them as relentlessly as no doubt my sheepskin-clad ancestor did his wild boar. But being an unmarried woman, with the handicap of my sex, my first acquaintance with crime will probably be my last. Indeed it came near enough to being my last acquaintance with anything.

The property was owned by Paul Armstrong, the president of the Traders' Bank, who at the time we took the house was in the West with his wife and daughter and a Doctor Walker, the Armstrong family physician. Halsey knew Louise Armstrong, had been rather attentive to her the winter before, but as Halsey was always attentive to somebody I had not thought of it seriously, although she was a charming girl. I knew of Mr Armstrong only through his connection with the bank, where the children's money was largely invested, and through an ugly story about the son, Arnold Armstrong, who was reported to have forged his father's name for a considerable amount to some bank paper. However, the story had had no interest for me.

I cleared Halsey and Gertrude away to a house party, and moved out to Sunnyside the first of May. The roads were bad but the trees were in leaf, and there were still tulips in the borders around the house. The arbutus was fragrant in the woods under the dead leaves, and on the way from the station, a short mile, while the car stuck in the mud, I found a bank showered with tiny forget-me-nots. The birds–don't ask me what kind; they all look alike to me, unless they have a hallmark of some bright color–the birds were chirping in the hedges, and everything breathed of peace. Liddy, who was born and bred on a brick pavement, got a little bit down-spirited when the crickets began to chirp, or scrape their legs together, or whatever it is they do, at twilight.

The first night passed quietly enough. I have always been grateful for that one night's peace. It shows what the country might be, under favorable circumstances. Never after that night did I put my head on my pillow with any assurance how long it would be there; or on my shoulders, for that matter.

On the following morning Liddy and Mrs Ralston, my own housekeeper, had a difference of opinion, and Mrs Ralston left on the eleven-o'clock train. Just after luncheon Burke, the butler, was taken unexpectedly with a pain in his right side, much worse when I was within hearing distance, and by afternoon he too was started cityward. That night the cook's sister had a baby–the cook, seeing indecision in my face, made it twins on second thought–and, to be short, by noon the next day the household staff was down to Liddy and myself. And this in a house with twenty-two rooms and five baths!

Liddy wanted to go back to the city at once, but the milk boy said that Thomas Johnson, the Armstrongs' colored butler, was working as a waiter at the Greenwood Club and might come back. I have the usual scruples about coaxing people's servants away, but few of us have any conscience regarding institutions or corporations–witness the way we beat railroads and streetcar companies when we can–so I called up the club, and about eight o'clock Thomas Johnson came to see me. Poor Thomas!

Well, it ended by my engaging Thomas on the spot, at outrageous wages and with permission to sleep in the gardener's lodge, empty since the house was rented. The old man–he was white-haired and a little stooped, but with an immense idea of his personal dignity–gave me his reasons hesitatingly.

"I ain't sayin' nothin', Mis' Innes," he said, with his hand on the doorknob, "but there's been goin's-on here this las' few months as ain't natchal. 'Tain't one thing an' 'tain't another–it's jest a door squealin' here an' a winder closin' there, but when doors an' winders gets to cuttin' up capers and there's nobody nigh 'em it's time Thomas Johnson sleep somewhar's else."

Liddy, who seemed to be never more than ten feet away

from me that night, and was afraid of her shadow in that great barn of a place, screamed a little, and turned a yellow-green. But I am not easily alarmed.

It was entirely in vain I represented to Thomas that we were alone, and that he would have to stay in the house that night. He was politely firm, but he would come over early the next morning and if I gave him a key he would come in time to get some sort of breakfast. I stood on the huge veranda and watched him shuffle along down the shadowy drive, with mingled feelings, irritation at his cowardice and thankfulness at getting him at all. I am not ashamed to say that I double-locked the hail door when I went in.

"You can lock up the rest of the house and go to bed, Liddy," I said severely. "You give me the creeps standing there. A woman of your age ought to have better sense." It usually braces Liddy to mention her age: she owns to forty, which is absurd. Her mother cooked for my grandfather, and Liddy must be at least as old as I. But that night she refused to brace.

"You're not going to ask me to lock up, Miss Rachel!" she quavered. "Why, there's a dozen French windows in the drawing-room and the billiard-room wing, and every one opens on a porch. And Mary Anne said that last night there was a man standing by the stable when she locked the kitchen door."

"Mary Anne was a fool," I said sternly. "If there had been a man there, she would have had him in the kitchen and been feeding him what was left from dinner inside of an hour, from force of habit. Now don't be ridiculous. Lock up the house and go to bed. I'm going to read."

But Liddy set her lips tight and stood still.

"I'm not going to bed," she said. "I am going to pack up, and tomorrow I am going to leave."

"You'll do nothing of the sort," I snapped. Liddy and I often desire to part company, but never at the same time. "If you are afraid I will go with you, but for goodness' sake don't try to hide behind me."

The house was a typical summer residence on an extensive scale. Wherever possible on the first floor the architect had done away with partitions, using arches and columns instead. The effect was cool and spacious, but scarcely cozy. As Liddy and I went from one window to another, our voices echoed back at us uncomfortably. There was plenty of light–the electric plant down in the village supplied us–but there were long vistas of polished floor, and mirrors which reflected us from unexpected corners until I felt some of Liddy's foolishness communicate itself to me.

The house was very long, a rectangle in general form, with the main entrance in the center of the long side. The brick-paved entry opened into a short hall, to the right of which, separated only by a row of pillars, was a huge living room. Beyond that was the drawing room, and in the end the billiard room. Off the billiard room, in the extreme right wing, was a den or cardroom with a small hail opening on the east veranda, and from there went up a narrow circular staircase. Halsey had pointed it out with delight.

"Just look, Aunt Rachel," he had said with a flourish. "The architect that put up this joint was wise to a few things. Arnold Armstrong and his friends could sit here and play cards all night and stumble up to bed in the early morning, without having the family send in a police call."

Liddy and I got as far as the cardroom and turned on all the lights. I tried the small entry door there, which opened on the veranda, and examined the windows. Everything was secure and Liddy, a little less nervous now, had just pointed out to me the disgracefully dusty condition of the hardwood floor, when suddenly the lights went out. We waited a moment. I think Liddy was stunned with fright, or she would have screamed. And then I clutched her by the arm and pointed to one of the windows opening on the porch. The sudden change threw the window into relief, an oblong of grayish light, and showed us a figure standing close, peering in. As I looked it darted across the veranda and out of sight in the darkness.

2

Liddy's knees seemed to give way under her. Without a sound she sank down, leaving me staring at the window in petrified amazement. She began then to moan under her breath, and in my excitement I reached down and shook her.

"Stop it," I whispered. "It's only a woman, maybe a maid of the Armstrongs'. Get up and help me find the door." She groaned again. "Very well," I said, "then I'll have to leave you here. I'm going."

She moved at that, and with her holding to my sleeve we felt our way, with numerous collisions, to the billiard room and from there to the drawing room. The lights came on then, and with the long French windows unshuttered I had a creepy feeling that each one sheltered a peering face. In fact, in the light of what happened afterward, I am pretty certain we were under surveillance during the entire ghostly evening. We hurried over the rest of the locking up and got upstairs as quickly as we could. I left the lights all on, and our footsteps echoed cavernously. Liddy had a stiff neck the next morning from looking back over her shoulder, and that night she refused to go to bed.

"Let me stay in your dressing room, Miss Rachel," she begged. "If you don't I'll sit in the hall outside the door. I'm not going to be murdered with my eyes shut."

"If you're going to be murdered," I retorted, "it won't make any difference whether they are shut or open. But you may stay in the dressing room, if you will lie on the couch. When you sleep in a chair you snore."

She was too far gone to be indignant, but after a while she came to the door and looked in to where I was composing myself for sleep with Drummond's *Spiritual World*.

"That wasn't a woman, Miss Rachel," she said, with her shoes in her hand. "It was a man in a long coat."

"What woman was a man?" I discouraged her without looking up, and she went back to the couch.

It was eleven o'clock when I finally prepared for bed. In spite of my assumption of indifference I locked the door into the hail, and finding the transom did not catch I put a chair cautiously before the door– it was not necessary to rouse Liddy–and climbing up put on the ledge of the transom a small dressing mirror, so that any movement of the frame would send it crashing down. Then secure in my precautions I went to bed.

I did not go to sleep at once. Liddy disturbed me just as I was growing drowsy, by coming in and peering under the bed. She was afraid to speak, however, because of her previous snubbing, and went back, stopping in the doorway to sigh dismally.

Somewhere downstairs a clock with a chime sang away the hours, eleven-thirty, forty-five, twelve. And then the lights went out to stay. The Casanova Electric Company shuts up shop and goes home to bed at midnight. When one has a party I believe it is customary to fee the company, which will drink hot coffee and keep awake a couple of hours longer. But the lights were out for good that night. Liddy had gone to sleep, as I knew she would. She was a very unreliable person, always awake and ready to talk when she wasn't wanted and dozing off to sleep when she was. I called her once or twice, the only result being an explosive snore that threatened her very windpipe; then I got up and lighted a bedroom candle.

My bedroom and dressing room were above the big living room on the first floor. On the second floor a long corridor ran the length of the house, with rooms opening from both sides. In the wings were small corridors crossing the main one, so the plan was simplicity itself. And just as I got back into bed I heard a sound from the east wing apparently, that made me stop frozen, with one bedroom slipper half off, and listen. It was a rattling metallic sound, and it reverberated along the empty halls like the crash of doom.

It was for all the world as if something heavy, perhaps a piece of steel, had rolled clattering and jangling down the hardwood stairs leading to the cardroom.

In the silence that followed Liddy stirred and snored again. I was exasperated. First she kept me awake by silly alarms, then when she was needed she slept like Joe Jefferson, or Rip Van Winkle; they are always the same to me. I went in and shook her, and I give her credit for being wide awake the minute I spoke.

"Get up," I said, "if you don't want to be murdered in your bed."

"Where? How?" she yelled vociferously, and jumped up.

"There's somebody in the house," I said. "Get up. We'll have to get to the telephone."

"Not out in the hail!" she gasped. "Oh, Miss Rachel, not out in the hail!" She was trying to hold me back, but I am a large woman and Liddy is small. We got to the door somehow and Liddy held a brass andiron, which it was all she could do to lift, let alone brain anybody with. I listened and, hearing nothing, opened the door a little and peered into the hall. It was a black void, full of terrible suggestion, and my candle only emphasized the gloom. Liddy squealed and drew me back again, and as the door slammed the mirror I had placed on the transom came down and hit her on the head. That completed our demoralization. It was some time before I could persuade her she had not been attacked from behind by a burglar, and when she found the mirror smashed on the floor she wasn't much better.

"There's going to be a death!" she wailed. "Oh, Miss Rachel, there's going to be a death!"

"There will be," I said grimly, "if you don't keep quiet, Liddy Allen." And so we sat there until morning, wondering if the candle would last until dawn, and arranging what trains we could take back to town. If we had only stuck to that decision and gone back before it was too late!

The sun came finally, and from my window I watched the trees along the drive take shadowy form, gradually lose their ghostlike appearance, become gray and then green. The Greenwood Club showed itself a dab of white against the hill across the valley, and an early robin or two hopped around in the dew. Not until the milk boy and the sun came, about the same time, did I dare to open the door into the hail and look around. Everything was as we had left it. Trunks were heaped here and there, ready for the trunk room, and through an end window of stained glass came a streak of red and yellow daylight that was eminently cheerful. The milk boy was pounding somewhere below, and the day had begun.

Thomas Johnson came ambling up the drive about half past six and we could hear him clattering around on the lower floor, opening shutters. I had to take Liddy to her room upstairs, however, she was quite sure she would find something uncanny there, and in fact when she did not, having now the courage of daylight, she was actually disappointed.

Well, we did not go back to town that day.

The discovery of a small picture fallen from the wall of the drawing room was quite sufficient to satisfy Liddy that the alarm had been a false one, but I was anything but convinced. Allowing for my nerves and the fact that small noises magnify themselves at night, there was still no possibility that the picture had made the series of sounds I heard. To prove it however I dropped it again. It fell with a single muffled crash of its wooden frame, and incidentally ruined itself beyond repair. I justified myself by reflecting that if the Armstrongs chose to leave pictures in unsafe positions, and to rent a house with a family ghost, the destruction of property was their responsibility, not mine.

I warned Liddy not to mention what had happened to anybody, and telephoned to town for servants. Then after a breakfast which did more credit to Thomas's heart than his head I went on a short tour of investigation. The sounds had come from the east wing, and not without some qualms I began there. At first I found nothing. Since then I have developed my powers of observation, but at that time I was a novice. The small cardroom seemed undisturbed. I looked for footprints, which is I believe the conventional thing to do, although my experience has been that as clues both footprints and thumbmarks are more useful in fiction than in fact. But the stairs in that wing offered something.

At the top of the flight had been placed a tall wicker hamper, packed with linen which had come from town. It stood at the edge of the top step, almost barring passage, and on the step below it was a long fresh scratch. For three steps the scratch was repeated, gradually diminishing, as if some object had fallen, striking each one as it dropped. Then for four steps nothing. On the fifth step below was a round dent in the hard wood. That was all, and it seemed little enough, except that I was positive the marks had not been there the day before.

It bore out my theory of the sound, which had been for all the world like the bumping of a metallic object down a flight of steps. The four steps had been skipped. I reasoned that an iron bar for instance would do something of the sort, strike two or three steps end down, then turn over, jumping a few steps and landing with a thud.

Iron bars, however, do not fall downstairs in the middle of the night alone. Coupled with the figure on the veranda, the agency by which it climbed might be assumed. But–and here was the thing which puzzled me most–the doors were all fastened that morning, the windows unmolested, and the particular door from the cardroom to the outside veranda had a combination lock of which I held the key, and which had not been tampered with.

I fixed on an attempt at burglary as the most natural explanation, an attempt frustrated by the falling of the object, whatever it was, which had roused me. Two things however I could not understand: how the intruder had escaped with everything locked, and why he had left the small silver which, in the absence of a butler, had remained downstairs overnight.

Under pretext of learning more about the place that morning Thomas Johnson led me through the house and the cellars, without result. Everything was in good order and repair. Money had been spent lavishly on construction and plumbing, the house was full of conveniences, and I had no reason to repent my bargain save the fact that in the nature of things night must come again. And other nights must follow–and we were a long way from a police station.

In the afternoon a taxi came up from Casanova with a fresh relay of servants. The driver took them with a flourish to the servants' entrance, and then drove around to the front of the house, where I was awaiting him.

"Two dollars," he said in reply to my question. "I don't charge full rates, because, bringin' 'em up all summer as I do it pays to make a special price. When they got off the train, I sez to myself: 'There's another bunch for Sunnyside, cook, parlormaid and all.' Yes'm, six summers and a new lot never less than once a month. They won't stand for the country and the lonesomeness, I reckon."

But with the presence of the "bunch" of servants my courage revived, and late in the afternoon came a message from Gertrude that she and Halsey would arrive that night at about eleven o'clock, coming in the car from Richfield. Things were looking up, and when Beulah, my cat and a most intelligent animal, found some early catnip on a bank near the house and rolled in it in a feline ecstasy, I decided that getting back to nature was the thing to do.

While I was dressing for dinner Liddy rapped at the door. She was hardly herself yet, but privately I think she was worrying about the broken mirror and its augury more than anything else. When she came in she was holding something in her hand, and she laid it on the dressing table carefully.

"I found it in the linen hamper," she said. "It must be Mr Halsey's, but it seems queer how it got there."

It was the half of a link cuff button of unique design, and I looked at it carefully.

"Where was it? In the bottom of the hamper?" I asked.

"On the very top," she replied. "It's a mercy it didn't fall out on the way."

When Liddy had gone I examined the fragment attentively. I had never seen it before, and I was certain it was not Halsey's. It was of Italian workmanship and consisted of a mother-of-pearl foundation encrusted with tiny seed pearls, strung on horsehair to hold them. In the center was a small ruby. The trinket was odd enough but not intrinsically of great value. Its interest for me lay in this: Liddy had found it lying in the top of the hamper which had blocked the east wing stairs.

That afternoon the Armstrongs' housekeeper, a youngish good-looking woman, applied for Mrs Ralston's place and I was glad enough to take her. She looked as though she might be equal to a dozen of Liddy, with her snapping black eyes and heavy jaw. Her name was Anne Watson, and I dined that evening for the first time in three days.

3

I had dinner served in the breakfast room. Somehow the huge dining room depressed me and Thomas, cheerful enough all day, had allowed his spirits to go down with the sun. He had a habit of watching the corners of the room, left shadowy by the candles on the table, and altogether it was not a festive meal.

Dinner over I went into the living room. I had three hours before the children could possibly arrive, and I got out my knitting. I had brought along two dozen pairs of slipper soles in assorted sizes–I always send knitted slippers to the Old Ladies' Home at Christmas– and now I sorted over the wools with a grim determination not to think about the night before. But my mind was not on my work. At the end of a half hour I found I had put a row of blue scallops on Sally Klinefelter's lavender slippers, and I put them away.

I got out the cuff link and went with it to the pantry. Thomas was wiping silver and the air was heavy with tobacco smoke. I sniffed and looked around, but there was no pipe to be seen.

"Thomas," I said, "you have been smoking."

"No, ma'am." He was injured innocence itself. "It's on my coat, ma'am. Over at the club the gentlemen–"

But Thomas did not finish. The pantry was suddenly filled with the odor of singeing cloth. Thomas gave a clutch at his coat, whirled to the sink, filled a tumbler with water and poured it into his right pocket with the celerity of practice.

"Thomas," I said, when he was sheepishly mopping the floor, "smoking is a filthy and injurious habit. If you must smoke you must, but don't stick a lighted pipe in your pocket again. Your skin's your own. You can blister it if you like. But this house is not mine, and I don't want a conflagration. Did you ever see this cuff link before?"

No, he never had, he said, but he looked at it oddly.

"I picked it up in the hall," I added indifferently. The old man's eyes were shrewd under his bushy eyebrows.

"There's strange goin's-on here, Mis' Innes," he said, shaking his head. "Somethin's goin' to happen sure. You ain't took notice that the big clock in the hail is stopped, I reckon?"

"Nonsense," I said. "Clocks have to stop, don't they, if they're not wound?"

"It's wound up all right, and it stopped at three o'clock last night," he answered solemnly. "More'n that, that there clock ain't stopped for fifteen years, not since Mr Armstrong's first wife died. And that ain't all–no, ma'am. Last three nights I slep' in this place, after the electrics went out I had a token. My oil lamp was full of oil, but it kep' goin' out, do what I would. Minute I shet my eyes out that lamp'd go. There ain't no surer token of death. The Bible sez, Let yer light shine! When a hand you can't see puts yer light out, it means death, sure."

The old man's voice was full of conviction. In spite of myself I had a chilly sensation in the small of my back, and I left him mumbling over his dishes. Later on I heard a crash from the pantry and Liddy reported that my cat Beulah, who is coal black, had darted in front of Thomas just as he picked up a tray of dishes; that the bad omen had been too much for him, and he had dropped the tray.

The roar of the motor as the car climbed the hill was the most we!come sound I had heard for a long time, and with Gertrude and Halsey actually before me, my troubles seemed over for good. Gertrude stood smiling in the hail, with her hat quite over one ear, and her hair in every direction over her shoulders. Gertrude is a very pretty girl no matter how her hair is, and I was not surprised when Halsey presented a good-looking young man, who bowed at me and looked at Trude– that is the ridiculous nickname Gertrude brought from school.

"I've brought a guest, Aunt Ray," Halsey said. "I want you to adopt him into your affections and your Saturday-to-Monday list. Let me present John Bailey, only you must call him Jack. In twelve hours he'll be calling you 'aunt': I know him."

We shook hands and I got a chance to look at Mr Bailey. He was a tall fellow, perhaps thirty, and he wore a small mustache. I remember wondering why. He seemed to have a good mouth and when he smiled his teeth were above the average. One never knows why certain men cling to a messy upper lip that must get into things, any more than one understands some women building up their hair on wire atrocities. Otherwise, he was very good to look at, stalwart and tanned, with the direct gaze that I like. I am particular about Mr Bailey, because he was a prominent figure in what happened later.

Gertrude was tired from the trip and went up to bed very soon. I made up my mind to tell them nothing until the next day, and then to make as little of our excitement as possible. After all, what had I to tell? An inquisitive face peering in at a window, a crash in the night, a scratch or two on the stairs and half a cuff button! As for Thomas and his forebodings, it was always my belief that a Negro is at least one part superstition.

It was Saturday night. The two men carried their high-balls to the billiard room, and I could hear them talking as I went upstairs. It seemed that Halsey had stopped at the Greenwood Club for gasoline and found Bailey there with the Sunday golf crowd. Mr Bailey had not been hard to persuade–probably Gertrude knew why–and they carried him off triumphantly. I roused Liddy to get them something to eat–Thomas was beyond reach in the lodge–and paid no attention to her evident terror of the kitchen regions. Then I went to bed. The men were still in the billiard room when I finally dozed off and the last thing I remember was the howl of a dog in front of the house. It wailed a crescendo of woe that trailed off hopefully, only to break out afresh from a new point of the compass.

At three o'clock in the morning I was roused by a revolver shot. The sound seemed to come from just outside
my door. For a moment I could not move. Then I heard
Gertrude stirring in her room and the next moment she had
thrown open the connecting door.

"Aunt Ray! Aunt Ray!" she called hysterically. "Someone must have been killed! What on earth–"

"Thieves," I said shortly. "Thank goodness, there are
some men in the house tonight." I was getting into my
slippers and a bathrobe, and Gertrude with shaking hands
was lighting a lamp. Then we opened the door into the
hail where crowded on the upper landing of the stairs the
maids, white-faced and trembling, were peering down. I
was greeted by a series of low screams and questions, and I
tried to quiet them. Gertrude had dropped on a chair and
sat there limp and shivering.

I went at once across the hall to Halsey's room and
knocked, then I pushed the door open. It was empty. The
bed had not been occupied!

"He must be in Mr Bailey's room," I said excitedly, and
followed by Liddy we went there. Like Halsey's, it had
not been occupied. Gertrude was on her feet now, but she
leaned against the door for support.

"They have both been killed!" she gasped. She caught
me by the arm and dragged me toward the stairs. "They
may only be hurt. We've got to find them," she said, her
eyes dilated with excitement.

I don't remember how we got down the stairs. I do remember expecting every moment to be killed. The cook
was at the telephone upstairs calling the Greenwood Club,
and Liddy was behind me afraid to come and not daring
to stay behind. We found the living room and the drawing room undisturbed. Somehow I felt that whatever we
found would be in the cardroom or on the staircase, and
nothing but the fear that Halsey was in danger drove me
on; with every step my knees seemed to give way under

me. Gertrude was ahead and in the cardroom she stopped, holding her candle high. Then she pointed silently into the hall beyond. Huddled there on the floor, face down and with his arms extended, was a man.

Gertrude ran forward with a gasping sob. "Jack," she cried, "oh, Jack!"

Liddy had run, screaming, and the two of us were there alone. It was Gertrude who turned him over until we could see his white face, and then she drew a deep breath and dropped limply to her knees. It was the body of a man, in a dinner coat and white waistcoat, stained now with blood. The body of a man I had never seen before.

4

Gertrude gazed at the face in a kind of fascination. Then she put out her hands blindly and I thought she was going to faint.

"He's killed him!" she muttered almost inarticulately, and at that and because my nerves were going I gave her a good shake.

"What do you mean?" I said frantically. There was a depth of grief and conviction in her tone that was worse than anything she could have said. The shake braced her, anyhow, and she seemed to pull herself together. But not another word would she say. She stood gazing down at that gruesome figure on the floor while Liddy, ashamed of her flight and afraid to come back alone, drove before her three terrified women servants into the drawing room, which was as near as any of them would venture.

Once in the drawing room, Gertrude collapsed and went from one fainting spell into another. I had all I could do to keep Liddy from drowning her with cold water, while the maids huddled in a corner, as much use as so many sheep. In a short time, although it seemed hours, a car came rushing up, and Anne Watson, who had waited to dress, opened the door. Three men from the Greenwood Club in all kinds of improvised costumes hurried in. I recognized a Mr Jarvis, but the others were strangers.

"What's wrong?" the Jarvis man asked. We made a strange picture, no doubt. "Nobody hurt, is there?" He was looking at Gertrude.

"Worse than that, Mr Jarvis," I said. "I think it is murder."

At the word there was a commotion. The cook began to cry, and Mrs Watson knocked over a chair. The men were visibly impressed.

"Not any member of the family?" Mr Jarvis asked, when he had got his breath.

"No," I said. "Nobody I know." And motioning Liddy to look after Gertrude I led the way with a lamp to the card-room door. One of the men gave an exclamation, and they all hurried across the room. Mr Jarvis took the lamp from me–I remember that–and then, feeling myself getting dizzy and light-headed I closed my eyes. When I opened them their brief examination was over, and Mr Jarvis was trying to put me in a chair.

"You must get upstairs," he said firmly, "you and Miss Gertrude too. This has been a terrible shock. In his own home, of all things!"

I stared at him without comprehension. "Who is it?" I asked with difficulty. There was a band drawn tight around my throat.

"It's Arnold Armstrong," he said, looking at me oddly, "and he has been murdered, here in his father's house."

After a minute I gathered myself together and Mr Jarvis helped me into the living room. Liddy had got Gertrude upstairs, and the two strange men from the club stayed with the body. The reaction from the shock and strain was tremendous: I was collapsed–and then Mr Jarvis asked me a question that brought back my wandering faculties.

"Where's Halsey?" he asked.

"Halsey!" Suddenly Gertrude's stricken face rose before me, and the empty rooms upstairs. Where was Halsey?

"He was here, wasn't he?" Mr Jarvis persisted. "He stopped at the club on his way over."

"I don't know where he is," I said feebly.

One of the men from the club came in, asked for the telephone, and I could hear him excitedly talking, saying something about coroners and the police. Mr Jarvis leaned over to me.

"Why don't you trust me, Miss Innes?" he said. "If I can do anything I will. But tell me the whole thing."

I did finally from the beginning, and when I told of Jack Bailey's being in the house that night he gave a long whistle.

"I wish they were both here," he said when I finished. "Whatever took them away, it would look better if they were here. Especially–"

"Especially what?"

"Especially since Jack Bailey and Arnold Armstrong were notoriously bad friends. It was Bailey who got Arnold into trouble last spring. Something about the bank. And then, too–"

"Go on," I said. "If there is anything more, I ought to know."

"There's nothing more," he said evasively. "There's just one thing we may bank on, Miss Innes. Any court in the country will acquit a man who kills an intruder in his house, at night. If Halsey–"

"You can't think Halsey did it!" I mumbled. There was a queer feeling of physical nausea coming over me.

"No, no, not at all," he said, with forced cheerfulness. "Come, Miss Innes, you're a ghost of yourself. I'm going to help you upstairs and call your maid. This has been too much for you."

Liddy helped me back to bed, and under the impression that I was in danger of freezing to death put a hot-water bottle over my heart and another at my feet. Then she left me. It was early dawn now, and from voices under my window I surmised that Mr Jarvis and his companions were searching the grounds. As for me, I lay in bed with every faculty awake. Where had Halsey gone? How had he gone, and when? Before the murder, certainly, but who would believe that? If either he or Jack Bailey had heard an intruder in the house and shot him–as they might have been justified in doing–why had they run away? The whole thing was unheard of, outrageous, and perfectly damnable.

About six o'clock Gertrude came in. She was fully dressed, and I sat up nervously.

"Poor Rachel," she said. "What a shocking night you have had!" She came over and sat down on the bed, and I saw that she looked practically exhausted.

"Is there anything new?" I asked anxiously.

"Nothing. The car's gone, but Warner"–Warner was our chauffeur– "Warner is at the lodge and knows nothing about it."

"Well," I said "if I ever get my hands on Halsey Innes I shan't let go until I have told him a few things. When we get this cleared up I am going back to the city to be quiet. One more night like the last two will end me. Don't talk to me about the peace of the country."

Whereupon I told Gertrude of the noises the night before, and the figure on the veranda in the east wing. As an afterthought I brought out the pearl cuff link.

"I have no doubt now," I said, "that it was Arnold Armstrong the night before last too. He had a key, probably. But why he should steal into his father's house I can't imagine. He could have come with my permission easily enough. Anyhow whoever it was that night left this little souvenir."

Gertrude took one look at the cuff link and went as white as the pearls in it. She clutched at the foot of the bed, and stood staring. As for me I was quite as astonished as she was.

"Where did you find it?" she asked finally, with a desperate effort at calm. And while I told her she stood gazing out the window with a look I could not fathom on her face. It was a relief when Mrs Watson tapped at the door and brought me some tea and toast. The cook was in bed and completely demoralized, she reported; and Liddy, brave with the daylight, was looking for footprints around the house. The police and the coroner, having to come from a distance, had not yet arrived. And Mrs Watson herself was a wreck; she was blue-white around the lips, and she had one hand tied up. She said she had fallen downstairs in her excitement. It was natural of course that the thing would shock her, having been the Armstrongs' housekeeper for several years and knowing Mr Arnold well.

Gertrude had slipped out during my talk with Mrs Watson, and I dressed and went downstairs. The billiard and card rooms were locked until the police got there, and the men from the club had gone back for more conventional clothing.

I could hear Thomas in the pantry, alternately wailing for Mr Arnold, as he called him, and citing the tokens that had precursed the murder. The house seemed to choke me and slipping a shawl around me I went out on the drive. At the corner by the east wing I met' Liddy. Her skirts were draggled with dew to her knees, and her hair was still in crimps.

"Go right in an change your clothes," I said sharply. "You're a sight, and at your age!"

She had a golf stick in her hand, and she said she had found it on the lawn. There was nothing unusual about it, but it occurred to me that a golf stick with a metal end might have been the object that had scratched the stairs near the cardroom. I took it from her and sent her up for dry garments. Her daylight courage and self-importance and her shuddering delight in the mystery irritated me beyond words. After I left her I made a circuit of the building. Nothing seemed to be disturbed. The house looked as calm and peaceful in the morning sun as it had the day I had been coerced into taking it. There was nothing to show that inside had been mystery and violence and sudden death.

In one of the tulip beds back of the house an early crow was pecking viciously at something that glittered in the light. I picked my way gingerly over through the dew and stooped. Almost buried in the soft ground was a revolver. I scraped the earth off it with the tip of my shoe and picking it up slipped it into my pocket. Not until I had got into my bedroom and double-locked the door did I venture to take it out and examine it. One look was all I needed. It was Halsey's own gun. I had unpacked it the day before and put it on his shaving stand, and there could be no mistake. His name was on a small silver plate on the handle.

I seemed to see a network closing around my boy, innocent as I knew he was. The revolver–I am afraid of them, but anxiety gave me courage to examine it–the revolver had still two bullets in it. I could only breathe a prayer of thankfulness that I had found it before any sharp-eyed detective had come around.

I decided to keep what clues I had–the cuff link, the golf stick and the revolver–in a secure place until I could see some reason for displaying them. The cuff link had been dropped into a little filigree box on my toilet table. I opened the box and felt around for it, but to my horror the box was empty. The cuff link had disappeared!

5

At eight o'clock that morning the Casanova hack brought up three men. They introduced themselves as the coroner of the county and two detectives from the city. The coroner led the way at once to the locked wing, and with the aid of one of the detectives examined the rooms and the body. The other detective, after a short scrutiny of the dead man, busied himself with the outside of the house. It was only after they had got a fair idea of things as they were that they sent for me.

I received them in the living room, and I had made up my mind exactly what to tell. I had taken the house for the summer, I said, while the Armstrongs were in California. In spite of a rumor among the servants about strange noises–I cited Thomas–nothing had occurred the first two nights. On the third night I believed that someone had been in the house. I had heard a crashing sound, but being alone with one maid had not investigated. The house had been locked in the morning and apparently undisturbed.

Then as clearly as I could I related how, the night before, a shot had roused us; that my niece and I had investigated and found a body, that I did not know who the murdered man was until Mr Jarvis from the club informed me, and that I knew of no reason why Mr Arnold Armstrong should steal into his father's house at night. I should have been glad to allow him entree there at any time.

"Have you reason to believe, Miss Innes," the coroner asked, "that any member of your household, imagining Mr Armstrong was a burglar, shot him in self-defense?"

"I have no reason for thinking so," I said quietly.

"Your theory is that Mr Armstrong was followed here by some enemy, and shot as he entered the house?"

"I don't think I have a theory," I said. "The thing that has puzzled me is why Mr Armstrong should enter his father's house two nights in succession, stealing in like a thief, when he needed only to ask entrance to be admitted."

The coroner was a very silent man. He listened to what I had to say, but he seemed anxious to make the next train back to town. He set the inquest for the following Saturday, gave Jamieson, the younger of the two detectives and the more intelligent looking, a few instructions, and after gravely shaking hands with me and regretting the unfortunate affair took his departure, accompanied by the other detective.

I was just beginning to breathe freely when Jamieson, who had been standing by the window, came over to me.

"The family consists of yourself alone, Miss Innes?"

"My niece is here," I said.

"There is no one but yourself and your niece?"

"My nephew." I had to moisten my lips.

"Oh, a nephew. I should like to see him, if he is here."

"He is not here just now," I said as quietly as I could. "I expect him at any time."

"He was here yesterday evening?"

"No–yes."

"Didn't he have a guest with him? Another man?"

"He brought a friend with him to stay over Sunday, a Mr Bailey."

"Mr John Bailey, the cashier of the Traders' Bank, I believe." And I knew that someone at the Greenwood Club had been talking. "When did they leave?"

"Very early. I don't know at just what time."

Jamieson turned suddenly and looked at me.

"Please try to be more explicit," he said. "You say your nephew and Mr Bailey were in the house last night, and yet you and your niece with some women servants found the body. Where was your nephew?"

I was entirely desperate by that time.

"I don't know," I said. "But be sure of this: Halsey knows nothing of this thing, and no amount of circumstantial evidence can make an innocent man guilty."

"Sit down," he said, pushing forward a chair. "There are some things I have to tell you, and in return please tell me all you know. Believe me, things always come out. In the first place, Mr Armstrong was shot from above. The bullet was fired at close range, entered below the shoulder and came out, after passing through the heart, well down the back. In other words, I believe the murderer stood on the stairs and fired down. In the second place, I found on the edge of the billiard table a charred cigar which had burned itself partly out, and a cigarette which had consumed itself to the cork tip. Neither one had been more than lighted, then put down and forgotten. Have you any idea what it was that made your nephew and Mr Bailey leave their cigars and their game, take out the car without calling the chauffeur, and all this certainly before three o'clock in the morning?"

"I don't know," I said; "but depend on it, Mr Jamieson, Halsey will be back himself to explain everything."

"I sincerely hope so," he said. "Miss Innes, has it occurred to you that Mr Bailey might know something of this?"

Gertrude had come downstairs and as he spoke she came in. I saw her stop suddenly, as if she had been struck.

"He does not," she said in a tone that was not her own. "Mr Bailey and my brother know nothing of this. The murder was committed at three. They left the house at a quarter before three."

"How do you know that?" Jamieson asked oddly. "Do you know at what time they left?"

"I do," Gertrude answered firmly. "At a quarter before three my brother and Mr Bailey left the house, by the main entrance. I was there when they went."

"Gertrude," I said excitedly, "you're dreaming! Why, at a quarter to three–"

"Listen," she said. "At half past two the downstairs telephone rang. I hadn't gone to sleep and I heard it. Then I heard Halsey answer it, and in a few minutes he came upstairs and knocked at my door. I–we talked for a minute, then I put on my dressing gown and slippers, and went downstairs with him. Mr Bailey was in the billiard room. We all talked together for perhaps ten minutes. Then it was decided that they had to leave to attend to something–"

"Can't you be more explicit?" Jamieson asked. "What did they have to attend to?"

"I am only telling you what happened, not why it happened," she said evenly. "Halsey went for the car and instead of bringing it to the house and rousing people he went by the lower road from the stable. Mr Bailey was to meet him at the foot of the lawn. Mr Bailey left–"

"Which way?" Jamieson asked sharply.

"By the main entrance. He left at a quarter to three. I know exactly."

"The clock in the hall is stopped, Miss Innes," said Jamieson. Nothing seemed to escape him.

"He looked at his watch," she replied, and I could see Mr Jamieson's eyes snap as if he had made a discovery. As for myself, during the whole recital I had been plunged into the deepest amazement.

"Will you pardon me for a personal question?" The detective was a youngish man, and I thought he was somewhat embarrassed. "What are your relations with Mr Bailey?"

Gertrude hesitated. Then she came over and put her hand lovingly in mine.

"I am engaged to marry him," she said simply.

I had grown so accustomed to surprises that I could only gasp again. As for Gertrude, the hand that lay in mine was icy cold.

"And after that," Jamieson went on, "you went directly to bed?"

Gertrude hesitated.

"No," she said finally. "I'm not nervous, and after I had put out the light I remembered something I had left in the billiard room. I felt my way back there through the darkness."

"Will you tell me what it was you had forgotten?"

"I can't tell you," she said slowly. "But I didn't leave the billiard room at once–I waited awhile."

"Why?" The detective's tone was imperative. "This is very important, Miss Innes."

"I was crying," Gertrude said in a low tone. "When the French clock in the drawing room struck three I got up, and then I heard a step on the east porch, just outside the cardroom. Someone with a key was working with the latch. I thought of course of Halsey. When we took the house he called that his entrance, arid he had carried a key for it ever since. The door opened and I was about to ask what he had forgotten when there was a flash and a report. Some heavy body dropped, and I guess I was scared out of my wits. Anyhow I ran through the drawing room and got upstairs. I scarcely remember how."

"You didn't see the dead man?"

She dropped into a chair, and I thought Jamieson must have finished. But he was not through.

"You certainly clear your brother and Mr Bailey admirably," he said. "The testimony is important, especially in view of the fact that your brother and Mr Armstrong had quarreled rather seriously some time ago."

"Nonsense," I broke in. "Things are bad enough, Mr Jamieson, without inventing bad feeling where it doesn't exist. Gertrude, I don't think Halsey even knew young Armstrong, did he?"

But Jamieson was sure of his ground.

"The quarrel," he persisted, "was about Mr Armstrong's conduct to you, Miss Gertrude. He had been annoying you, paying you unwelcome attentions. That's the fact, isn't it?"

And I had never seen the man!

When she nodded a "yes" I saw the tremendous possibilities involved. If this detective could prove that Gertrude feared and disliked the murdered man and that young

Armstrong had been annoying her for some reason, all that added to Gertrude's confession of her presence in the billiard room at the time of the crime looked strange, to say the least. The prominence of his family assured a strenuous effort to find the murderer, and if we had nothing worse to look forward to we were sure of a disgusting publicity.

Jamieson shut his notebook with a snap, and thanked us.

"I have an idea," he said, with a grim sort of smile, "that at any rate the ghost is laid here. Whatever the rappings have been—and the colored man says they began when the family went west three months ago—they're likely to stop now."

Which shows how much he knew about it. The ghost was not laid; with the murder of Arnold Armstrong he or it only seemed to take on fresh vigor.

Jamieson left then and when Gertrude had gone upstairs, as she did at once, I sat and thought over what I had just heard. Her engagement, which had come as a surprise to me, paled now beside the significance of her story. If Halsey and Jack Bailey had left before the crime, why was Halsey's revolver in the tulip bed? What was the mysterious cause of their sudden flight? What had Gertrude left in the billiard room that she had gone back for? What was the significance of the cuff link? And where was it?

I was not left long in peace. For hours that morning police officers prowled the place, photographs were taken, and men were everywhere. In due time however the body was removed, and we had at least an interval of quiet. Gertrude was shut in her room, and Liddy should have been shut in a lunatic asylum.

But before the body was taken away I was asked to look at it. Whatever lines of dissipation had been in young Armstrong's face had been wiped away by death. But he had been handsome. And young. I felt a stab of pity for him.

6

When Jamieson left he had enjoined absolute secrecy on everybody in the household. The Greenwood Club promised the same thing, and as there are no Sunday afternoon papers the murder was not publicly known until Monday. The police however notified the Armstrong family lawyer, and early in the afternoon he came out.

Mr Harton was a small thin man, and he looked as if he did not relish his business that day.

"This is very unfortunate, Miss Innes," he said, after we had shaken hands. "Most unfortunate and mysterious. With the father and mother in the West, I find everything devolves on me, and as you can understand it is an unpleasant duty."

"No doubt," I said absently. "Mr Harton, I am going to ask you some questions, and I hope you will answer them. I feel that I am entitled to some knowledge, because my family and I myself are in a most ambiguous position."

I don't know whether he understood me or not. He took off his glasses and wiped them.

"I shall be very happy," he said with old-fashioned courtesy. "I know very little, of course."

"Thank you. Mr Harton, did Mr Arnold Armstrong know that Sunnyside had been rented?"

"I think–yes, he did. In fact, I myself told him about it."

"And he knew who the tenants were?"

"Yes."

"He had not been living with the family for some years, I believe?"

"No. Unfortunately there had been trouble between Arnold and his father. For the past two years he had lived in town."

"Then it would be unlikely that he came here last night to get possession of anything belonging to him?"

"I should think it hardly possible," he admitted. "To be perfectly frank, Miss Innes, I can't think of any reason whatever for his coming here as he did. He had been staying at the clubhouse across the valley for the last week, Jarvis tells me, but that only explains how he came here, not why."

He gave me a shrewd look through his spectacles. "I know him only slightly," he said, "but I understand he—well, he lived his own life. If he came back it was a case of the Prodigal Son, Miss Innes. That's all I can say."

He was greatly upset. I could see that. But he did not elaborate except to mutter something about the sins of the fathers being visited on the children, which left me pondering.

He asked to see the scene of the crime, and as we started Mrs Watson appeared at the cardroom door. Evidently he knew her, for he spoke to her.

"I'm sorry about this, Mrs Watson," he said. "Who would have expected such a thing?"

But she only shook her head and passed us without speaking. She went on, and Mr Harton viewed the spot where the body had been found without comment. Someone—perhaps Mrs Watson herself—had washed the blood from the carpet in the hall. I stepped over the place and going to the door at the foot of the circular staircase opened it and glanced out.

If I could only have seen Halsey coming at his usual harebrained pace up the drive, if I could have heard the throb of the motor, I would have felt that my troubles were over. But there was nothing to be seen. The countryside lay sunny and quiet in its peaceful Sunday afternoon calm, and far down the drive Jamieson was walking slowly, stooping now and then as if to examine the road. When I turned back Mr Harton was furtively wiping his spectacles.

"I have known him since he was a boy," he said. "Whatever he was he didn't deserve this."

Before he left he told me something of the Armstrong family. Paul Armstrong, the father, had been married twice. Arnold was a son by the first marriage. The second Mrs Armstrong had been a widow with a child, a little girl. This child, now perhaps twenty, was Louise Armstrong, having taken her stepfather's name, and was at present in California with the family.

"They will probably return at once," he concluded, "and part of my errand here today is to see if you will relinquish your lease here in their favor."

"We would better wait and see if they care to come," I said. "It seems unlikely, and my town house is being re-modeled." At that he let the matter drop, but it came up unpleasantly enough later.

At six o'clock the house had more or less settled down, and at seven-thirty, after an early dinner, Mr Harton went. Gertrude had not come down, and there was no news of Halsey. Jamieson had taken a lodging in the village, and I had not seen him since midafternoon. It was about nine o'clock, I think, when the bell rang and he was ushered into the living room.

"Sit down," I said grimly. "Have you found anything that will incriminate me, Mr Jamieson?"

He had the grace to look uncomfortable. "No," he said. "If you had killed Mr Armstrong, I imagine you would have left no clues. You are a very intelligent woman, Mrs Innes."

After that we got along better. I was knitting, while he was fishing in his pocket. After a minute he brought out two scraps of paper. "I have been to the clubhouse," he said, "and among Mr Armstrong's effects I found these. One is curious. The other is puzzling."

The first was a sheet of club note paPer on which was written over and over the name "Halsey B. Innes." It was Halsey's flowing signature to a dot, but it lacked Halsey's ease. The ones toward the bottom of the sheet were much better than the top ones. Jamieson smiled at my face.

"His old tricks," he said. "That one is merely curious. This one, as I said before, is puzzling."

The second scrap, folded and refolded into a compass so tiny that the writing had been partly obliterated, was part of a letter. The lower half of a sheet, not typed, but written in a cramped hand.

"........ by altering the plans for .... rooms may be possible. The best way, in my opinion, would be to .... the plan for .... in one of the ..... rooms .... chimney."

That was all.

"Well?" I said, looking up. "There is nothing in that, is there? A man ought to be able to change the plan of his house without becoming an object of suspicion."

"There is little in the paper itself," he admitted. "But why should Arnold Armstrong carry that around unless it meant something? He never built a house, you may be sure of that. If it is this house it may mean anything, from a secret room–"

"To an extra bathroom," I said scornfully. "Haven't you a thumbprint too?"

"I have," he said, with a smile, "and the print of a foot in a tulip bed, and a number of other things. The oddest part is, Miss Innes, that the thumbmark is probably yours and the footprint certainly."

His audacity was the only thing that saved me. His amused smile put me on my mettle, and I ripped out a perfectly good scallop before I answered.

"Why did I step into the tulip bed?" I asked, with interest.

"You picked up something," he said good-humoredly, "which you are going to tell me about later."

"Am I indeed?" I was politely curious. "With this remarkable insight of yours, I wish you would tell me where I shall find my four-thousand-dollar car."

"I was just coming to that," he said. "You will find it about thirty miles away at Andrews Station in a garage where it is being repaired."

I laid down my knitting then and looked at him. "And Halsey?" I managed to say.

"We are going to exchange information," he said. "I am going to tell you that, when you tell me what you picked up in the tulip bed."

We looked steadily at each other. It was not an unfriendly stare; we were only measuring weapons. Then he smiled a little and got up.

"With your permission," he said, "I am going to examine the cardroom and the staircase again. You might think over my offer in the meantime."

He went on through the drawing room, and I listened to his footsteps growing gradually fainter. I dropped my pretense at knitting and leaning back I thought over the last forty-eight hours. Here was I, Rachel Innes, a spinster, a granddaughter of old John Innes of Revolutionary days, a D.A.R., a Colonial Dame, mixed up with a vulgar and revolting crime and even attempting to hoodwink the law! Certainly I had left the strait and narrow way.

I was roused by hearing Mr Jamieson coming rapidly back through the drawing room. He stopped at the door.

"Miss Innes," he said quickly, "will you come with me and light the hall over here? I have locked somebody in the small room at the head of the cardroom stairs." I jumped up at once.

"You mean the murderer?" I gasped.

"Possibly," he said quietly, as we hurried together up the stairs. "Someone was hiding on the staircase when I went back. I spoke, but instead of an answer whoever it was turned and ran up. I followed but as I turned the corner at the top a figure darted through this door and closed it. The key was on my side and I turned it. It's a closet, I think." We were in the upper hall now. "If you will show me the electric switch, Miss Innes, you would better wait in your own room."

Trembling as I was, I was determined to see that door opened. I hardly knew what I feared, but so many terrible and inexplicable things had happened that suspense was worse than certainty.

"I'm perfectly cool," I said, "and I intend to stay right here."

The lights flashed up along that end of the corridor, throwing the doors into relief. At the intersection of the small hallway with the larger the circular staircase wound its way up, as if it had been an afterthought of the architect. And just around the corner in the small hallway was the door Jamieson had indicated. I was still unfamiliar with the house and I did not remember the door. My heart was thumping wildly in my ears, but I nodded to him to go ahead. I was perhaps eight or ten feet away when he turned the key. I think he had a gun in his hand.

"Come out," he said quietly. There was no response. "Come out," ne repeated. "I've got you." Then suddenly, he stepped aside and threw the door open.

From where I stood I could not see beyond the door, but I saw Jamieson's face change and heard him mutter something. Then he bolted down the stairs, three at a time. When my knees had stopped shaking, I moved forward, slowly, nervously, until I had a partial view of what was beyond the door. It seemed at first to be a closet, empty. After that I went close and examined it, to stop with a shudder. Where the floor should have been was black void and darkness, from which came the indescribable damp smell of the cellars.

Jamieson had locked somebody in the clothes chute. As I leaned over I fancied I heard a groan. Or was it the wind?

7

I was panic-stricken. As I ran along the corridor I was confident that the mysterious intruder and probable murderer had been found, and that he lay dead or dying at the foot of the chute. I got down the staircase somehow, and through the kitchen to the basement stairs. Jamieson had been before me and the door stood open. Liddy was standing in the middle of the kitchen, holding a frying pan by the handle as a weapon.

"Don't go down there," she yelled when she saw me moving toward the basement stairs. "Don't you do it, Miss Rachel. That Jamieson's down there now. There's only trouble comes of hunting ghosts. They lead you into bottomless pits and things like that. Please, Miss Rachel, don't–" as I tried to get past her.

She was interrupted by Jamieson's reappearance. He ran up the stairs two at a time, and his face was flushed and furious.

"The whole place is locked," he said angrily. "Where's the laundry key kept?"

"It's kept in the door," Liddy snapped. "That whole end of the cellar is kept locked, so nobody can get at the clothes. And then the key's left in the door, so that unless a thief was as blind as some detectives he could walk right in."

"Liddy," I said sharply, "come down with us and turn on all the lights."

She offered her resignation as usual on the spot, but I took her by the arm and she came along finally. She switched on all the lights and pointed to a door just ahead.

"That's the door," she said sulkily. "The key's in it."

The key was not in it, however. Mr Jamieson shook it, but it was a heavy door and well locked. Then he stooped and began punching around the keyhole with the end of a lead pencil, and when he stood up his face was exultant.

"It's locked on the inside," he said in a low tone. "There is somebody in there."

"Lord have mercy!" gasped Liddy, and turned to run.

"Liddy," I called, "go through the house at once and see who is missing, or if anyone is. We'll have to clear this thing at once. Mr Jamieson, if you will watch here I will go to the lodge and find Warner, the chauffeur. Thomas would be no use. Together you may be able to force the door."

"A good idea," he assented. "But there are windows, of course, and there is nothing to prevent whoever was in there from getting out that way."

"Then lock the door at the top of the basement stairs," I suggested, "and patrol the house from the outside."

We agreed to this, and I had a feeling that the mystery of Sunnyside was about to be solved. I ran down the steps and along the drive. Just at the corner I ran full tilt into somebody who seemed to be as much alarmed as I was. It was not until I had recoiled a step or two that I recognized Gertrude, and she me.

"Good gracious, Rachel," she exclaimed, "what is the matter?"

"There's somebody locked in the laundry," I panted. "That is unless– You didn't see anyone crossing the lawn or skulking around the house, did you?"

"I think we have mystery on the brain," Gertrude said wearily. "No, I haven't seen anyone except old Thomas, who looked for all the world as if he had been caught stealing the spoons. What on earth have you locked in the laundry?"

"I can't wait to explain," I replied. "I must get Warner from the lodge. If you came out for air you'd better change your shoes." That was when I noticed Gertrude was limping. Not much, but sufficiently to make her progress very slow and seemingly painful. "You've hurt yourself," I said sharply.

"I turned my ankle," she explained. "I thought perhaps I might see Halsey coming home. He ought to be back. I don't understand."

I hurried on down the drive. The lodge was some distance from the house, in a grove of trees where the drive met the country road. There were two white stone pillars to mark the entrance, but the iron gates, once closed and tended by the lodgekeeper, now stood permanently open. Times had changed, and the lodge at Sunnyside was merely a sort of supplementary servants' quarters. It was as convenient in its appointments as the big house and infinitely easier to care for.

As I went down the drive my thoughts were busy. Who could it be that Jamieson had trapped in the cellar? Would we find a body or someone badly injured? Scarcely either. Whoever had fallen had been able to lock the laundry door on the inside. But if the fugitive had come from outside the house, how did he get in? If it was some member of the household, who could it have been? That was when a feeling of horror almost overwhelmed me. Gertrude! Gertrude and her injured ankle. Gertrude limping slowly up the drive when I had thought she was in bed!

I tried to put the thought away, but it would not go. If Gertrude had been on the circular staircase that night why had she run from Jamieson? The idea, puzzling as it was, seemed borne out by this circumstance. Whoever had taken refuge at the head of the stairs could scarcely have been familiar with the house, or with the location of the chute. The mystery seemed to deepen constantly. What possible connection could there be between Halsey and Gertrude, and the murder of Arnold Armstrong? And yet every way I turned I seemed to find something that pointed to such a connection.

At the foot of the drive the road described a long sloping horseshoe-shaped curve around the lodge. There were lights there, streaming cheerfully out onto the trees, and from an upper room came wavering shadows, as if someone with a lamp was moving around. I had come almost silently in my evening slippers, and I had my second collision of the evening on the road just above the house. I ran full tilt into a man in a long coat who was standing in the shadow beside the drive, with his back to me and watching the lighted windows.

"What the hell!" he ejaculated furiously, and turned around. When he saw me, however, he did not wait for any retort on my part. He faded away–this is not slang; he did–he absolutely disappeared in the dusk without my getting more than a glimpse of his face. I had a vague impression of unfamiliar features and of a sort of cap with a visor. Then he was gone.

I went to the lodge and rapped. It required two or three poundings to bring Thomas to the door, and he opened it only an inch or so. "Where is Warner?" I asked.

"I think he's in bed, ma'am."

"Get him up," I said, "and for goodness' sake open the door, Thomas. I'll wait for Warner."

"It's kind o' close in here, ma'am," he said, obeying gingerly, and disclosing a cool and comfortable-looking interior. "Perhaps you'd keer to set on the porch an' rest yo'self."

It was so evident that Thomas did not want me inside that I went in.

"Tell Warner he is needed in a hurry," I repeated, and turned into the little sitting room. I could hear Thomas going up the stairs, could hear him rouse Warner, and the steps of the chauffeur as he hurriedly dressed. But my attention was busy with the room below.

On the center table, open, was a pigskin traveling bag. It was filled with gold-topped bottles, and it breathed opulence, luxury, femininity from every inch of surface. How did it get there? I was still asking myself the question when Warner came running down the stairs and into the room. He was completely but somewhat incongruously dressed, and his open, boyish face looked abashed. He was a country boy, absolutely frank and reliable, and of fair education and intelligence. One of the small army of American youths who turn a natural aptitude for mechanics into the special field of the automobile, and earn good salaries in a congenial occupation.

"What is it, Miss Innes?" he asked anxiously.

"There is someone locked in the laundry," I replied. "Mr Jamieson wants you to help him break the lock. Warner, whose bag is this?"

He was in the doorway by this time and he pretended not to hear.

"Warner," I called, "come back here. Whose bag is this?"

He stopped then, but he did not turn around.

"It's–I think it belongs to Thomas," he said, and hurried up the drive.

To Thomas! An English fitted bag with mirrors and cosmetic jars of which Thomas could not even have guessed the use! However, I put the bag in the back of my mind, which was fast becoming stored with absurd and apparently irreconcilable facts, and followed Warner to the house.

Liddy had come back to the kitchen. The door to the basement stairs was double-barred, and had a table pushed against it. And beside her on the table was most of the kitchen paraphernalia.

"Did you see if there was anyone missing in the house?" I asked, ignoring the array of saucepans, rolling pins, and the poker from the range.

"Rosie is missing," Liddy said with unction. She had objected to Rosie, the parlor maid, from the start. "Mrs Watson went into her room and found she had gone without her hat. People that trust themselves a dozen miles from the city, in strange houses, with servants they don't know, needn't be surprised if they wake up some morning and find their throats cut."

After which carefully veiled sarcasm Liddy relapsed into gloom. Warner came in then with a handful of small tools, and Jamieson went with him to the basement. Oddly enough I was not alarmed. With all my heart I wished for Halsey, but I was not frightened. At the door he was to force Warner put down his tools and looked at it. Then he turned the handle. Without the slightest difficulty the door opened, revealing the blackness of the drying room beyond!

Jamieson gave an exclamation of disgust. "Damnation!" he said. "Confound such careless work! I might have known."

It was true enough. We got the lights on finally and looked all through the three rooms that constituted this wing of the basement. Everything was quiet and empty. An explanation of how the fugitive had escaped injury was found in a heaped-up basket of clothes under the chute. The basket had been overturned but that was all. Jamieson examined the windows. One was unlocked and offered an easy escape. The window or the door to the yard outside? Which way had the fugitive escaped? The door seemed most probable, and I hoped it had been so. I could not have borne just then to think that it was my poor Gertrude we had been hounding through the darkness. And yet I had met Gertrude not far from that very door.

I went upstairs at last, tired and depressed. Mrs Watson and Liddy were making tea in the kitchen. In certain walks of life the teapot is the refuge in times of stress, trouble or sickness. They give tea to the dying and they put it in the baby's nursing bottle. Also Mrs Watson was fixing a tray to be sent in to me, and when I asked her about Rosie she confirmed her absence.

"She's not here," she said; "but I wouldn't think much of that, Miss Innes. Rosie is a pretty young girl, and perhaps she has a friend in the neighborhood. It will be a good thing if she has. The maids stay much better when they have something like that to hold them here."

Gertrude had gone back to her room, and while I was drinking my cup of hot tea Jamieson came in.

"Suppose we take up the conversation where we left off an hour and a half ago," he suggested. "But before we go on, I want to say this. The person who escaped from the laundry was a woman with a foot of moderate size and well arched. She wore nothing but a stocking on her right foot, and, in spite of the unlocked door she escaped by the window. Which seems rather curious."

Again I thought of Gertrude's sprained ankle. At least I was sure she was wearing slippers on both feet. Nevertheless I was uneasy. She *had* been limping.

8

"Miss Innes," Jamieson began, "what is your opinion of the figure you saw on the east veranda the night you and your maid were in the house alone?"

"It was a woman," I said positively.

"And yet your maid affirms with equal positiveness that it was a man."

"Nonsense," I broke in. "Liddy had her eyes shut. She always shuts them when she's frightened."

"You never thought then that the intruder who came later that night might be a woman? The woman in fact whom you saw on the veranda?"

"I had reasons for thinking it was a man," I said, remembering the pearl cuff link.

"Now we're getting down to business," he said, smiling. "What were your reasons for thinking that?"

I hesitated, and his smile faded.

"Listen," he said. "If you have any reason for believing that your midnight guest was Mr Armstrong, other than his visit here the next night, you ought to tell me. We can take nothing for granted. If for instance the intruder who dropped the bar and scratched the staircase–yes, of course I know about that–if this visitor was a woman, why should not the same woman have come back the following night, met Mr Armstrong on the circular staircase, and either in alarm or for some other reason shot him?"

"It was a man," I reiterated stubbornly. And then, because I could think of no other reason for my statement, I told him about the broken pearl cuff link. He was more than interested.

"Will you give me the link," he said, when I finished, "or, at least, let me see it? It may be most important."

"Won't the description do?"

"Not so well as the original." He eyed me suspiciously.

"Well, I'm very sorry," I said, as calmly as I could. "The thing is lost. It must have fallen out of a box on my dressing table. Anyhow I can't find it."

Whatever he thought of my explanation, and I knew he doubted it, he made no sign. He asked me to describe the link accurately and I did so, while he glanced at a list he took from his pocket.

"One set monogram cuff links," he read, "one set plain dinner links with small pearl, one set cuff links, antique with woman's head set with diamonds and emeralds. There is no mention of such a link as you describe, and yet if your theory is right Mr Armstrong must have worn back that night to the club one complete cuff link, and a half perhaps of the other."

The idea was new to me. If it had not been the murdered man who had entered the house that night, who had it been?

"There are a number of unusual things connected with this case," the detective went on. "Miss Gertrude Innes testified that she heard someone fumbling with the lock last night, that the door opened, and that almost immediately the shot was fired. Now, Miss Innes, here is the strange part of that. Arnold Armstrong had no key with him. There was no key in the lock or on the floor. In other words, the evidence points absolutely to the fact that Mr Armstrong was admitted to the house from within."

"It's impossible," I broke in. "Mr Jamieson, do you know what your words imply? Do you know that you are practically accusing Gertrude Innes of admitting that man?"

"Not quite that," he said, with his friendly smile. "In fact, Miss Innes, I am quite certain she didn't do anything of the sort. But as long as I learn only bits of the truth from both you and her what can I do? I know you picked up something in the flower bed, but you refuse to tell me what it was. I know Miss Gertrude went back to the billiard room to get something, yet she refuses to say what. You suspect what happened to the cuff link after you found it, but you won't tell me. So far, all I am sure of is this: I do not believe Arnold Armstrong was the midnight visitor who so alarmed you by dropping–shall we say?–a golf stick. And I believe that when he did come he was admitted by someone in the house. Who was that person? Liddy?"

I stirred my tea angrily.

"I have always heard," I said, "that undertakers' assistants are jovial young men. A man's sense of humor seems to be in inverse proportion to the gravity of his profession."

"A man's sense of humor is often a barbarous and a cruel thing," he admitted. "It is to the feminine as the hug of a bear is to the scratch of something with claws. I don't know which is worse." He glanced up abruptly. "Is that you, Thomas? Come in."

Thomas stood in the doorway. He looked alarmed and apprehensive, and I remembered the pigskin traveling bag in the lodge. Thomas came just inside the door and stood with his arms hanging and his eyes under their shaggy gray brows fixed on Jamieson.

"Thomas," said the detective, not unkindly, "I sent for you to tell us what you told Sam Bohannon at the club, the day before Mr Arnold was found here dead. Let me see. You came here Friday night to see Miss Innes, didn't you? And came to work here Saturday morning?"

For some unexplained reason Thomas looked relieved.

"Yas, suh," he said. "You see it were like this: When Mistah Armstrong and the fam'ly went away Mis' Watson an' me we was lef' in charge till the place was rented. Mis' Watson, she've bin here a good while an' she warn't skeery. So she slep' in the house. I'd bin havin' tokens–I tol' Mis' Innes some of 'em–an' I slep' in the lodge. Then one day Mis' Watson she came to me an' she sez, 'Thomas, you'll hey to sleep up in the big house. I'm too nervous to do it any more.' But I jes' reckon to myself that ef it's too skeery fer her it's too skeery fer me. We had it then sho' nuff, and it ended up with Mis' Watson stayin' in the lodge nights an' me lookin' fer work at de club."

"Did Mrs Watson say that anything had happened to alarm her?"

"No, suh. She was jes' natchally skeered. Well, that was all, far's I know, until the night I come over to see Mis' Innes. I come across the valley, along the path from the clubhouse, and I goes home that way. Down in the creek bottom I almost run into a man. He wuz standin' with his back to me, an' he was workin' with one of these yere electric light things that fit in yer pocket. He was havin' trouble. One minute it'd flash out an' the flex' it'd be gone. I hed a view of 'is dress shirt an' tie as I passed. I didn't see his face. But I know it warn't Mr Arnold. It was a taller man than Mr Arnold. Beside that Mr Arnold was playin' cards when I got back to the clubhouse, same's he'd been doin' all day."

"And the next morning you came back along the same path," pursued Jamieson relentlessly.

"The nex' mornin' I come back along the path, an' down where I dun see the man night befoh I picked up this here." The old man held out a tiny object, and Jamieson took it. Then he held it on his extended palm for me to see. It was the other half of the pearl cuff link.

But Jamieson was not quite through questioning him. "And so you showed it to Sam, at the club, and asked him if he knew anyone who owned such a link, and Sam said–what did Sam say?"

"Wal, Sam, he 'lowed he'd seen such a pair of cuff buttons in a shirt belongin' to Mr Bailey. Mr Jack Bailey, sub."

"I'll keep this link, Thomas, for a while," the detective said. "That's all I wanted to know. Good night."

As Thomas shuffled out Jamieson watched me sharply.

"You see, Miss Innes," he said, "Mr Bailey insists on mixing himself with this thing. If Mr Bailey came here that Friday night expecting to meet Arnold Armstrong, and missed him–If, as I say, he had done this, might he not, seeing him enter the following night, have struck him down as he had intended before?"

"But the motive?" I gasped. "Why on earth would he do it?"

"There could be motive proved, I think. Arnold Armstrong and John Bailey have been on bad terms since Bailey, as cashier of the Traders' Bank, brought Arnold almost into the clutches of the law. Then don't forget that both men have been paying attention to your niece. Bailey's flight looks bad, too."

"And you think Halsey helped him to escape?"

"What do you think? Suppose I reconstruct that evening as I see it. Bailey and Armstrong had quarreled at the club. I learned this today. After that your nephew brought Bailey over here. And it looks as though Armstrong, prompted by jealous, insane fury followed them both, coming across by the path. He entered the billiard-room wing, perhaps rapping and being admitted by your nephew. And just inside he was shot by someone on the circular staircase. The shot fired, your nephew and Bailey left the house at once, going toward the garage and the car. They drove off by the lower road, which prevented their being heard, and when you got downstairs everything was quiet."

"That's not what Gertrude says," I objected.

He lit a cigarette before he spoke.

"Miss Gertrude only brought forward her explanation the following morning. Quite frankly I don't believe it, Miss Innes. It's the story of a loving and frightened woman."

"And this thing tonight? The clothes chute."

"It may upset my whole view of the case," he admitted. "I have no idea of jumping to any conclusion yet. We may, for instance, come back to the figure on the porch. If it was a woman you saw that night through the window we might start with other premises. Or your nephew's explanation when we find him may turn us in a new direction. It's possible he shot Arnold Armstrong as a burglar and then escaped, shocked at what he had done. In any case however I feel confident that the body was here when he left. Mr Armstrong left the club, ostensibly for a moonlight saunter, about half after eleven o'clock. It was three when the shot was fired."

I leaned back bewildered. It seemed to me that the evening had been full of significant happenings, had I only had the brains to understand them. Had Gertrude been the fugitive in the clothes chute? In that case who was the man on the drive near the lodge? And whose gold-mounted dressing bag had I seen in the lodge sitting room?

It was late when Jamieson finally got up to go. I went with him to the door, and together we stood looking out over the valley. Below lay the small village of Casanova with its Old World houses, its blossoming trees and its peace. Above on the hill across the valley were the lights of the Greenwood Club. It was even possible to see the curving row of parallel lights which marked the carriage road. Rumors about the club came back to me. Founded by a group of wealthy men from the city, a good bit more took place there than the golf which was its ostensible purpose. There was, I knew, a good bit of drinking and gambling, and once a year ago there had been a suicide under those very lights.

Jamieson left soon, taking a short cut to the village, and I still stood there. It must have been after eleven, and the monotonous tick of the big clock on the stairs behind me was the only sound. Then I was conscious that someone was running up the drive. In a minute a woman darted into the area of light made by the open door, and caught me by the arm. It was Rosie, a Rosie in a state of collapse from terror and, not the least important, clutching one of my Coalport plates and a silver spoon.

She stood staring into the darkness behind, still holding the plate. I got her into the house and took the plate from her. Then I stood and looked down at her where she crouched tremblingly against the doorway.

"Well," I asked, "didn't your young man enjoy his meal?"

She couldn't speak. She looked at the spoon she still held as if she was unconscious of it. Then she stared at me.

"I appreciate your desire to have everything nice for him," I went on, "but the next time you might take the Limoges china. It's more easily duplicated and less expensive."

"I haven't a young man. Not here." She had got her breath now, and dropped into a chair. "I've been chased by somebody, Miss Innes."

"Did he chase you out of the house and back again?" I asked dryly.

She began to cry, not silently but noisily, hysterically. I stopped her by giving her a good shake. "What in the world is the matter with you?" I snapped. "Has the day of good common sense gone by?–Sit up and tell me the whole thing."

Rosie sat up then and sniffled. "I was coming up the drive–" she began.

"You'd better start with when you went down the drive, with my dishes and my silver," I interrupted. But seeing more signs of hysteria I gave in. "Very well, you were coming up the drive–"

"I had a basket of–of silver and dishes on my arm, and I was carrying the plate, because I was afraid I'd break it. Part way up the road a man stepped out of the bushes and held his arm like this, spread out, so I couldn't get past. He said 'Not so fast, young lady; I want you to let me see what's in that basket.'"

She got up in her excitement and took hold of my arm.

"It was like this, Miss Innes," she said, "and say you was the man. When he said that, I screamed and ducked under his arm like this. He caught at the basket and I dropped it. I ran as fast as I could, and he came after me as far as the trees. Then he stopped. Oh, Miss Innes, I know it was the murderer. I'm sure of it."

"Don't be foolish," I said. "Whoever killed Mr Armstrong would put as much space between himself and this house as he could."

But she was hysterical again. I saw it was no use asking her about the basket and its contents, or why she had been out. She was shaking all over, and I doubt if she even heard what I said.

"Get on up to your bed," I told her. "And remember this. If I hear of your telling this cock-and-bull story to the other maids I'll deduct from your wages for every broken dish I find in the drive."

I listened to her as she went upstairs, running past the shadowy places and slamming her door. Then I sat down and looked at the Coalport plate and the silver spoon. I had brought from town my own china and silver, and from all appearances I would have little enough to take back. But though I might jeer at Rosie as much as I wished, the fact remained that someone had been on the drive that night who had no business there. Although neither had Rosie, for that matter.

I could fancy Liddy's face when she missed the extra pieces of china. She had opposed Rosie from the start, and if Liddy once finds a prophecy fulfilled, especially an unpleasant one, she never allows me to forget it. It seemed to me that it was absurd to leave that china dotted along the road for her to find the next morning; so with a sudden resolution I opened the door again and stepped out into the darkness. As the door closed behind me I half regretted my impulse. Then I shut my teeth and went on.

I have never been a nervous woman, as I have said before. Moreover, a minute or two in the darkness enabled me to see things fairly well. Beulah gave me rather a start by rubbing unexpectedly against my feet. Then we two side by side went down the drive.

There were no fragments of china, but where the trees began I picked up a silver spoon. So far Rosie's story was borne out. But I began to wonder if it was not indiscreet, to say the least, this midnight prowling in a neighborhood with such a deservedly bad reputation. Then I saw something gleaming which proved to be the handle of a cup, and a step or two farther on I found a V-shaped bit of a plate. But the most surprising thing of all was to find the basket sitting comfortably beside the road with the rest of the broken crockery piled neatly within, and a handful of small silver, spoons, forks, and the like on top. I could only stand and stare. Evidently Rosie's story was true. But where had she carried her basket? And why had the thief, if he was a thief, picked up the broken china out of the road and left it along with his booty?

It was with my nearest approach to a nervous collapse that I heard the familiar throbbing of a motor, and as it came closer I recognized the outline of my car.

Halsey had come back.

Strange enough it must have seemed to Halsey too, to come across me in the middle of the night, with the long skirt of my gray silk dress over my shoulders to keep off the dew, while holding a red and green basket under one arm and a black cat under the other. What with relief and joy I began to cry right there, and very nearly wiped my eyes on Beulah in the excitement.

9

"Good God, Ray!" Halsey said from the gloom behind the lamps. "What in the world are you doing here?"

"Taking a walk," I said, trying to be composed. I don't think the answer struck either of us as being ridiculous at the time. "Where have you been? I've been slowly losing my mind."

"Get in and let me take you up to the house." He was in the road, and had Beulah and the basket out of my arms in a moment. I could see the car plainly now and Warner was at the wheel, Warner in an ulster and a pair of slippers over Heaven knows what. Jack Bailey was not there. I got in, and we went slowly and cautiously up to the house.

We did not talk. What we had to say was too important to commence there, and besides it took all kinds of coaxing to get the car up the last grade. It was apparently almost out of gas. Only when we had closed the front door and stood facing each other in the hail did Halsey say anything. Then he slipped his strong young arm around my shoulders and turned me so I faced the light.

"Poor Rachel!" he said gently. And I nearly wept again. "Look here, I have to see Gertrude. I have a lot to say to her."

Then Gertrude herself came down the stairs. She had not been to bed evidently, for she still wore the white negligee she had worn earlier in the evening, and she limped somewhat. During her slow progress down the stairs I had time to notice one thing. Jamieson had said the woman who escaped from the cellar had worn no shoe on her right foot. Gertrude's right ankle was the one she had sprained.

The meeting between brother and sister was tense but without tears Halsey kissed her, and there were signs of strain and anxiety in both young faces.

"Is everything all right?" she asked.

"Right as can be," Halsey said with forced cheerfulness.

I lighted the living room and we went in there. Only a half hour before I had sat with Jamieson in that very room, listening while he overtly accused both Gertrude and Halsey of at least a knowledge of the death of Arnold Armstrong. Now Halsey was here to speak for himself. I should learn everything that had puzzled me.

"I saw it in the paper tonight for the first time," he was saying. "It knocked me silly. When I think of this houseful of women, and a thing like that occurring! What happened? Who did it?"

Gertrude's face was still set and white. "We don't know, Halsey," she said. "You and Jack left almost at the time it happened. The police think that you, that all of us, know something about it. The detective thinks so too."

"The hell he does!" Halsey's eyes were fairly starting from his head. "Sorry, Aunt Ray, but the fellow's a lunatic."

"It's up to you to explain a lot of things," I said dryly. "Where you went that night, or rather morning, and why you went as you did. This has been a terrible time for all of us."

He stood staring at me, and I could see indecision and something like alarm in his face.

"I can't tell you where I went, Aunt Ray," he said, after a moment. "As to why, you'll learn that soon enough. But Gertrude knows that Jack and I left the house before this thing happened."

"Mr Jamieson doesn't believe me," Gertrude said drearily. "Halsey, if the worst comes, if they should arrest you, you must talk. You'll have to."

"I'm not talking to anyone, not yet," he said, with a new sternness in his voice. "Aunt Ray, it was necessary for Jack and me to leave that night. I cannot tell you why. It was essential. That's all. As to where we went, if I have to depend on that as an alibi I still won't talk. The whole thing is absurd, a trumped-up charge that cannot possibly be serious."

"Has Jack Bailey gone back to the city," I demanded, "or to the club? You can tell that much, can't you?"

"Neither," he said defiantly. "At the present moment I don't know where he is."

"Halsey," I asked gravely, leaning forward, "have you the slightest suspicion who killed Arnold Armstrong? The police think he was admitted by someone in this house, and that he was shot down from above by someone on the circular staircase."

"Well, I didn't do it, nor did Jack," he maintained. But I fancied I caught a sudden glance at Gertrude, a flash of something that looked like a warning.

After that, as quietly and calmly as I could, I went over the whole story from the night Liddy and I had been alone to the finding of the body, including the curious experience of Rosie and her pursuer that same evening. The basket still stood on the table, a mute witness to this last mystifying occurrence.

"There's something else," I said hesitatingly, at the last. "Halsey, I've never told this even to Gertrude, but the morning after the crime I found, outside in the garden, a revolver. It was yours, Halsey."

For an appreciable moment he stared at me. Then he turned to Gertrude, looking bewildered.

"My gun, Trude!" he exclaimed. "Jack took it with him, didn't he?" To my amazement she did not answer. Instead she got up and taking a cigarette from a box proceeded to light it. I was near enough to see that her hands were shaking.

"If he did, you'd better not say so," I said tartly. "Jamieson will be sure Jack came back and shot him. He thinks one of you did now."

"He didn't come back," Halsey said stiffly. "Gertrude, when you brought down a revolver that night for Jack to take with him, what one did you bring? Mine?"

Gertrude had recovered by that time.

"No," she said. "Yours was loaded, and I knew the state Jack was in. I gave him one I have had for a year or two. It wasn't loaded."

Halsey threw up both hands.

"If that isn't like a girl!" he said. "Why didn't you do what I asked you to? You send Bailey off with an empty gun and throw mine in a tulip bed, of all places on earth! Mine was a thirty-eight caliber. The inquest will show of course that the bullet that killed Armstrong was a thirty-eight and that it came from my gun. Where the hell does that leave me?"

"You forget," I broke in, "that I have the revolver, and that no one knows about it."

But Gertrude flushed with anger.

"I cannot stand it any more," she said. "I didn't throw your revolver into the tulip bed. I think you did it yourself!"

They glared at each other across the big library table, with young eyes all at once hard and suspicious. Then Gertrude held out both hands to him.

"We can't quarrel," she said brokenly. "Just now, with so much at stake. It's shameful. I know you are as innocent as I am. Make me believe it, Halsey."

He soothed her as best he could, and the breach seemed to be healed. But long after I went to bed he sat downstairs in the living room alone, and I knew he was going over the case as he had learned it. Some things were clear to him that were dark to me. He knew, and Gertrude knew too, why Jack Bailey and he had gone away that night as they had. He knew where they had been, and why Jack had not returned with him. It seemed to me that without fuller confidence from both the children–they are always children to me–I should never be able to learn anything.

As I was finally getting ready for bed, Halsey came upstairs and knocked at my door. When I had got into a negligee–I used to say wrapper before Gertrude came back from school–I let him in. He stood in the doorway a moment, and then to my amazement he went into agonies of silent mirth. I sat down on the side of the bed and waited in severe silence for him to stop, but he only seemed to grow worse. When he had recovered he took me by the elbow and pulled me in front of the mirror.

" 'How to be beautiful,' " he quoted. " 'Advice to maids and matrons,' by the Lady Who Knows." And then I saw myself. I had neglected to remove my wrinkle eradicators and I presume my appearance was odd. I believe that it is a woman's duty to care for her looks, but it is much like telling a necessary lie. One ought not to be found out. By the time I had jerked the things off Halsey was serious again, and I listened to his story.

"Look, old girl," he began, extinguishing his cigarette on the back of my ivory hairbrush, "I would give a hell of a lot to tell you the whole thing. But I can't, for a day or so anyhow. Only one thing I might have told you a long time ago. If you had known it, you wouldn't have suspected me for a moment of–of having anything to do with killing Armstrong. God only knows what I might do to a fellow like that if there was enough provocation, and if I had a gun in my hand–under ordinary circumstances. But I care a great deal about Louise Armstrong, Rachel. I hope to marry her someday. Is it likely I would kill her brother?"

"Her stepbrother," I corrected. "No, of course it isn't likely, or possible. Why didn't you tell me, Halsey?"

"Well, there were two reasons," he said slowly. "One was that you had a girl already picked out for me–"

"Nonsense," I broke in, and felt myself growing red. "I merely showed her to you. She was a nice girl, Halsey."

But he ignored that.

"And the second reason," he pursued, "was that the Armstrongs would have none of me."

I sat bolt upright at that and gasped.

"The Armstrongs!" I repeated. "With old Peter Armstrong driving a stage across the mountains while your grandfather was governor during the War between the States!"

"Well, the war governor's dead and out of the matrimonial market," Halsey interrupted. "And the present Innes admits himself he isn't good enough for Louise. But of course–"

"Exactly," I said despairingly, "and naturally you're taken at your own valuation. The Inneses are not always so self-depreciatory."

"Not always, no," he said, looking at me with his boyish smile. "Fortunately Louise doesn't agree with her family. She's willing to take me, war governor or no, provided her mother consents. She isn't overly fond of her stepfather but she adores her mother. And now, can't you see where this thing puts me? Down and out with all of them."

"But the whole thing is outrageous," I argued. "And besides, Gertrude's sworn statement that you left before Arnold Armstrong came would clear you at once."

Halsey got up and began to pace the room, and his air of cheerfulness dropped like a mask.

"She can't swear it," he said finally. "Gertrude's story was true as far as it went, but she didn't tell everything. Armstrong came here at two-thirty that night, came into the billiard room and stayed about five minutes. We were all here. He came to bring something."

"Halsey," I cried, "you must tell me the whole truth. Every time I see a way for you to escape you block it yourself with this wall of mystery. What did he bring?"

"A telegram for Bailey," he said. "It came by special messenger from town. Bailey had started for here, and the messenger had gone back to the city. The steward gave it to Arnold, who had been drinking all day and couldn't sleep, and was coming for a stroll in this direction anyhow."

"And he brought it and then left?"

"Yes."

"What was in the telegram?"

"I can tell you as soon as certain things are made public. It is only a matter of days now," he added gloomily.

"And Gertrude's story of a telephone message?"

"Poor Trude!" he said. "She's a loyal kid. Aunt Ray, there was no such message. I expect your detective already knows that and discredits all Gertrude told him."

"And when she went back, it was to get the telegram? Did you leave it there?"

"We may have. We were pretty well excited. Or she may have thought we had. When you get to thinking about it, Aunt Ray, it looks bad for all three of us, doesn't it? And yet I'll swear none of us even inadvertently killed that poor devil."

I looked at the closed door into Gertrude's dressing room, and lowered my voice.

"The same horrible thought keeps troubling me," I said, lowering my voice. "Halsey, Gertrude probably had your revolver. She must have examined it anyhow that night. After you and Jack had gone, what if that ruffian came back, and she–"

I couldn't finish. Halsey stood looking at me with shut lips. "She might have heard him fumbling at the door–he had no key, the police say–and thinking it was you or Jack she admitted him. When she saw her mistake she ran up the stairs a step or two and because she was afraid of him she fired at him."

"Don't even think it," he said sharply. "It's nonsense."

"What about your gun? It was almost buried in that flower bed. What about her ankle? How did she sprain it?"

"What about her ankle? Any girl can do a thing like that. Look at the heels they wear."

But I had to tell him, if only to have him say I was crazy.

"I think she fell down the clothes chute," I half whispered. And to my dismay he looked as if I had signed a death warrant.

10

The morning after Halsey's return was Tuesday. Arnold Armstrong had been found dead at the foot of the circular staircase at three o'clock on Sunday morning. There was to be a funeral service that day, the inquest having been deferred to the end of the week. But the internment of the body was to wait until the Armstrongs arrived from California. No one, I think, was very sorry that Arnold Armstrong was dead, but the manner of his death aroused some sympathy and an enormous amount of curiosity. Mrs Ogden Fitzhugh, a cousin, took charge of the arrangements and everything, I believe, was as quiet as possible. I gave Thomas Johnson and Mrs Watson permission to go into town to pay their last respects to the dead man, but for some reason they did not care to go.

Halsey spent part of the day with the detective, Jamieson, but he said nothing of what happened. He looked grave and anxious, and he had a long conversation with Gertrude late in the afternoon.

Tuesday evening found us quiet, with the quiet that precedes an explosion. Gertrude and Halsey were both gloomy and distracted, and as Liddy had already discovered that some of the china was broken-it is impossible to have any secrets from an old servant–I was not in a pleasant humor myself. When Warner brought up the afternoon mail and the evening papers at seven I was curious to know what the papers said of the murder. We had turned away at least a dozen reporters. But I read over the headline that ran halfway across the top of the *Gazette* twice before I comprehended it. Halsey had opened the *Chronicle* and was staring at it fixedly.

"The Traders' Bank closes its doors" was what I read. I put down the paper and looked across the table. "Did you know about this?" I asked Halsey. "I expected it. But not so soon," he replied. "And you?" to Gertrude.

"Jack told us something," Gertrude said, her voice flat. "It looks bad for him now, Halsey, doesn't it?"

"Jack!" I said scornfully. "Your Jack's flight is easy enough to explain now. And you helped him, both of you, to get away! You get that from your mother. It isn't an Innes trait. Do you know that every dollar you have, both of you, is in that bank?"

Gertrude tried to speak, but Halsey stopped her.

"That isn't all, Gertrude," he said quietly; "Jack's under arrest."

"Under arrest!" She leaped to her feet and tore the paper out of his hand. She glanced at the heading, then she crumpled the newspaper into a ball and flung it to the floor. While Halsey, looking stricken and white, was trying to smooth it out and read it, she dropped her head on the table and sobbed stormily.

I have the clipping somewhere, but just now I can remember only the essentials.

On the afternoon before, while the Traders' Bank was in the rush of closing hour, between two and three, Mr Jacob Trautmnan, president of the Pearl Brewing Company, came into the bank to pay off a loan. As security for the loan he had deposited some three hundred International Steamship Company 5's, in total value three hundred thousand dollars. Mr Trautman went to the loan clerk and, after certain formalities had been gone through, the loan clerk went to the vault. Mr Trautman, who was a large and genial Jewish gentleman, waited for a time, whistling under his breath. The loan clerk did not come back, and after an interval Mr Trautman saw him emerge from the vault and go to the assistant cashier. The two went hurriedly to the vault. A lapse of another ten minutes, and the assistant cashier came out and approached Mr Trautman. He was noticeably white and trembling. Mr Trautman was told that through an oversight the bonds had been misplaced, and was asked to return the following morning, when everything would be made all right.

Mr Trautman, however, was a shrewd businessman, and he did not like the appearance of things. He left the bank apparently satisfied, and within thirty minutes he had called up three different members of the Traders' Board of Directors. At three-thirty there was a hastily convened board meeting, with some stormy scenes, and late in the afternoon a national bank examiner was in possession of the books. The bank had not opened for business on Tuesday. The article went on:

At twelve-thirty o'clock the Saturday before, as soon as the business of the day was closed, Mr John Bailey, the cashier of the defunct bank, had taken his hat and departed. During the afternoon he had called up Mr Aronson, a member of the board, saying he was ill and might not be at the bank for a day or two. As Bailey was highly thought of, Mr Aronson merely expressed regret. From that time until Monday night, when Mr Bailey had surrendered to the police, little was known of his movements. Sometime after one o'clock on Saturday he had entered the Western Union office at Cherry and White streets and had sent two telegrams. He was at the Greenwood Country Club on Saturday night, and appeared unlike himself. Nothing was said as to where he had been in the interval. It was reported that he would be released under heavy bond sometime that day, Tuesday.

The article closed by saying that, while the officers of the bank refused to talk until the examiner had finished his work, it was known that securities aggregating a million and a quarter were missing. Then there was a diatribe on the possibility of such an occurrence; on the folly of a one-man bank, and of a Board of Directors that met only to lunch together and to listen to a brief report from the cashier, and on the poor policy of a government that arranges a three- or four-day examination twice a year.

The mystery, it insinuated, had not been cleared by the

arrest of the cashier. Before now minor officials had been used to cloak the misdeeds of men higher up. Inseparable as the words "speculation" and "peculation" have grown to be, John Bailey was not known to be in the stock market. His only words after his surrender had been "Send for Mr Armstrong at once." The telegraph message which had finally reached the president of the Traders' Bank, in an interior town in California, had been responded to by a telegram from Doctor Walker, the young physician who was traveling with the Armstrong family, saying that Paul Armstrong was very ill and unable to travel.

That was how things stood that Tuesday before dinner. The Traders' Bank had suspended payment, and John Bailey was under arrest, charged with wrecking it. Paul Armstrong lay very ill in California, and his only son had been murdered two days before. I sat dazed and bewildered. The children's money was gone. That was bad enough, though I had plenty if they would let me share it. But Gertrude's grief was beyond any power of mine to comfort. The man she was in love with stood accused of a colossal embezzlement and even worse. For in the instant that I sat there I seemed to see the coils closing around John Bailey as the murderer of Arnold Armstrong.

Gertrude lifted her head at last and stared across the table at Halsey. "Why did he do it?" she said bleakly. "Couldn't you stop him, Halsey? It was suicidal to go back."

Halsey was looking steadily through the windows of the breakfast room, but it was evident he saw nothing.

"It was the only thing he could do, Trude," he said at last. "Aunt Ray, when I found Jack at the Greenwood Club last Saturday night he was frantic. I can't talk until Jack tells me I may, but he is absolutely innocent of all this. I thought, Trude and I thought, we were helping him. But it was the wrong way. He came back. Isn't that the act of an innocent man?"

"Then why did he leave at all?" I asked, unconvinced.

"What innocent man would run away from here at three o'clock in the morning? Doesn't it look as though he thought it was impossible to escape?"

Gertrude rose angrily. "You are not even just!" she flamed. "You don't know anything about it, and you think he is guilty."

"I know we have all lost a great deal of money," I said. "I shall believe Mr Bailey innocent the moment he is shown to be. You profess to know the truth, but you won't tell me! What am I to think?"

Halsey leaned over and patted my hand.

"You must take us on faith," he said. "Jack Bailey hasn't a penny that doesn't belong to him. The truth will come out in a day or so."

"I'll believe that when it's proved," I said grimly. "In the meantime, I take no one on faith. The Inneses never do."

Gertrude, who had been standing aloof at a window, turned suddenly. "But when the bonds are offered for sale, Halsey, won't the thief be detected at once?"

Halsey turned with a superior smile.

"It wouldn't be done that way," he said. "They would be taken out of the vault by someone who had access to it, and used as collateral for a loan in other banks. It would be possible to realize eighty per cent of their face value."

"In cash?"

"In cash."

"But the man who did it, he would be known?"

"Yes. I tell you both, as sure as I stand here, I believe that Paul Armstrong looted his own bank. I believe he has a million at least as the result, and that he will never come back. I'm worse than a pauper now. I can't ask Louise to share nothing a year with me, and when I think of this disgrace for her I'm crazy."

The most ordinary events of life seemed pregnant with possibilities that evening, and when Halsey was called to the telephone I ceased all pretense at eating. When he came back from the telephone his face showed that something had occurred. He waited, however, until Thomas left the dining room. Then he told us.

"Paul Armstrong is dead," he announced gravely. "He died this morning in California. Whatever he did, he is beyond the law now."

Gertrude turned pale.

"And the only man who could have cleared Jack can never do it!" she said despairingly.

"Also," I replied coldly, "Mr Armstrong is forever beyond the power of defending himself. When your Jack comes to me with some two hundred thousand dollars in his hands, which is about what you've lost, I'll believe him innocent."

Halsey threw his cigarette away and turned on me.

"There you go!" he exclaimed. "If he were the thief he could return the money, of course. If he's innocent he probably hasn't a tenth of that amount in the world. In his hands! That's like a woman."

Gertrude, who had been pale and despairing during the early part of the conversation, had flushed an indignant red. She got up and drew herself to her slender height, looking down at me with the scorn of the young and positive.

"You are the only mother I ever had," she said tensely. "I had given you all I would have given my mother had she lived, my love and trust. And now when I need you most you fail me. I tell you, John Bailey is a good man, an honest man. If you say he's not, you–you–"

"Gertrude," Halsey broke in sharply. She dropped beside the table and burying her face in her arms broke into a storm of tears.

"I love him so much," she sobbed, in a surrender that was totally unlike her. "I never thought it would be like this. I can't bear it. I can't."

Halsey and I stood helpless before the storm. I would have tried to comfort her, but she had put me away, and there was something aloof in her grief, something new and strange. When at last her sorrow had subsided to the dry shaking sobs of a tired child, without raising her head she put out one groping hand.

"Aunt Ray!" she whispered. In a moment I was on my knees beside her, her arm around my neck and her cheek against my hair.

"Where am I in all this?" Halsey said suddenly, and tried to put his arms around us both. It was a welcome distraction, and Gertrude was soon herself again. The little storm had cleared the air. Nevertheless, my opinion remained unchanged. There was much to be cleared up before I would consent to any renewal of my acquaintance with John Bailey. And Halsey and Gertrude knew it, knowing me.

11

It was about half past eight when we left the dining room, and still engrossed with one subject, the failure of the bank and its attendant evils, Halsey and I went out into the grounds for a stroll. Gertrude followed us shortly. "The light was thickening," to appropriate Shakespeare's description of twilight, and once again the tree toads and the crickets were making night throb with their tiny life.

It was almost oppressively lonely in spite of its beauty, and I felt a sickening pang of homesickness for my city at night, for the clatter of horses' feet on cemented paving, for the lights, the voices, the sound of children playing. The country after dark oppresses me. The stars, quite eclipsed in the city by the electric lights, here become insistent, assertive. Whether I want to or not I find myself looking for the few I know by name and feeling ridiculously new and small by contrast, always an unpleasant sensation.

After Gertrude joined us we avoided any further mention of the murder. To Halsey as to me there was ever present, I am sure, the thought of our conversation of the night before. As we strolled back and forth along the drive Jamieson unexpectedly emerged from the shadow of the trees.

"Good evening," he said, managing to include Gertrude in his bow. Gertrude had never been even ordinarily courteous to him, and she nodded coldly. Halsey was more cordial, although we were all constrained enough. He and Gertrude went on together, leaving the detective to walk with me. As soon as they were out of earshot he turned to me.

"Do you know, Miss Innes," he said, "the deeper I go into this thing the more strange it seems to me. I am very sorry for Miss Gertrude. It looks as if Bailey, whom she has tried so hard to save, is guilty as hell. After her plucky fight for him it seems hard." I looked through the dusk to where Gertrude's light dinner dress gleamed among the trees. She *had* made a plucky fight, poor child. Whatever she might have been driven to do,' I could find nothing but a deep sympathy for her. If she had only come to me with the whole truth then!

"Miss Innes," Jamieson was saying, "in the last three days, have you seen any suspicious figures around the grounds? Any woman, for instance."

"No," I replied. "I have a houseful of maids who will bear watching, one and all. But there has been no strange woman near the house or Liddy would have seen her, you may be sure. She has a telescopic eye."

Jamieson looked thoughtful.

"It may not amount to anything," he said slowly. "It is difficult to get any perspective on things around here, because everyone down in the village is sure he saw the murderer, either before or since the crime. And half of them will stretch a point or two as to facts to be obliging. But the man who drives the taxi down there tells a story that may possibly prove to be important."

"I've heard it, I think. Was it the one the parlormaid brought up yesterday, about a ghost wringing its hands on the roof? Or perhaps it's the one the milk boy saw, a tramp washing a dirty shirt, presumably bloody, in the creek below the bridge?"

I could see the gleam of his teeth as he smiled.

"Neither," he said. "But Matthew Geist, which is our friend's name, claims that on Saturday night at nine-thirty a lady in black, with a heavy black veil over her face, as though she was in mourning–"

"I knew it would be a veiled lady," I broke in.

"A veiled lady," he persisted, "who was apparently young and beautiful, engaged his taxi and asked to be driven to Sunnyside. Near the gate however she made him stop, in spite of his remonstrances, saying she preferred to walk to the house. She paid him and he left her there. Now, Miss Innes, you had no such visitor, I believe?"

"None," I said decidedly.

"Geist thought it might be another member of the family, or even a new maid, as you had got a supply that day. But he said her getting out near the gate puzzled him. Anyhow, we have now one veiled lady who, with the ghostly intruder of Friday night, makes two assets I hardly know what to do with."

"It is mystifying," I admitted, "although I can think of one possible explanation. The path from the Greenwood Club to the village enters the road near the lodge gate. A woman who wished to reach the Country Club without being seen might choose such a method. There are plenty of women there."

I think this gave him something to ponder, for in a short time he said good night and left. But I myself was far from satisfied. I was determined on one thing. If my suspicions, for I had suspicions, were true, I would make my own investigations and Jamieson should learn only what was good for him to know.

We went back to the house and Gertrude, who was more like herself since her talk with Halsey, sat down at the mahogany desk in the lIving room to write a letter. Halsey prowled up and down the entire east wing, and after a little I joined him in the billiard room and together we went over the details of the discovery of the body.

The cardroom was quite dark. Where we sat in the billiard room only one of the side brackets was lighted and we spoke in subdued tones, as the hour and the subject seemed to demand. When I spoke of the figure Liddy and I had seen on the porch through the cardroom window Friday night Halsey sauntered into the darkened room, and together we stood there, much as Liddy and I had done that other night.

The window was the same grayish rectangle in the blackness as before. A few feet away in the hall was the spot where the body of Arnold Armstrong had been found. I was a bit nervous, and I put my hand on Halsey's sleeve. Suddenly from the top of the staircase above us came the sound of a cautious footstep. At first I was not sure, but Halsey's attitude told me he had heard and was listening. The step, slow, measured, infinitely cautious, was nearer now. Halsey tried to loosen my fingers, but I was in a paralysis of fright.

The swish of a body against the curving rail as if for guidance was plain enough, and now whoever it was had reached the foot of the staircase and had caught a glimpse of our rigid silhouettes against the billiard room doorway. Halsey threw me off then and strode forward.

"Who's there?" he called, and took a half dozen rapid strides toward the foot of the staircase. Then I heard him mutter something, there was the crash of a falling body and the slam of the outer door. I screamed, I think. Then I remember turning on the lights and finding Halsey, white with fury, trying to untangle himself from something warm and fleecy. He had cut his forehead on the lowest step of the stairs, and he was a ghastly sight. He flung the white object at me and jerking open the outer door raced outside into the darkness.

Gertrude had come on hearing the noise, and now we stood, staring at each other over—of all things on earth—a white silk and wool blanket, exquisitely fine! It was the most unghostly thing in the world, with its lavender border and its faint scent. Gertrude was the first to speak.

"What happened? Who had it?" she asked.

"Halsey tried to stop someone on the stairs and fell. Gertrude, that blanket isn't mine. I have never seen it before."

She held it up and looked at it. After that she went to the door to the veranda and threw it open. Perhaps a hundred feet from the house were two figures who moved slowly toward us as we looked. When they came within range of the light I recognized Halsey, and with him Mrs Watson, the housekeeper.

12

The most commonplace incident takes on a new appearance if the attendant circumstances are unusual. There was no reason on earth why Mrs Watson should not have carried a blanket down the east wing staircase, if she so desired. But to take a blanket down at eleven o'clock at night, with every precaution as to noise, and when discovered to fling it at Halsey and bolt–Halsey's word, and a good one– into the grounds, this made the incident more than significant.

They moved slowly across the lawn and up the steps. Halsey was talking quietly, and Mrs Watson was looking down and listening. She was a woman of a certain amount of dignity, most efficient, so far as I could tell, although Liddy would have found fault if she had dared. But just now Mrs Watson's face was an enigma. She was defiant, I think, under her mask of submission, and she still showed the effect of nervous shock.

"Mrs Watson," I said severely, "will you be so good as to explain this rather unusual occurrence?"

"I don't think it so unusual, Miss Innes." Her voice was deep and very clear, but just now it was somewhat shaky. "I was taking a blanket down to Thomas, who isn't well, and I used this staircase as being nearer the path to the lodge. When Mr Innes called and then rushed at me I was alarmed and flung the blanket at him."

Halsey was examining the cut on his forehead in a small mirror on the wall. It was not much of an injury, but it had bled freely and his appearance was rather terrifying.

"Thomas ill?" he said, over his shoulder. "Why, I thought I saw Thomas out there as you made that cyclonic break out the door and across the porch."

I could see that under pretense of examining his injury he was watching her through the mirror.

"Is this one of the servants' blankets, Mrs Watson?" I asked, holding up its luxurious folds to the light.

"Everything else is locked away," she replied. Which was true enough, no doubt. I had rented the house without bed furnishings.

"If Thomas is ill," Halsey said, "some member of the family ought to go down to see him. You needn't bother, Mrs Watson. I will take the blanket."

She drew herself up quickly as if in protest, but she found nothing to say. She stood smoothing the folds of her dead-black dress, her face as white as chalk above it. Then she seemed to make up her mind.

"Very well, Mr Innes," she said. "Perhaps you'd better go. I have done all I could."

She turned and went up to the circular staircase, moving slowly and with a certain dignity. Below, the three of us stared at one another across the intervening white blanket.

"Upon my word," Halsey broke out, "this place is a walking nightmare. I have the feeling that we three outsiders, who have paid our money for the privilege of staying in this spook factory, are living on the very top of things. We're on the lid, so to speak. Now and then we get a sight of the things inside, but we are not a part of them."

"Do you suppose," Gertrude asked doubtfully, "that she really meant that blanket for Thomas?"

"Thomas was standing beside that magnolia tree," Halsey replied, "when I ran after Mrs Watson. It's down to this, Aunt Ray. Rosie's basket and Mrs Watson's blanket can mean only one thing: there is somebody hiding or being hidden in the lodge. It wouldn't surprise me if we hold the key to the whole situation now. Anyhow, I'm going to the lodge to investigate."

Gertrude wanted to go too, but she looked so shaken that I insisted she should not. I sent for Liddy to help her to bed, and then Halsey and I started for the lodge. The grass was heavy with dew, and manlike Halsey chose the shortest way across the lawn. Halfway there, however, he stopped.

"We'd better go by the drive," he said. "This isn't a lawn; it's a field. Where's the gardener these days?"

"There isn't any," I said meekly. "We have been thankful enough so far to have our meals prepared and served and the beds made. The gardener who belongs here is working at the club."

"Remind me tomorrow to send out a man from town," he said. "I know the very fellow."

I record this scrap of conversation, just as I have tried to put down anything and everything that had a bearing on what followed, because the gardener Halsey sent the next day played an important part in the events of the next few weeks. Events which culminated as you know by stirring the country profoundly. At that time, however, I was busy trying to keep my feet dry, and paid little or no attention.

Along the drive I showed Halsey where I had found Rosie's basket with the bits of broken china piled inside. He was rather skeptical. Or at least he so pretended.

"Warner probably," he said when I had finished. "Began it as a joke on Rosie and ended by picking up the broken china out of the road, knowing it would play hob with the tires of the car." Which shows how near one can come to the truth and yet miss it altogether.

At the lodge everything was quiet. There was a light in the sitting room downstairs, and a faint gleam as if from a shaded lamp in one of the upper rooms. Halsey stopped and examined the place with calculating eyes.

"I don't know, Aunt Ray," he said dubiously; "this is hardly a woman's affair. If there's a scrap of any kind, you scram in a hurry." Which was Halsey's solicitous care for me put into vernacular.

"I shall stay right here," I said, and crossing the small veranda, now shaded and fragrant with honeysuckle, I hammered the knocker on the door.

Thomas opened the door himself, Thomas, fully dressed and in his customary health. I had the blanket over my arm.

"I brought the blanket, Thomas," I said; "I am sorry you are so ill." The old man stood staring at me and then at the blanket. His confusion under other circumstances would have been ludicrous.

"What! Not sick?" Halsey said from the step. "Thomas, I'm afraid you've been malingering."

Thomas seemed to have been debating something with himself. Now he stepped out on the porch and closed the door gently behind him.

"I reckon you bettah come in, Mis' Innes," he said, speaking cautiously. "It's got so I dunno what to do, and it's boun' to come out some time er ruther."

He threw the door open then and I stepped inside, Halsey close behind. In the sitting room the old Negro turned with quiet dignity to Halsey.

"You bettah sit down, suh," he said. "It's a place for a woman, sub." Things were not turning out the way Halsey expected. He sat down near the center table with his hands thrust in his pockets, and watched me as I followed Thomas up the narrow stairs. At the top a woman was standing, and a second glance showed me it was Rosie. She shrank back a little, but I said nothing. And then Thomas motioned to a partly open door, and I went in.

The lodge boasted three bedrooms upstairs, all comfortably furnished. In this one, the largest and airiest, a night lamp was burning, and by its light I could make out a plain white metal bed. A girl was asleep there, or in a half stupor, for she muttered something now and then. Rosie had taken her courage in her hands and on coming in had turned up the light. It was only then that I knew. Fever-flushed, ill as she was, I recognized Louise Armstrong.

I stood gazing down at her in a stupor of amazement. Louise here, hiding at the lodge, ill and alone! Rosie came up to the bed, smoothed the white counterpane, and turned down the light.

"I am afraid she's worse tonight," she ventured at last. I put my hand on the sick girl's forehead. It was burning with fever, and I turned to where Thomas lingered in the hallway.

"Will you tell me what you mean, Thomas Johnson, by not telling me this before?" I demanded indignantly.

Thomas quailed.

"Mis' Louise wouldn' let me," he said earnestly. "I wanted to. She ought to 'a' had a doctor the night she came, but she wouldn' hear to it. Is she–is she very bad, Mis' Innes?"

"Bad enough," I said coldly. "Send Mr Innes up."

Halsey came up the stairs slowly, looking rather interested and inclined to be amused. For a moment he could not see anything distinctly in the darkened room. He stopped, glanced at Rosie and at me, and then his eyes fell on the restless head on the pillow. I think he felt who it was before he really saw her, for he crossed the room in a couple of strides and bent over the bed.

"Louise!" he said softly. But she did not reply, and her eyes showed no recognition. Halsey was young, and illness was new to him. He straightened himself slowly, still watching her, and caught my arm.

"She's dying, Aunt Ray!" he said huskily. "Dying! Why, she doesn't know me!"

"Fudge!" I snapped, being apt to grow irritable when my sympathies are aroused. "She's doing nothing of the sort. And don't pinch my arm. If you want something to do, go and choke Thomas."

But at that moment Louise roused from her stupor to cough, and at the end of the paroxysm, as Rosie laid her back exhausted, she knew us. That was all Halsey wanted. To him consciousness was recovery. He dropped on his knees beside the bed, and tried to tell her she was all right, and that we would bring her around in a hurry, and how beautiful she looked–only to break down utterly and have to stop. And at that I came to my senses, and put him out.

"This instant!" I ordered, as he hesitated. "And send Rosie here."

He did not go far. He sat on the top step of the stairs, only leaving to telephone for a doctor and getting in everybody's way in his eagerness to fetch and carry. I got him away finally, by sending him to fix up the car as a sort of ambulance, in case the doctor would allow the sick girl to be moved. He sent Gertrude down to the lodge loaded with all manner of impossible things, including an armful of Turkish towels and a box of mustard plasters, and as the two girls had known each other somewhat before Louise brightened perceptibly when she saw her.

When the doctor from Englewood–the Casanova doctor, Doctor Walker, being away–had started for Sunnyside, and I had got Thomas to stop trying to explain what he did not understand himself, I had a long talk with the old man, and this is what I learned.

On the Saturday evening before, about ten o'clock, he had been reading in the sitting room downstairs when someone rapped at the door. The old man was alone and at first he was uncertain about opening the door. He did so finally, and was amazed at being confronted by Louise Armstrong. Thomas was an old family servant, having been with the present Mrs Armstrong since she was a child, and he was overwhelmed at seeing Louise.

He saw that she was excited and tired, and he drew her into the sitting room and made her sit down. After a while he went to the house and brought Mrs Watson, and they talked until late. The old man said Louise was in trouble, and seemed frightened. Mrs Watson made some tea and Louise drank it, but she made them both promise to keep her presence a secret. She had not known that Sunnyside was rented, and whatever her trouble was this complicated things. She seemed puzzled. Her stepfather and her mother were still in California. That was all she would say about them. Why she had run away no one could imagine. Arnold Armstrong was at the Greenwood Club and at last Thomas, not knowing what else to do, went over there along the path. It was almost midnight. Part way over he met Armstrong himself and brought him to the lodge. Mrs Watson had gone to the house for some bed linen, it having been arranged that under the circumstances Louise would be better at the lodge until morning. Arnold Armstrong and Louise had a long conference, during which he was heard to storm and become very violent. When he left it was after two. He had gone up to the house–Thomas did not know why–and at three o'clock he was shot at the foot of the circular staircase.

The following morning Louise had been ill. She had asked for Arnold, and was told he had left town. Thomas had not the moral courage to tell her of the crime. She refused a doctor, and shrank morbidly from having her presence known. Mrs Watson and Thomas had had their hands full, and at last Rosie had been enlisted to help them. She carried necessary provisions to the lodge, and helped to keep the secret.

Thomas told me quite frankly that he had been anxious to keep Louise's presence hidden for the reason that they had all seen Arnold Armstrong that night, and he himself for one was known to have had no very friendly feeling for the dead man. As to the reason for Louise's flight from California, or why she had not gone to the Fitzhughs' or to some of her people in town, he had no more information than I had. With the death of her stepfather and the prospect of the immediate return of the family things had become more and more impossible. I gathered that Thomas was as relieved as I at the turn events had taken. No, she did not know of either of the deaths in the family.

Taken all around, I had only substituted one mystery for another. If I knew now why Rosie had taken the basket of dishes, I did not know who had spoken to her and followed her along the drive. If I knew that Louise was in the lodge, I did not know why she was there. If I knew that Arnold Armstrong had spent some time there the night before he was murdered, I was still no nearer the solution of the crime.

Who was the midnight intruder who had so alarmed Liddy and myself? Who had fallen down the clothes chute? Was Jack Bailey a rascal or a victim of circumstance? Time was to answer all these things, but not too soon. Not soon enough.

13

The doctor from Englewood came very soon, and I went up with him to see the sick girl. Halsey had gone to supervise the fitting of the car with blankets and pillows, and Gertrude was opening and airing Louise's own rooms at the house. Her private sitting room, bedroom and dressing room were as they had been when we came. They occupied the end of the east wing, near the circular staircase, and we had not even opened them.

The girl herself was too ill to notice what was being done. When with the help of the doctor, who was a fatherly man with a family of girls at home, we got her to the house and up the stairs into bed, she dropped into a feverish sleep, which lasted until morning. Doctor Stewart–that was the Englewood doctor–stayed almost all night, giving the medicine himself and watching her closely. Afterwards he told me that she had had a narrow escape from pneumonia, arid that the cerebral symptoms had been rather alarming. I said I was glad it wasn't an "itis" of some kind, anyhow, and he smiled solemnly.

He left after breakfast, saying that he thought the worst of the danger was over, and that she must be kept very quiet.

"The shock of two deaths I suppose has done this," he remarked, picking up his case. "It has been most deplorable. She is certainly suffering from shock."

I set him right at once.

"She doesn't know of either one, doctor," I said. "So don't mention them to her."

He looked as surprised as a medical man ever does.

"I don't know the family," he said, preparing to get into his car. "Young Walker down in Casanova has been attending them. I understand he is going to marry this girl."

"You have been misinformed," I said stiffly. "Miss Armstrong is going to marry my nephew."

He smiled as he turned on the ignition.

"Young ladies are changeable these days," he said. "We thought the wedding was to occur soon. Well, I'll stop in this afternoon to see how she's getting along. Just keep her warm and quiet."

He drove away then, and I stood looking after him. He was a doctor of the old school, of the class of family practitioner that is fast dying out. A loyal and honorable gentleman who was at once physician and confidential adviser to his patients. When I was a girl we called in the doctor either when we had the measles or when mother's sister died in the far West. He cut out redundant tonsils and brought the babies with the same air of inspiring self-confidence. Nowadays it requires a different specialist for each of these occurrences. When babies cried, old Doctor Wainwright gave them peppermint and dropped warm sweet oil in their ears, with sublime faith that if it was not colic it was earache. When, at the end of a year, Father met him on the street and asked for a bill, he used to go home, estimate what his services were worth for that period, divide it in half—I don't think he kept any books—and send Father a statement in a cramped hand on a sheet of ruled white paper. He was an honored guest at all the weddings, christenings, and funerals—yes, funerals—for everyone knew he had done his best, and there was no gainsaying in the ways of Providence.

Ah well, Doctor Wainwright is gone, and I am an elderly woman with an increasing tendency to live in the past. The contrast between my old doctor at home and the Casanova doctor, Frank Walker, always rouses me to wrath and digression.

Some time about noon of that day, Wednesday, Mrs Ogden Fitzhugh telephoned me. I had the barest acquaintance with her, and that only because she managed to be put on the governing board of the Old Ladies' Home, where she ruins their digestions by sending them ice cream and cake on every holiday. Beyond that and her reputation at bridge, which was insufferably bad–she was the worst player at the bridge club–I knew little of her. It was she who had taken charge of Arnold Armstrong's funeral, however, and I went at once to the telephone.

"Yes," I said, "this is Miss Innes."

"Miss Innes," she said volubly, "I have just received a very Strange telegram from my cousin, Mrs Armstrong. Her husband died yesterday in California and– Wait, I will read you the message."

I knew what was coming, and I made up my mind at once. If Louise Armstrong had a good and sufficient reason for leaving her people and coming home, a reason moreover which kept her from going at once to Mrs Ogden Fitzhugh and that brought her to the lodge at Sunnyside instead, it was not my intention to betray her. Louise herself must notify her people. I do not justify myself now, but I was in a peculiar position toward the Armstrong family. I was connected most unpleasantly with a cold-blooded crime, and my niece and nephew were practically beggared, either directly or indirectly, through the head of the family.

Mrs Fitzhugh had found the message.

" 'Paul died yesterday. Heart disease,' " she read. " 'Wire at once if Louise is with you.' You see, Miss Innes, Louise must have started east and Fanny is alarmed about her."

"Yes," I said.

"Louise is not here," Mrs Fitzhugh went on, "and none of her friends–the few who are still in town–has seen her. I called you because Sunnyside was not rented when she went away, and Louise might have gone there."

"I am sorry, Mrs Fitzhugh, but I can't help you," I said, and was immediately filled with compunction. Suppose Louise grew worse? Who was I to play Providence in this case? The anxious mother certainly had a right to know that her daughter was in good hands. So I broke in on Mrs Fitzhugh's voluble excuses for disturbing me.

"Mrs Fitzhugh," I said. "I was going to let you think I knew nothing about Louise Armstrong, but I have changed my mind. Louise is here, with me." There was a clatter of ejaculations at the other end of the wire. "She is very ill and not able to be moved. Moreover, she is unable to see anyone. I wish you would wire her mother that she is with me, and tell her not to worry. No. I do not know why she came east."

"But, my dear Miss Innes–" Mrs Fitzhugh began. I cut in ruthlessly.

"I will send for you as soon as she can see you," I said. "No, she is not in a critical state now, but the doctor says she must have absolute quiet."

When I had hung up the receiver I sat down to think. So Louise had fled from her people in California, and had come east alone. It was not a new idea, but why had she done it? It occurred to me that Doctor Walker might be concerned in it, might possibly have bothered her with unwelcome attentions. But it seemed to me that Louise was hardly a girl to take refuge in flight under such circumstances. She had always been high-spirited, with the build and outspokenness of the outdoor girl. It would have been much more in keeping with Louise's character as I knew it to resent vigorously any unwelcome attentions from anyone. It was the suitor whom I should have expected to see in headlong flight, not the girl in the case.

The puzzle was no clearer at the end of a half hour. I picked up the morning papers, which were still full of the looting of the Traders' Bank, the interest at fever height again because of Paul Armstrong's death. The bank examiners were still working on the books and said nothing for publication. John Bailey had been released on bail. The body of Paul Armstrong would arrive Sunday and would be buried from the Armstrong town house. There were rumors that the dead man's estate had been a comparatively small one. But the last paragraph was the important one.

Walter P. Broadhurst of the Marine Bank had produced a

large number of American Traction bonds, which had been placed as security with the Marine Bank for a loan of one hundred and sixty thousand dollars, made to Paul Armstrong just before his California trip. The bonds were a part of the missing bonds from the Traders' Bank. While this involved the late president of the wrecked bank, to my mind it by rio means cleared its cashier.

The gardener mentioned by Halsey came out about two o'clock in the afternoon, and walked up from the station. I was favorably impressed by him. His references were good–he had been employed by the Brays until they went to Europe, and he looked young and vigorous. He asked for one assistant, and I was glad enough to get off so easily. He was a pleasant-faced young fellow, although rather shabbily dressed. He had black hair and blue eyes, and his name was Alexander Graham. I have been particular about Alex, because as I said before he played an important part later.

That afternoon I had a new insight into the character of the dead banker. I had my first conversation with Louise. She sent for me, and against my better judgment I went. There were so many things she could not be told, in her weakened condition, that I dreaded the interview. It was much easier than I expected, however, because she asked no questions.

Gertrude had gone to bed, having been up almost all night, and Halsey was absent on one of those mysterious absences of his that grew more and more frequent as time went on, until it culminated in the event of the night of June the tenth. Liddy was in attendance in the sickroom. There being little or nothing to do, she seemed to spend her time smoothing the wrinkles from the counterpane. Louise lay under a field of virgin white, folded back at an angle of geometrical exactness and necessitating a readjustment every time the sick girl turned.

Liddy heard my approach and came out to meet me. She seemed to be in a perpetual state of goose flesh, and she had got in the habit of looking past me when she talked, as if she saw things. It had the effect of making me look over my shoulder to see what she was staring at, and was intensely irritating.

"She's awake," Liddy said, looking uneasily down the circular staircase, which was beside me. "She was talkin' in her sleep something awful. About dead men and coffins."

"Liddy," I said sternly, "did you breathe a word about everything not being right here?"

Liddy's gaze had wandered to the door of the clothes chute, now bolted securely.

"Not a word," she said, "beyond asking her a question or two, which there was no harm in. She says there never was a ghost known here."

I glared at her, speechless, and closing the door into Louise's dressing room, to Liddy's great disappointment, I went on to the bedroom beyond.

Whatever Paul Armstrong had been, he had been lavish with his stepdaughter. Gertrude's rooms at home were always beautiful, but the three rooms in the east wing at Sunnyside, set apart for the daughter of the house, were much more expensive. From the walls to the rugs on the floor, from the furniture to the appointments of the bath with its pool sunk into the floor instead of the customary unlovely tub, everything was luxurious. In the bedroom Louise was watching for me. It was easy to see that she was much improved. The flush was going, and the peculiar gasping breathing and coughing of the night before were now a comfortable and easy respiration.

She held out her hand and I took it between both of mine.

"What can I say to you, Miss Innes?" she said slowly. "To have come like this–"

I thought she was going to break down, but she did not.

"You're not to think of anything but of getting well," I said, patting her hand. "When you're better I am going to scold you for not coming here at once. This is your home, my dear, and of all people in the world Halsey's old aunt ought to make you welcome."

She smiled a little, sadly, I thought.

"I ought not to see Halsey," she said. "Miss Innes, there are a great many things you will never understand, I'm afraid. I am an impostor on your sympathy, because I stay here and let you lavish care on me, and all the time I know you are going to despise me."

"Nonsense!" I said briskly. "Why, what would Halsey do to me if I even ventured such a thing? He is in such a state that if I dared to be anything but rapturous over you he would throw me out a window. He would be quite capable of it."

She seemed scarcely to hear me. She had eloquent brown eyes–the Inneses are fair, and are prone to a grayish-green optic that is better for use than appearance–and they seemed now to be clouded with trouble.

"Poor Halsey!" she said softly. "Miss Innes, I can't marry him, and I am afraid to tell him. I am a coward–a coward!"

I sat beside the bed and stared at her. She was too ill to argue with, and besides sick people take queer fancies.

"We'll talk about that when you are stronger," I said gently.

"But there are some things I must tell you," she insisted. "You must wonder how I came here, and why I stayed hidden at the lodge. Dear old Thomas has been almost crazy, Miss Innes. I didn't know that Sunnyside was rented. I knew my mother wanted to rent it, without telling my stepfather, but the news must have reached her after I left. When I started east I had only one idea, to be alone, to bury myself here. Then I must have taken a cold on the train."

"You came east in clothing suitable for California," I said, "and like all girls nowadays I don't suppose you wear much." But she was not listening.

"Miss Innes," she said, "has my stepbrother Arnold gone away?"

"What do you mean?" I asked, startled. But Louise was literal.

"He didn't come back to the lodge that night," she said, "and it was frightfully important that I should see him again."

"I believe he has gone away," I replied uncertainly. "Isn't it something we could attend to instead?"

But she shook her head. "I must do it myself," she said dully. "My mother must have rented Sunnyside without telling my stepfather, and—Miss Innes, did you ever hear of anyone being wretchedly poor in the midst of luxury? Did you ever long and long for money, money to use without question, money that no one would take you to task about? My mother and I have been surrounded for years with every indulgence, everything that would make a display. But we have never Lad any money, Miss Innes. That must have been why Mother rented this house. Mv stepfather pays our bills but that's all. It's the most maddening, humiliating existence in the world. I could take honest poverty better."

"Never mind," I said. "When you and Halsey are married you can be as honest as you like, and you will certainly be poor."

She looked puzzled at that. I had no time to explain, however, for Halsey came to the door at that moment and I could hear him coaxing Liddy.

"Shall I bring him in?" I asked Louise, uncertain what to do. The girl seemed to shrink back among her pillows at the sound of his voice. I was vaguely irritated with her. There are few young fellows like Halsey, straightforward, honest, and willing to sacrifice everything for the one woman. I knew one once, more than thirty years ago, who was like that. He died a long time ago, and sometimes I take out his picture with its cane and its queer silk hat and look at it. But of late years it has grown too painful. He is always young and I am an old woman. I would not bring him back if I could.

Perhaps it was some such memory that made me call out sharply.

"Come in, Halsey." And then I took my sewing and went into the dressing room beyond to play propriety. I did not try to hear what they said, but every word came through the open door with curious distinctness. Halsey had evidently gone over to the bed, and I suppose he kissed her. There was silence for a moment, as if words were superfluous things.

"I have been almost wild, darling".–Halsey's voice. "Why didn't you trust me and send for me before?"

"It was because I couldn't trust myself," she said in a low tone. "I'm too weak to struggle today. I've wanted you so dreadfully."

There was something I did not hear, then Halsey again.

"We could go away," he was saying. "What does it matter about anyone in the world but just the two of us? To be always together like this, hand in hand. Louise darling, don't tell me it isn't going to be. I won't believe you."

"You don't know; you don't know," she repeated dully. "Halsey, I care. You know that. But not enough to marry you the way things are."

"That is not true, Louise," he said sternly. "You can't look at me with your honest eyes and say that."

"I can't marry you," she repeated miserably. "It's bad enough, isn't it? Don't make it worse. Someday before long, you'll be glad."

"Then it's because you have never really cared for me." There were depths of hurt pride in his voice. "You saw how much I loved you, and you let me think you cared. That isn't like you, Louise. There is something you haven't told me. Is it because there is someone else?"

"Yes," almost inaudibly.

"Louise! Hell, I don't believe it."

"It's true," she said. "Halsey, you mustn't try to see me again. As soon as I can I am going away from here, where you are all so much kinder than I deserve. And whatever you hear about me try to think as well of me as you can. I'm going to marry another man. Just try not to hate me, won't you?"

I could hear him cross the room to the window. Then after a pause he went back to her. I could hardly Sit still. I wanted to go in and give her a good spanking, weak as she was. The dratted little fool!

"Then it's all over," he was saying with a long breath. "Everything goes into the discard. All the things we planned and hoped shot to bits. Well, I'm no crybaby, and I'll give up the minute you say you're in love with the other fellow."

"I haven't said that. But nevertheless I'm going to marry him."

I could hear Halsey's low triumphant laugh.

"To hell with him," he said. "Sweetheart, as long as you care for me I am not afraid. And you do care. I know it."

The wind slammed the door between the two rooms just then, and I could hear nothing more although I moved my chair quite close. After a discreet interval I went into the other room, and found Louise alone. She was staring at the cherub painted on the ceiling over the bed, and because she looked exhausted I did not disturb her.

14

We had discovered Louise at the lodge Tuesday night. It was Wednesday I had my interview with her. Thursday and Friday were uneventful, save as they marked improvement in our patient. Gertrude spent almost all the time with her, and the two had grown to be great friends. But certain things hung over me constantly: the coroner's inquest on the death of Arnold Armstrong, to be held Saturday, and the arrival of Mrs Armstrong and young Doctor Walker, bringing the body of the dead president of the Traders' Bank. We had not told Louise of either death.

Then, too, I was anxious about the children. With their mother's inheritance swept away in the wreck of the bank, and with their love affairs in a disastrous condition, things could scarcely be worse. Added to that the cook and Liddy had a flare-up over the proper way to make beef tea for Louise, and of course the cook left.

Mrs Watson had been glad enough, I think, to turn Louise over to our care, and Thomas went upstairs night and morning to greet his young mistress from the doorway. Poor Thomas! He had the faculty– found still in some old Negroes–of making his employer's interest his. It was always "we" with Thomas. I miss him sorely, pipe-smoking, obsequious, not over-reliable but kindly old man!

On Thursday Mr Harton, the Armstrongs' attorney, called up from town. He had been advised, he said, that Mrs Armstrong was coming east with her husband's body and would arrive Monday. He came with some hesitation, he went on, to the fact that he had been further instructed to ask me to relinquish my lease on Sunnyside, as it was Mrs Armstrong's desire to come directly there.

I was aghast.

"Leave?" I said. "Surely you are mistaken, Mr Harton. And come here! I should think, after what happened here only a few days ago, she would never wish to come back!"

"Nevertheless," he replied, "she is most anxious to come. This is what she says: 'Use every possible means to have Sunnyside vacated. Must go there at once.'"

"Mr Harton," I said testily, "I am not going to do anything of the kind. We have suffered enough at the hands of this family. I rented the house at an exorbitant figure and I have moved out here for the summer. My city home is dismantled and in the hands of decorators. I have been here one week, during which I have not had a single night of uninterrupted sleep, and I intend to stay until I have recuperated. Moreover, if Mr Armstrong died insolvent, as I believe was the case, his widow ought to be glad to be rid of so expensive a piece of property."

The lawyer cleared his throat.

"I am very sorry you have made this decision," he said. "Miss Innes, Mrs Fitzhugh tells me Louise Armstrong is with you."

"She is."

"Has she been informed of this–double bereavement?"

"Not yet," I said. "She has been very ill. Perhaps tonight she can be told."

"It is very sad. Very sad," he said. "I have a telegram for her, Mrs Hines. Shall I send it out?"

"Better open it and read it to me," I suggested. "If it's important that will save time."

There was a pause while Mr Harton opened the telegram. Then he read it slowly, judicially.

"'Watch for Nina Carrington. Home Monday. Signed F.L.W.'"

"Humph!" I grunted. "Watch for Nina Carrington. Home Monday. Very well, Mr Harton, I will tell her, whoever Nina is. But she is not in condition to watch for anyone."

"Well, Miss Innes, if you decide to–er–relinquish the lease, let me know," the lawyer said.

"I will not relinquish it," I replied, and I imagined his irritation from the way he hung up the receiver.

I wrote the telegram down word for word, afraid to trust my memory, and decided to ask Doctor Stewart how soon Louise might be told the truth. The closing of the Traders' Bank I considered unnecessary for her to know, but the death of her stepfather and stepbrother must be broken to her soon or she might hear it in some unexpected and shocking manner.

Doctor Stewart came about four o'clock, bringing his leather bag into the house with a great deal of care, and opening it at the foot of the stairs to show me a dozen big yellow eggs nesting among the bottles.

"Real eggs," he said proudly. "None of your anemic store eggs but the real thing, some of them still warm. Feel them! Eggnog for Louise."

He was beaming with satisfaction, and before he left he insisted on going back to the pantry and making an eggnog with his own hands. Somehow all the time he was doing it I had a vision of Doctor Willoughby, my nerve specialist in the city, trying to make an eggnog. I wondered if he ever prescribed anything so plebeian and so delicious. And while Doctor Stewart whisked the eggs he talked.

"I said to Mrs Stewart," he confided, a little red in the face from the exertion, "after I went home the other day, that you would think me an old gossip for saying what I did about Walker and Louise."

"Nothing of the sort," I protested.

"The fact is," he went on, evidently justifying himself, "I got that piece of information just as we get a lot of things, through the kitchen end of the house. Young Walker's chauffeur–Walker's more fashionable than I am, and he goes around the country in a big car–well, his chauffeur comes to see our maid, and he told her the whole thing. I thought it was probable, because Walker spent a lot of time up here last summer when the family was here. And besides Riggs, that's Walker's man, had a very pat little story about the doctor's building a house on this property at the foot of the hill. The sugar, please."

The eggnog was finished. Drop by drop the liquor had cooked the egg and now with a final whisk, a last toss in the shaker, it was ready, a symphony in gold and white. The doctor sniffed it,

"Real eggs, real milk, and a touch of real Kentucky bourbon," he said.

He insisted on carrying it up himself, but at the foot of the stairs he paused.

"Riggs said the plans were drawn for the house," he said, harking back to the former subject. "Drawn by Huston, the architect in town. So I naturally believed him."

When the doctor came down I was ready with a question.

"Doctor," I asked, "is there anyone in the neighborhood named Carrington? Nina Carrington?"

"Carrington?" He wrinkled his forehead. "Carrington? No, I don't remember any such family. There used to be Covingtons down the creek."

"The name was Carrington," I said, and the subject lapsed.

Gertrude and Halsey went for a long walk that afternoon, and Louise slept. Time hung heavy on my hands, and I did as I had fallen into a habit of doing lately–I sat down and thought things over. One result of my meditations was that I got up abruptly and went to the telephone. I had taken the most intense dislike to this Doctor Walker, whom I had never seen and who was being talked of in the countryside as the fiance of Louise Armstrong.

I knew Sam Houston well. There had been a time, when Sam was a good deal younger than he is now and before he married Anne Endicott, when I knew him even better. So now I felt no hesitation in calling him over the telephone. But when his office boy had given way to his confidential clerk, and that functionary had condescended to connect his employer's desk telephone, I was somewhat at a loss as to how to begin.

"Why, how are you, Rachel?" Sam said sonorously. "Going to build that house at Rock View?" It was a twenty-year-old joke of his.

"Sometime, perhaps," I said. "Just now I want to ask you a question about something that is none of my business."

"I see you haven't changed an iota in a quarter of a century." This was intended to be another jest. "Ask ahead. Everything but my domestic affairs is at your service."

"Try to be serious," I said. "And tell me this: has your firm made any plans for a house recently, for a Doctor Walker at Casanova?"

"Yes, we have. Why?"

"Where was it to be built? I have a reason for asking."

"It was to be on the Armstrong place. Mr Armstrong himself consulted me, and the inference was–in fact, I'm quite certain–the house was to be occupied by Mr Armstrong's daughter, who was engaged to marry Walker."

When Sam had inquired for the different members of my family and had finally rung off I was certain of one thing. Louise Armstrong was in love with Halsey, and the man she was going to marry was Doctor Walker. Moreover, this decision was not new. Marriage had been contemplated for some time. There must certainly be some explanation, but what was it?

That day I repeated to Louise the telegram Mr Harton had opened. She seemed to understand, but an unhappier face I have never seen. She looked like a criminal whose reprieve is over, with the day of execution approaching.

15

The next day, Friday, Gertrude broke the news of her step-father's death to Louise. She did it as gently as she could, telling her first that he was very ill and finally that he was dead. Louise received the news in the most unexpected manner, and when Gertrude came out to tell me how she had stood it I think she was almost shocked.

"She just lay and stared at me, Aunt Ray," she said. "Do you know, I believe she's glad! And she's too honest to pretend anything else. What sort of man was Paul Armstrong anyhow?"

"He was a bully as well as a rascal, Gertrude," I said. "But I am convinced of one thing, Louise will send for Halsey now, and they will make it all up."

For Louise had steadily refused to see Halsey all that day, and the boy was frantic.

We had a quiet hour, Halsey and I, that evening, and I told him several things: about the request that we give up the lease to Sunnyside, about the telegram to Louise, about the rumors of an approaching marriage between the girl and Doctor Walker, and last of all about my own interview with her the day before.

He sat back in a big chair, with his face in the shadow, and my heart fairly ached for him. He was so big and so boyish. When I had finished he drew a long breath.

"Whatever Louise does," he said, "nothing will convince me that she doesn't care for me. And up to two months ago, when she and her mother went west, I was the happiest fellow on earth. Then something made a difference. She wrote me that her people were opposed to the marriage, that her feeling for me was what it had always been, but that something had happened which had changed her ideas as to the future. I was not to write until she wrote me, and whatever occurred I was to think the best I could of her. It sounded like a puzzle. When I saw her yesterday, it was the same thing, only perhaps worse."

"Halsey," I asked, "have you any idea of the nature of the interview between Louise and Arnold the night he was murdered?"

"It was stormy. Thomas says once or twice he almost broke into the room, he was so scared for Louise."

"Another thing," I said. "Have you ever heard Louise mention a woman named Carrington, Nina Carrington?"

"Never," he said positively.

Try as we would, our thoughts always came back to that fatal Saturday night, and the murder. Every conversational path led to it, and we all felt that Jamieson was tightening the threads of evidence around John Bailey. The detective's absence was hardly reassuring. He must have had something to work on in town, or he would have returned.

The papers reported that the cashier of the Traders' Bank was ill in his apartment at the Knickerbocker, a situation not surprising, everything considered. The guilt of the defunct president was no longer in doubt. The missing bonds had been advertised and some of them discovered. In every instance they had been used as collateral for large loans, and the belief was current that not less than a million and a half dollars had been realized. Practically everyone connected with the bank had been placed under arrest and then released on heavy bond.

Was Armstrong alone in his guilt, or was the cashier his accomplice? Where was the money? The estate of the dead man was comparatively small, a city house on a fashionable street, Sunnyside, which was largely mortgaged, an insurance policy of fifty thousand dollars, and some personal property–this was all. The rest lost in speculation probably, the papers said. There was one thing that looked uncomfortable for Jack Bailey. He and Paul Armstrong together had promoted a railroad company in New Mexico, and it was rumored that together they had sunk large sums of money there.

The business alliance between the two men added to the belief that Bailey knew something of the looting. His unexplained absence from the bank on Monday lent color to the suspicion against him. The strange thing seemed to be his surrendering himself as he had. To me it seemed the shrewd calculation of a clever crook. I was not actively antagonistic to Gertrude's lover, but I meant to be convinced, one way or the other. I took no one on faith.

That night the Sunnyside ghost began to walk again. Liddy had been sleeping in Louise's dressing room on a couch, and the approach of dusk was a signal for her to barricade the entire suite. Situated as it was beyond the circular staircase nothing but an extremity of excitement would have made her pass it after dark. I confess myself that the place seemed to me to have a sinister appearance; but we kept that wing well lighted, and until the lights went out at midnight it was really cheerful, if one did not know its history.

On Friday night then I had gone to bed, resolved to go at once to sleep. Thoughts that insisted on obtruding themselves I pushed resolutely to the back of my mind, and I systematically relaxed every muscle. I fell asleep soon, and was dreaming that Doctor Walker was building his new house immediately in front of my windows. I could hear the thump-thump of the hammers, and finally I awakened to a knowledge that somebody was pounding on my door.

I was up at once and with the sound of my footstep on the floor the low knocking ceased, to be followed immediately by sibilant whispering through the keyhole.

"Miss Rachel! Miss Rachel!" somebody was saying, over and over.

"Is that you, Liddy?" I asked, my hand on the knob.

"For the love of mercy let me in!" she said in a low tone.

She must have been leaning against the door, for when I opened it she fell in. She was greenish-white, and had a red-and-black barred flannel petticoat over her shoulders.

"Listen," she said, standing in the middle of the floor and holding on to me. "Oh, Miss Rachel, it's the ghost of that dead man hammering to get in!"

Sure enough, there was a dull thud–thud–thud from some place near. It was muffled. One felt rather than heard it, and it was impossible to locate. One moment it seemed to come, three taps and a pause, from the floor under us. The next, thud–thud–thud, it came apparently from the wall.

"It's not a ghost," I said decidedly. "If it was a ghost it wouldn't rap: it would come through the keyhole." Liddy looked at the keyhole. "But it sounds very much as though someone is trying to break into the house."

Liddy was shivering violently. I told her to get me my slippers and she brought me a pair of kid gloves, so I found my things myself and prepared to call Halsey. As before, the night alarm had found the electric lights gone. The hall save for its night lamp was in darkness as I went across to Halsey's room, and it was a relief to find him there, very sound asleep and with his door unlocked.

"Wake up, Halsey," I said, shaking him.

He stirred a little. Liddy was half in and half out the door, afraid as usual to be left alone and not quite daring to enter. Her scruples seemed to fade all at once, however. She gave a suppressed yell, bolted into the room, and stood tightly clutching the footboard of the bed. Halsey was gradually waking.

"I've seen it," Liddy wailed. "A woman in white down the hall!"

I paid no attention.

"Halsey," I persevered, "someone is breaking into the house! For heaven's sake, get up."

"It isn't our house," he said sleepily. And then he roused to the exigency of the occasion. "All right, Ray," he said, still yawning. "If you'll let me get into something–"

It was all I could do to get Liddy out of the room. The demands of the occasion had no influence on her. She had seen the ghost, she persisted, and she wasn't going into the hail. But I got her over to my room at last, more dead than alive, and made her lie down on the bed.

The tappings which seemed to have ceased for a while had commenced again but they were fainter. Halsey came over in a few minutes, and stood listening and trying to locate the sound.

"Persistent devil, isn't he?" he said. "Where's my gun, Aunt Rachel?" As will have been noticed, both Gertrude and Halsey seldom call me "aunt" at all–I am Ray or Rachel, but in real emergency I become Aunt Rachel. This was such a time. And I got the revolver in a hurry. While I was locating it he saw Liddy and realized that Louise was alone.

"You let me attend to this fellow, whoever it is, Aunt Rachel, and go to Louise, will you? She may be awake and having a fit."

So in spite of her protests I left Liddy alone and went back to the east wing. Perhaps I went a little faster than usual past tl?e yawning blackness of the circular staircase, and I could hear Halsey creaking cautiously down the main staircase. The rapping, or pounding, had ceased, and the silence was almost painful. Then suddenly from apparently under my very feet there rose a woman's scream, a cry of terror that broke off as suddenly as it came. I stood frozen and still. Every drop of blood in my body seemed to leave the surface and gather around my heart. In the dead silence that followed, it throbbed as if it would burst. More dead than alive I stumbled into Louise's bedroom.

She was not there.

16

I stood looking at the empty bed. The coverings had been thrown back, and Louise's silk dressing gown was gone from the foot, where it had been lying. The night lamp burned dimly, revealing the emptiness of the place. I picked it up, but my hand shook so that I put it down again, and got somehow to the door.

There were voices in the hail and Gertrude came running toward me. "What is it?" she cried. "What was that noise? Where is Louise?"

"She is not in her room," I said stupidly. "I think she must have been the one who screamed."

Liddy had joined us now, carrying a light. We stood huddled together at the head of the circular staircase, looking down into its shadows. There was nothing to be seen, and it was absolutely quiet down there. Then we heard Halsey running up the main staircase. He came quickly down the hall to where we were standing.

"There's no sign of anyone trying to get in," he said. "I thought I heard someone shriek. Who was it?"

Our stricken faces told him the truth.

"Someone did scream down there," I said. "And Louise is not in her room."

With a jerk Halsey took the light from Liddy and ran down the circular staircase. I followed him, more slowly. My legs seemed to be paralyzed, for I could scarcely walk. At the foot of the stairs Halsey gave an exclamation and put down the light.

"Aunt Rachel!" he called sharply.

At the foot of the staircase, huddled in a heap with her head on the lower step, was Louise Armstrong. She lay limp and white, her dressing gown dragging loose from one sleeve of her pajamas, and her heavy dark hair spread above her as if she had slipped down.

She was not dead. Halsey put her down on the floor and began to rub her cold hands, while Gertrude and Liddy ran for stimulants. As for me, I sat there at the foot of that ghostly staircase–sat, because my knees wouldn't hold me–and wondered where it would all end. Louise was still unconscious but she was breathing better, and I suggested that we get her back to bed before she came to. There was something grisly and horrible to me, seeing her there in almost the same attitude and in the same place where we had found her brother's body. And to add to the similarity, just then the hail clock, far off, struck faintly three o'clock.

It was four before Louise was able to talk, and the first rays of dawn were coming through her windows, which faced the east, before she could tell us coherently what had occurred. I give it as she told it. She lay propped up in bed, and Halsey sat beside her and held her hand while she talked.

"I was not sleeping well," she began, "partly, I think, because I had slept during the afternoon. Liddy brought me some hot milk at ten o'clock and I slept until twelve. Then I wakened and I got to thinking about things and worrying, so I could not go to sleep.

"I was wondering why I had not heard from Arnold since I saw him that night at the lodge. I was afraid he was ill, because he was to have done something for me, and he had not come back. It must have been three when I heard someone rapping down below. I sat up and listened to be quite sure, and the rapping kept up. It was cautious, and I was about to call Liddy. Then suddenly I thought I knew what it was. The east entrance and the circular staircase were always used by Arnold when he was out late, and sometimes when he forgot his key he would rap and I would go down and let him in.

"I thought he had come back to see me–I didn't think about the time, for his hours were always erratic. But I was afraid I was too weak to get down the stairs. The knocking kept up, and just as I was about to call Liddy she ran through the room and out into the hall. I got up then, feeling weak and dizzy, and put on my dressing gown. If it was Arnold, I knew I had to see him.

"It was very dark everywhere, but of course I knew my way. I felt along for the stair rail and went down as quickly as I could. The knocking had stopped, and I was afraid I was too late. I got to the foot of the staircase and over to the door onto the east veranda. I had never thought of anything but that it was Arnold, until I got to the door. It was unlocked and opened about an inch, and everything was black. It was perfectly dark outside, and I felt queer and shaky. Then I thought perhaps Arnold had used his key. He did strange things sometimes when he had been drinking, so I turned around. Just as I reached the foot of the staircase I thought I heard someone coming. My nerves were going anyhow there in the dark, and I could scarcely stand. I got up as far as the third or fourth step. Then I felt that some one was coming toward me on the staircase. The next instant a hand met mine on the stair rail, and someone brushed past me. That was when I screamed. Then I must have fainted."

That was Louise's story. There could be no doubt of its truth, and the thing that made it inexpressibly awful to me was that the poor girl had crept down to answer the summons of a brother who would never need her kindly offices again. Twice now without apparent reason someone had entered the house by means of the east entrance, had apparently gone his way unhindered through the house, and gone out again as he had entered. Had this unknown visitor been there a third time, the night Arnold Armstrong was murdered? Or a fourth, the time Jamieson had locked someone in the clothes chute?

Sleep was impossible, I think, for any of us. We dispersed finally to bathe and dress, leaving Louise little the worse for her experience. But I determined that before the day was over she must know the true state of affairs. Another decision I made, and I put it into execution immediately after breakfast. I had one of the unused bedrooms in the east wing, back along the small corridor, prepared for occupancy; and from that time on Alex, the gardener, slept there. One man in that barn of a house was an absurdity, with things happening all the time, and I must say that Alex was as unobjectionable as anyone could possibly have been.

The next morning Halsey and I made an exhaustive examination of the circular staircase, the small entry at its foot, and the cardroom opening from it. There was no evidence of anything unusual the night before, and had we not ourselves heard the rapping noises I should have felt that Louise's imagination had run away with her. The outer door was closed and locked, and the staircase curved above us, for all the world like any other staircase of the sort.

Halsey, who had never taken seriously my account of the night Liddy and I were there alone, was grave enough now. He examined the paneling of the wainscoting above and below the stairs, looking for a secret door, and suddenly there flashed into my mind the recollection of a scrap of paper that Jamieson had found among Arnold Armstrong's effects. As nearly as possible I repeated its contents to him while Halsey took them down in a notebook.

"I wish you had told me that before," he said, as he put the memorandum carefully away. However, we found nothing at all in the house, and I expected little from any examination of the porch and grounds. But as we opened the outer door something fell into the entry with a clatter. It was a cue from the billiard room.

Halsey picked it up with an exclamation.

"That's careless enough," he said. "Some of the servants must have been amusing themselves."

I was far from convinced. Not one of the servants would go into that wing at night unless driven by dire necessity. And a billiard cue! As a weapon of either offense or defense it was an absurdity, unless one accepted Liddy's hypothesis of a ghost. Even then, as Halsey pointed out, a billiard-playing ghost would be a very modern evolution of an ancient institution.

That afternoon Gertrude, Halsey and I attended the coroner's inquest in town. Doctor Stewart had been summoned also, it transpiring that in that early Sunday morning, when Gertrude and I had gone to our rooms, he had been called to view the body. We went, the four of us, in the car, preferring the execrable roads to the matinee train with half of Casanova staring at us. And on the way we decided to say nothing about Louise and her interview with her stepbrother the night he died. The girl was in trouble enough as it was.

17

In giving the gist of what happened at the inquest, I have only one excuse, to recall to the reader the events of the night of Arnold Armstrong's murder. Many things had occurred which were not brought out at the inquest and some things were told there which were new to me. Altogether it was a gloomy affair, and the six men in the corner who constituted the coroner's jury were evidently the merest puppets in the hands of that all-powerful gentleman, the coroner.

Gertrude and I sat well back, for there were a number of people we knew: Barbara Fitzhugh, in extravagant mourning–she always went into black on the slightest provocation, because it was becoming–and Mr Jarvis, the man who had come over from the Greenwood Club the night of the murder. Mr Harton was there, too, looking impatient as the inquest dragged, but alive to every particle of evidence. From a corner Jamieson was watching the proceedings intently.

Doctor Stewart was called first. His evidence was told briefly, and amounted to this: on the Sunday morning previous, at a quarter before five, he had been called to the telephone. The message was from a Mr Jarvis, who asked him to come at once to Sunnyside, as there had been an accident there and Mr Arnold Armstrong had been shot. He had dressed hastily, gathered up some instruments, and driven to Sunnyside.

He was met by Mr Jarvis, who took him at once to the east wing. There, just as he had fallen, was the body of Arnold Armstrong. There was no need of the instruments. The man was dead. In answer to the coroner's question he said the body had not been moved, save to turn it over. It lay at the foot of the circular staircase. Yes, he believed

death had been instantaneous. The body was still somewhat warm and rigor mortis had not set in. It occurred late
in cases of sudden death. No, he believed the probability of
suicide might be eliminated; the wounds could have been
self-inflicted, but with difficulty, and no weapon had been
found.

The doctor's examination was over, but he hesitated and
cleared his throat.

"Mr Coroner," he said. "at the risk of taking up valuable
time, I would like to speak of an incident that may or may
not throw some light on this matter."

The audience was alert at once.

"Kindly proceed, doctor," the coroner said.

"My home is in Englewood, two miles from Casanova,"
the doctor began. "In the absence of Doctor Walker a number of Casanova people have been consulting me. A month
ago–five weeks, to be exact–a woman whom I had never
seen came to my office. She was in deep mourning and kept
her veil down, and she brought for examination a child, a
boy of six. The little fellow was ill. It looked like typhoid,
and the mother was frantic. She wanted a permit to admit the youngster to the Children's Hospital in town here,
where I am a member of the staff, and I gave her one. The
incident would have escaped me, but for a curious thing.
Two days before Mr Armstrong was shot I was sent for to
go to the Country Club. Someone had been struck with a
golf ball that had gone wild. It was late when I left–I was on
foot, and about a mile from the club on the Claysburg road
I met two people. They were disputing violently, and I had
no difficulty in recognizing Mr Armstrong. The woman, beyond doubt, was the one who had consulted me about the
child."

At this hint of scandal Mrs Ogden Fitzhugh sat up very
straight. Jamieson was looking slightly skeptical, and the
coroner made a note.

"The Children's Hospital, you say, doctor?" he asked.

"Yes. But the child, who entered as Lucien Wallace, was taken away by his mother two weeks ago. I have tried to trace them and failed."

All at once I remembered the telegram sent to Louise by someone signed F.L.W., presumably Doctor Walker. Could this veiled woman be the Nina Carrington of the message? But it was only idle speculation. I had no way of finding out, and the inquest was proceeding.

The report of the coroner's physician came next. The post-mortem examination showed that the bullet had entered the chest in the fourth left intercostal space and had taken an oblique course downward and backward, piercing both heart and lungs. The left lung was collapsed, and the exit point of the ball had been found in the muscles of the back to the left of the spinal column. It was improbable that such a wound had been self-inflicted, and its oblique downward course pointed to the fact that the shot had been fired from above. In other words, as the murdered man had been found dead at the foot of a staircase, it was probable that the shot had been fired by someone higher up on the stairs. There were no marks of powder. The bullet, a thirty-eight caliber, had been found in the dead man's clothing and was shown to the jury.

Mr Jarvis was called next, but his testimony amounted to little. He had been summoned by telephone to Sunnyside, had come over at once with the steward and Mr Winthrop, at present out of town. They had been admitted by the housekeeper, and had found the body lying at the foot of the staircase. He had made a search for a weapon, but there was none around. The outer entry door in the east wing had been unfastened and was open about an inch.

I had been growing more and more nervous. When the coroner called Mr John Bailey, the room was filled with suppressed excitement. Jamieson went forward and spoke a few words to the coroner, who nodded. Then Halsey was called.

"Mr Innes," the coroner said, "will you tell under what

circumstances you saw Mr Arnold Armstrong the night he died?"

"I saw him first at the Country Club," Halsey said quietly. He was rather pale, but very composed. "I stopped there with my automobile for gasoline. Mr Armstrong had been playing cards. When I saw him there, he was coming out of the cardroom, talking to John Bailey."

"The nature of the discussion–was it amicable?"

Halsey hesitated.

"They were having a dispute," he said. "I asked Mr Bailey to leave the club with me and come to Sunnyside over Sunday.".

"Isn't it a fact, Mr Innes, that you took Mr Bailey away from the clubhouse because you were afraid there would be blows?"

"The situation was unpleasant," Halsey said evasively.

"At that time had you any suspicion that the Traders' Bank had been wrecked?"

"No."

"What occurred next?"

"Mr Bailey and I talked in the billiard room until two-thirty."

"And Mr Arnold Armstrong came there, while you were talking?"

"Yes. He came just before half past two. He rapped at the east door, and I admitted him."

The silence in the room was intense. Jamieson's eyes never left Halsey's face.

"Will you tell us the nature of his errand?"

"He brought a telegram which had come to the club for Mr Bailey."

"He was sober?"

"Perfectly, at that time. Not earlier."

"Was not his apparent friendliness a change from his former attitude?"

"Yes. I didn't understand it."

"How long did he stay?"

"About five minutes. Then he left, by the east entrance."

"What occurred then?"

"We talked for a few minutes, discussing a plan Mr Bailey had in mind. Then I went to the stables where I kept my car, and got it out."

"Leaving Mr Bailey alone in the billiard room?"

Halsey hesitated. "My sister was there." Mrs Ogden Fitzhugh had the audacity to turn and stare at Gertrude. "And then?"

"I took the car along the lower road, not to disturb the household. Mr Bailey came down across the lawn, through the hedge, and got into the car on the road."

"Then you know nothing of Mr Armstrong's movements after he left the house?"

"Nothing. I read of his death Monday evening for the first time."

"Mr Bailey did not see him on his way across the lawn?"

"I think not. If he had seen him he would have spoken of it."

"Thank you. That is all. Miss Gertrude Innes."

Gertrude's replies were fully as concise as Halsey's. Mrs Fitzhugh subjected her to a sharp inspection, commencing with her hat and ending with her shoes. I flatter myself she found nothing wrong with either her clothes or her manner, but poor Gertrude's testimony was the reverse of comforting.

She had been summoned, she said, by her brother after Mr Armstrong had gone. She had waited in the billiard room with Mr Bailey until the automobile was ready. Then she had locked the door at the foot of the staircase, and taking a lamp had accompanied Mr Bailey to the main entrance of the house, and had watched him cross the lawn. Instead of going at once to her room she had gone back to the billiard room for something which had been left there. The cardroom and billiard room were in darkness.

She had groped around, found the article she was looking for, and was on the point of returning to her room when she had heard some-one fumbling at the east outer door. She had thought it was probably her brother, and had been about to go to the door when she heard it open. Almost immediately there was a shot, and she had run panic-stricken through the drawing room and had roused the house.

"You heard no other sound?" the coroner asked. "There was no one with Mr Armstrong when he entered?"

"It was perfectly dark. There were no voices and I heard nothing. There was just the opening of the door, the shot, and the sound of somebody falling."

"Then, while you went through the drawing room and upstairs to alarm the household, the criminal, whoever it was, could have escaped by the east door?"

"Yes."

"Thank you. That will do."

I flatter myself that the coroner got little enough out of me. I saw Jamieson smiling to himself, and the coroner gave me up after a time. I admitted I had found the body, said I had not known who it was until Mr Jarvis told me, and ended by looking up at Barbara Fitzhugh and saying that in renting the house I had not expected to be involved in any family scandal. At which she turned purple.

The verdict was that Arnold Armstrong had met his death at the hands of a person or persons unknown, and we all prepared to leave. Barbara Fitzhugh flounced out without waiting to speak to me, but Mr Harton came, as I knew he would.

"You have decided to give up the house, I hope, Miss Innes," he said. "Mrs Armstrong has wired me again."

"I am not going to give it up," I maintained, "until I understand some things that are puzzling me. The day the murderer is discovered I will leave."

"Then, judging by what I have heard, you will be back in the city very soon," he said. And I knew that he suspected the discredited cashier of the Traders' Bank.

Jamieson came up to me as I was about to leave the coroner's office.

"How is your patient?" he asked, with his odd little smile.

"I have no patient," I replied, startled.

"I will put it in a different way, then. How is Miss Armstrong?"

"She–she is doing very well," I stammered.

"Good," cheerfully. "And our ghost? Is it laid?"

"Mr Jamieson," I said suddenly, "I wish you would do one thing. I wish you would come to Sunnyside and spend a few days there. The ghost is not laid. I want you to spend one night at least watching the circular staircase. The murder of Arnold Armstrong was a beginning, not an end, I'm sure of that."

He looked serious.

" Perhaps I can do it," he said. "I have been doing something else, but–well, I'll come out tonight."

We were very silent during the trip back to Sunnyside. I watched Gertrude closely and somewhat sadly. To me there was one glaring flaw in her story, and it seemed to stand out for everyone to see. Arnold Armstrong had had no key, and yet she said she had locked the east door. He must have been admitted from within the house: over and over I repeated it to myself.

That night, as gently as I could, I told Louise the story of her step-brother's death. She sat in her big pillow-filled chair and heard me through without interruption. It was clear that she was shocked beyond words, but if I had hoped to learn anything from her expression, I had failed. She was as much in the dark as we were.

18

My asking the detective out to Sunnyside raised an unexpected storm of protest from Gertrude and Halsey. I was not prepared for it, and I scarcely knew how to account for it. To me Jamieson was far less formidable under my eyes where I knew what he was doing than he was off in the city, twisting circumstances and motives to suit himself, and learning what he wished to know about events at Sunnyside in some occult way. I was glad enough to have him there, when excitements began to come thick and fast.

A new element was about to enter into affairs. Monday, or Tuesday at the latest, would find Doctor Walker back in his green-and-white house in the village, and Louise's attitude to him in the immediate future would signify Halsey's happiness or wretchedness, as it might turn out. Then too the return of her mother would mean of course that she would have to leave us, and I had become greatly attached to her.

From the day Jamieson came to Sunnyside there was a subtle change in Gertrude's manner to me. It was elusive, difficult to analyze, but it was there. She was no longer frank with me, although I think her affection never wavered. At the time I laid the change to the fact that I had forbidden all communication with John Bailey, and had refused to acknowledge any engagement between the two. Gertrude spent much of her time wandering through the grounds, or taking long cross-country walks. Halsey played golf at the Country Club day after day, and after Louise left, as she did the following week, Jamieson and I were much together. He played a fair game of cribbage, but he cheated at solitaire.

The night the detective arrived, Saturday, I had a talk with him. I told him of the experience Louise Armstrong had had the night before, on the circular staircase, and about the man who had so frightened Rosie on the drive. I saw he thought the information was important, and to my suggestion that we put an additional lock on the east wing door he opposed a strong negative.

"I think it probable," he said, "that our visitor will be back again, and the thing to do is to leave things exactly as they are, to avoid rousing suspicion. Then I can watch for at least a part of each night and probably Mr Innes will help us out. I would say as little to Thomas as possible. The old man knows more than he's willing to admit."

I suggested that Alex, the gardener, would probably be willing to help, and Jamieson undertook to make the arrangement. For one night, however, he preferred to watch alone. Apparently nothing occurred. The detective sat in absolute darkness on the lower step of the stairs, dozing, he said afterwards, now and then. Nothing could pass him in either direction, and the door in the morning remained as securely fastened as it had been the night before. And yet one of the most inexplicable occurrences of the whole affair took place that very night.

Liddy came to my room on Sunday morning with a face as long as the moral law. She laid out my things as usual, but I missed her customary garrulousness. I was not regaled with the new cook's extravagance as to eggs, and she even forbore to mention "that Jamieson," on whose arrival she had looked with silent disfavor.

"What's the matter, Liddy?" I asked at last. "Didn't you sleep last night?"

"No, ma'am," she said stiffly.

"Did you have two cups of coffee with your dinner?" I inquired.

"No, ma'am," indignantly.

I sat up and almost upset my hot water. I always take a cup of hot water with a pinch of salt before I get up. It tones the stomach.

"Liddy Allen," I said, "stop combing that switch and tell me what is wrong with you."

Liddy heaved a sigh.

"Girl and woman," she said, "I've been with you twenty-five years, Miss Rachel, through good temper and bad–" The idea! and what I have taken from her in the way of sulks!–"but I guess I can't stand it any longer. My trunk's packed."

"Who packed it?" I asked, expecting from her tone to be told she had wakened to find it done by some ghostly hand.

"I did; Miss Rachel, you won't believe me when I tell you this house is haunted. Who was it fell down the clothes chute? Who was it scared Miss Louise almost into her grave?"

"I'm doing my best to find out," I said. "What in the world are you driving at?"

She drew a long breath. "There is a hole in the trunk-room wall, dug out since last night. It's big enough to put your head in, and the plaster's all over the place."

"Nonsense!" I said. "Plaster is always falling."

But Liddy merely looked superior.

"Just ask Alex," she said. "When he put the new cook's trunk there last night the wall was as smooth as this. This morning it's dug out, and there's plaster on the cook's trunk. Miss Rachel, you can get a dozen detectives and put one on every stair in the house, and you'll never catch anything. There's some things you can't handcuff."

Liddy was right. As soon as I could I went up to the trunk room, which was directly over my bedroom. The plan of the upper story of the house was like that of the second floor, generally speaking. But one end–over the east wing–had been left only roughly finished, the intention having been to convert it into a ballroom; and various storerooms, including a large airy linen room, opened from a long corridor like that on the second floor. And in the trunk room, as Liddy had said, was a fresh break in the plaster.

Not only in the plaster, but through the lathing the aperture extended. I reached into the opening, and three feet away, perhaps, I could touch the bricks of the partition wall. For some reason the architect in building the house had left a space there that struck me, even in the surprise of the discovery, as a considerable waste of room.

"You're sure the hole wasn't here yesterday?" I asked Liddy, whose expression was a mixture of satisfaction and alarm. In answer she pointed to the new cook's trunk–that necessary adjunct of the migratory domestic. The top was covered with fine white plaster, as was the floor. But there were no large pieces of mortar lying around, no bits of lathing. When I mentioned this to Liddy she merely raised her eyebrows. Being quite confident that the gap was of unholy origin, she did not concern herself with such trifles as a bit of mortar and lath. No doubt they were even then heaped neatly on a gravestone in the Casanova churchyard!

I brought Jamieson up to see the hole in the wall, directly after breakfast. His expression was very odd when he looked at it, and the first thing he did was to try to discover what object, if any, such a hole could have. He got a piece of candle, and by enlarging the aperture a little was able to examine what lay beyond. The result was nil. The trunk room, although heated by steam heat like the rest of the house, boasted of a fireplace and mantel as well. The opening had been made between the flue and the outer wall of the house. On inspection there was revealed, however, only the brick of the chimney on one side and the outer wall of the house on the other; in depth the space extended only to the flooring. The breach had been made about four feet from the floor, and inside were all the missing bits of plaster. It had been a methodical ghost.

It was very much of a disappointment. I had expected a secret room, at the very least, and I think even Jamieson had fancied he might at last have a clue to the mystery. There was evidently nothing more to be discovered. Liddy reported that everything was serene among the servants, and that none of them had been disturbed by the noise. The maddening thing, however, was that the nightly visitor had evidently more than one way of gaining access to the house, and we made arrangements to redouble our vigilance as to windows and doors that night.

Halsey was inclined to pooh-pooh the whole affair. He said a break in the plaster might have occurred months ago and gone unnoticed, and that the dust had probably been stirred up the day before. After all we had to let it go at that, but we put in an uncomfortable Sunday. Gertrude went to church, and Halsey took a long walk in the morning. Louise was able to sit up, and she allowed Halsey and Liddy to assist her downstairs late in the afternoon. The east veranda was shady, green with vines and plants, cheerful with cushions and lounging chairs. We put Louise in a steamer chair and she sat there passively enough, her hands clasped in her lap.

We were very silent. Halsey sat on the rail with a pipe, openly watching Louise as she looked broodingly across the valley to the hills. There was something baffling in the girl's eyes, and gradually Halsey's boyish features lost their glow at seeing her about again, and settled into grim lines. He was like his father just then.

We sat until late afternoon, Halsey growing more and more moody. Shortly before six he got up and went into the house, and in a few minutes he came out and called me to the telephone. It was Anna Whitcomb, in town, and she kept me for twenty minutes, telling me the children had had the measles, and how Madame Sweeny had botched her new gown. Only she used an i instead of an o.

When I finished Liddy was behind me, her mouth a thin line.

"I wish you would try to look cheerful, Liddy," I groaned. "Your face would sour milk." But Liddy seldom replied to my gibes. She folded her lips a little tighter.

"He called her up," she said oracularly. "He called her up, and asked her to keep you at the telephone, so he could talk to Miss Louise. A thankless child is sharper than a serpent's tooth."

"Nonsense!" I said brusquely. "I might have known enough to leave them. It's a long time since you and I were in love, Liddy, and I suppose we forget."

Liddy sniffed.

"No man ever made a fool of me," she replied virtuously.

"Well, something did," I retorted.

19

"Mr Jamieson," I said, when we found ourselves alone after dinner that night, "the inquest yesterday seemed to me the merest recapitulation of things that were already known. It developed nothing new beyond Doctor Stewart's story, and that was volunteered."

"An inquest is only a necessary formality, Miss Innes," he replied. "Unless a crime is committed in the open, the inquest does nothing beyond getting evidence from witnesses while events are still in their minds. The police step in later. You and I both know ho .v many important things never transpired. For instance, the dead man had no key, and yet Miss Gertrude testified to a fumbling at the lock and then the opening of the door. The piece of evidence you mention, Doctor Stewart's story, is one of those things we have to take cautiously. The doctor has a patient who wears black and does not raise her veil. So it is the typical mysterious lady! Then the good doctor comes across Arnold Armstrong, who was a graceless scamp–de mortuis, what's the rest of it?–and he is quarreling with a lady in black. Behold, says the doctor, they are one and the same."

"Why was Mr Bailey not present at the inquest?"

The detective's expression was peculiar.

"Because his physician testified that he is ill, and unable to leave his bed."

"Ill!" I exclaimed. "Neither Halsey nor Gertrude has told me it was serious."

"There are more things than that, Miss Innes, that are puzzling. Bailey gives the impression that he knew nothing of the crash at the bank until he read it in the paper Monday night, and that he went back and surrendered himself immediately. I do not believe it. Jonas, the watchman at the Traders' Bank, tells a different story. He says that on the

Thursday night before, about eight-thirty, Bailey went back to the bank. Jonas admitted him, and he says the cashier was in a state almost of collapse. Bailey worked until midnight, then he closed the vault and went away. The occurrence was so unusual that the watchman pondered over it all the rest of the night.

"Then what did Bailey do when he went back to the Knickerbocker Apartments that night? He packed a suitcase ready for instant departure. But he held off too long, waiting for something. My personal opinion is that he waited to see Miss Gertrude before getting out of the country. Then, when he had shot down Arnold Armstrong that night, he had to choose between two evils. He did the thing that would immediately turn public opinion in his favor, and surrendered himself as an innocent man. The strongest thing against him is his preparation for flight, and his deciding to come back after the murder of Arnold Armstrong. He was shrewd enough to disarm suspicion as to the graver charge."

The evening dragged along slowly. Mrs Watson came to my bedroom before I went to bed and asked if I had any iodine. She showed me a badly swollen hand, with reddish streaks running up toward the elbow; she said it was the hand she had hurt the night of the murder a week before, and that she had not slept well since. It looked to me as if it might be serious, and I told her to let Doctor Stewart see it.

The next morning she went up to town on the eleven-o'clock train and was admitted to the Emergency Hospital, suffering from blood poisoning. I fully meant to go up and see her there, but other things later drove her entirely from my mind. I telephoned to the hospital that day, however, and ordered a private room for her and whatever comforts she might be allowed.

Mrs Armstrong arrived Monday evening with her husband's body, and the services were set for the next day. The house on Chestnut Street in town had been opened, and Tuesday morning Louise left us to go home. She sent for me before she went, and I saw she had been crying.

"How can I thank you, Miss Innes?" she said. "You have taken me on faith, and you haven't asked me any questions. Sometime perhaps I can tell you. And when that time comes you will all despise me, Halsey too."

I tried to tell her how glad I was to have had her, but there was something else she wanted to say. She said it finally, when she had bade a constrained good-bye to Halsey and the car was waiting at the door.

"Miss Innes," she said in a low tone, "if they–if there is any attempt made to have you give up the house, do it if you possibly can. I'm afraid to have you stay."

I didn't like it. It was a definite warning, but if she knew what it was all about she should have told me. I wondered if Halsey had not made a mistake, after all. But I could do nothing. Gertrude went into town with her that day and saw her safely home. She reported a decided coolness in the greeting between Louise and her mother, and that Doctor Walker was there, apparently in charge of the arrangements for the funeral. Halsey disappeared shortly after Louise left and came home about nine that night, muddy and tired. As for Thomas, he went around dejected and sad, and I saw the detective watching him closely at dinner. Even now I wonder. What did Thomas know? What did he suspect?

At ten o'clock the household had settled down for the night. Liddy, who was taking Mrs Watson's place, had finished examining the tea towels and the corners of the shelves in the refrigerator and had gone to bed. Alex, the gardener, had gone heavily up the circular staircase to his room, and Jamieson was examining the locks of the windows. Halsey dropped into a chair in the living room and stared moodily ahead. Once he roused.

"What sort of looking chap is Walker, Gertrude?" he asked.

"Rather tall, very dark and smooth-shaven. Not bad-looking," Gertrude said, putting down the book she had been pretending to read. Halsey kicked a coffee table viciously.

"Lovely place this village must be in the winter," he said irrelevantly. "A girl would be buried alive here."

It was then someone rapped at the knocker on the heavy front door. Halsey got up leisurely and opened it, admitting Warner. He was out of breath from running, and he looked half abashed.

"I am sorry to disturb you," he said, "but I didn't know what else to do. It's about Thomas."

"What about Thomas?" I asked. Jamieson had come into the hall and we all stared at Warner.

"He's acting queer," Warner explained. "He's sitting down there on the edge of the porch, and he says he has seen a ghost. The old man looks bad, too. He can scarcely speak."

"He's as full of superstition as an egg is of meat," I said. "Halsey, bring some whisky and we will all go down."

He got a bottle from the side board in the dining room. Gertrude threw a shawl around my shoulders, and we all started down over the hill. I had made so many nocturnal excursions around the place that I knew my way perfectly. But Thomas was not on the veranda nor was he inside the house. The men exchanged significant glances and Warner got a lantern.

"He can't have gone far," he said. "He was trembling so that he couldn't stand when I left."

Jamieson and Halsey together made the rounds of the lodge, occasionally calling the old man by name. But there was no response. No Thomas came, bowing and showing his white teeth through the darkness. I began to be vaguely uneasy for the first time. Gertrude, who was never nervous in the dark, outside, went alone down the drive to the gate and stood there looking along the yellowish line of the road, while I waited on the tiny veranda.

Warner was puzzled. He came around to the edge of the steps and stood looking at them as if they ought to know and explain.

"He might have stumbled into the house," he said, "but he couldn't have climbed the stairs. Anyhow, he's not inside or outside that I can see." The other members of the party had come back now, and no one had found any trace of the old man. His pipe, still warm, rested on the edge of the rail, and inside on the table his old gray hat showed that its owner had not gone far.

He was not far, after all. From the table my eyes traveled around the room, and stopped at the door of a closet. I hardly know what impulse moved me, but I went in and turned the knob. It burst open with the impetus of a weight behind it, and something fell partly forward in a heap on the floor. It was Thomas, Thomas without a mark of injury on him. And dead.

20

Warner was on his knees in a moment, fumbling at the old man's collar to loosen it. But Halsey caught his hand.

"Let him alone," he said. "You can't help him. He's dead."

We stood there, each avoiding the other's eyes. We spoke low and reverently in the presence of death, and we tacitly avoided any mention of the suspicion that was in every mind. When Jamieson had finished his cursory examination he got up and dusted the knees of his trousers.

"There is no wound," he said, and I know I for one drew a long breath of relief. "From what Warner says and from his hiding in the closet, I should say he was scared to death. Fright and a weak heart, together."

"But what could have done it?" Gertrude asked. "He was all right this evening at dinner. Warner, what did he say when you found him on the porch?"

Warner looked shaken. His honest, boyish face was colorless.

"Just what I told you, Miss Innes. He'd been reading the paper downstairs. I had put up the car, and feeling sleepy I came down to the lodge to go to bed. As I went upstairs Thomas put down the paper and taking his pipe went out on the porch. Then I heard an exclamation from him."

"What did he say?" demanded Jamieson.

"I couldn't hear, but his voice was strange. It sounded startled. I waited for him to call out again, but he didn't, so I went downstairs. He was sitting on the porch step, looking straight ahead, as if he saw something among the trees across the road. And he kept mumbling about having seen a ghost. He looked queer and I tried to get him inside, but he wouldn't move. Then I thought I'd better go up to the house."

"Didn't he say anything else you could understand?" I asked.

"He said something about the grave giving up its dead."

Jamieson was going through the old man's pockets and Gertrude was composing his arms folding them across his white shirt bosom, always so spotless.

Jamieson looked up at me.

"What was that you said to me, Miss Innes, about the murder at the house being a beginning and not an end? By Jove, I believe you were right!" In the course of his investigations the detective had come to the inner pocket of the dead butler's black coat. Here he found some things that interested him. One was a small flat key with a red cord tied to it, and the other was a bit of white paper, on which was written something in Thomas's cramped hand. Jamieson read it: then he gave it to me. It was an address in fresh ink–

LUCIEN WALLACE, 14 Elm Street, Richfield.

As the card went around, I think both the detective and I watched for any possible effect it might have, but beyond perplexity there seemed to be none.

"Richfield!" Gertrude exclaimed. "Why, Elm Street is the main street; don't you remember, Halsey?"

"Lucien Wallace," Halsey said. "That is the child Stewart spoke of at the inquest."

Warner, with his mechanic's instinct, had reached for the key. What he said was not a surprise.

"Yale lock," he said. "Probably a key to the east entry."

There was no reason why Thomas, an old and trusted servant, should not have had a key to that particular door, although the servants' entry was in the west wing. But I had not known of this key, and it opened up a new field of conjecture. Just now, however, there were many things to be attended to, and leaving Warner with the body we all went back to the house. Jamieson walked with me, while Halsey and Gertrude followed.

"I suppose I shall have to notify the Armstrongs," I said. "They will know if Thomas had any people and how to reach them. Of course I expect to defray the expenses of the funeral, but his relatives must be found. What do you think frightened him, Mr Jamieson?"

"It's hard to say," he replied slowly, "but I think we may be certain it was fright, and that he was hiding from something. I am sorry in more than one way. I have always believed that Thomas knew or suspected something that he wouldn't tell. Do you know how much money there was in that worn-out wallet of his? Nearly a hundred dollars! Almost two months' wages, yet those darkies seldom have a penny. Well, what Thomas knew will probably be buried with him." Halsey suggested that the grounds be searched, but Jamieson vetoed the suggestion.

"You would find nothing," he said. "Anybody clever enough to get into Sunnyside and tear a hole in the wall while I watched downstairs is not to be found by going around the shrubbery with a lantern."

With the death of Thomas I felt that a climax had come in affairs at Sunnyside. The night that followed was quiet enough. Halsey watched at the foot of the staircase, and a complicated system of bolts on the other doors seemed to be effectual.

Once in the night I wakened and thought I heard the tapping again. But all was quiet, and I had reached the stage where I refused to be disturbed for minor occurrences.

The Armstrongs were notified of Thomas's death, and I had my first interview with Doctor Walker as a result. He came up early the next morning, just as we finished breakfast, in a professional-looking black car. I found him striding up and down the living room, and in spite of my preconceived dislike I had to admit that the man was presentable. A big fellow he was, tall and dark, as Gertrude had said, smooth-shaven and erect, with prominent features and a square jaw. He was painfully spruce in his appearance, and his manner was almost obtrusively apologetic.

"I must make a double excuse for this early visit, Miss Innes," he said as he sat down. The chair was lower than he expected, and his dignity required collecting before he went on. "My professional duties are urgent and long neglected, and"–a fall to the everyday manner–"something must be done about the butler's body."

"Yes," I said, sitting on the edge of my chair. "I merely wished the address of Thomas's people. You might have telephoned if you were busy."

He smiled.

"I wanted to see you about something else," he said. "As for Thomas, it is Mrs Armstrong's wish that you allow her to attend to the expense. About his relatives, I have already notified his brother in the village. It was heart disease, I think. Thomas always had a bad heart."

"Heart disease and fright," I said, still on the edge of my chair. But the doctor had no intention of leaving.

"I understand you have a ghost up here, and that you have the house filled with detectives to exorcise it," he said, smiling faintly. For some reason I felt I was being pumped, as Halsey says. "You have been misinformed," I replied.

"What, no ghost, no detectives!" he said, still with his smile. "What a disappointment to the village!"

I resented his attempt at playfulness. It had been anything but a joke to us.

"Doctor Walker," I said tartly, "I fail to see any humor in the situation. Since I came here one man has been shot and another one has died from shock. There have been intruders in the house and strange noises. If that is funny, there is something wrong with my sense of humor."

"You miss the point," he said, still good-naturedly. "The thing that is funny to me is that you insist on remaining here, under the circumstances. I should think nothing would keep you."

"You are mistaken. Everything that occurs only confirms my resolution to stay until the mystery is cleared."

"I have a message for you, Miss Innes," he said, rising at last. "Mrs Armstrong asked me to thank you for your kindness to Louise, whose trip east, coming at the time it did, put her to great inconvenience. Also–and this is a delicate matter–she asked me to appeal to your natural sympathy for her at this time, and to ask you if you would not reconsider your decision about the house. Sunnyside is her home. She loves it dearly, and just now she wants to come here for quiet and peace."

"She must have had a change of heart," I said, ungraciously enough. "Louise told me her mother despised the place. Besides this is no place for quiet and peace just now. Anyhow, doctor, while I don't care to force an issue, I shall certainly remain here, for a time at least."

"For how long?" he asked.

"My lease is for six months. I shall stay until some explanation is found for certain things. My own family is involved now, and I shall do everything to clear the mystery of Arnold Armstrong's murder."

The doctor stood looking down, slapping his gloves thoughtfully against the palm of a well-looked-after hand.

"You say there have been intruders in the house?" he asked. "You are sure of that, Miss Innes?"

"Certain."

"In what part?"

"In the east wing."

"Can you tell me when these intrusions occurred, and what the purpose seemed to be? Was it robbery?"

"No," I said decidedly. "As to time, once on Friday night a week ago, again the following night, when Arnold Armstrong was murdered, and again last Friday night."

The doctor looked serious. He seemed to be debating some question in his mind, and to reach a decision.

"Miss Innes," he said, "I am in a peculiar position: I understand your attitude, of course; but do you think you are wise? Ever since you have come here there have been hostile demonstrations against you and your family. I'm not a croaker, but wouldn't it be safer to go back to town? To leave before anything occurs that will cause you lifelong regret."

"I am willing to take the responsibility," I said coldly. "Warnings don't scare me."

I think he gave me up then as a poor proposition. He asked to be shown where Arnold Armstrong's body had been found, and I took him there. He scrutinized the whole place carefully, examining the stairs and the lock. When he had taken a formal farewell I was confident of one thing. Doctor Walker would do anything he could to get me away from Sunnyside.

21

It was Monday evening when we found the body of poor old Thomas. Monday night had been uneventful; things were quiet at the house and the peculiar circumstances of the old man's death had been carefully kept from the servants. Rosie took charge of the dining room and pantry, in the absence of a butler, and except for the warning of the Casanova doctor everything breathed of peace.

Affairs at the Traders' Bank were progressing slowly. The failure had hit small stockholders very hard, the minister of the little Methodist chapel in Casanova among them. He had received as a legacy from an uncle a few shares of stock in the Traders' Bank, and now his joy was turned to bitterness. He had to sacrifice everything he had in the world, and his feeling against Paul Armstrong, dead as he was, must have been bitter in the extreme. He was asked to officiate at the simple services when the dead banker's body was interred in Casanova churchyard, but the good man providentially took cold and a substitute was called in.

A few days after the services he called to see me, a kindly-faced little man in a shabby suit and an ancient tie. I think he was uncertain as to my connection with the Armstrong family, and dubious whether I considered Mr Armstrong's taking away a matter for condolence or congratulation. He was not long in doubt.

I liked the little man. He had known Thomas well, and had promised to officiate at the services in the rickety African Zion Church. He told me more of himself than he knew, and before he left I astonished him—and myself, I admit—by promising a new carpet for his church. He was much affected, and I gathered that he had yearned over his ragged chapel as a mother over a half-clothed child.

"You are laying up treasure, Miss Innes," he said brokenly, "where neither moth nor rust corrupt, nor thieves break through and steal."

"It is certainly a safer place than Sunnyside," I admitted. And the thought of the carpet permitted him to smile. He stood just inside the doorway, looking from the luxury of the house to the beauty of the view.

"The rich ought to be good," he said wistfully. "They have so much that is beautiful, and beauty is ennobling. And yet while I ought to say nothing in view of this lovely spot, to him these trees and lawns were not the work of God. They were property, at so much an acre. He loved money, Miss Innes. He offered up everything to his golden calf. Not power, not ambition, was his fetish. It was money." Then he dropped his pulpit manner and turned to me with his engaging smile.

"In spite of all this luxury," he said, "the country people here have a saying that Mr Paul Armstrong could sit on a dollar and see all around it. Unlike the summer people, he gave neither to the poor nor to the church. He loved money for its own sake."

"And there are no pockets in shrouds!" I said cynically.

I sent him home in the car, with a bunch of hothouse roses for his wife, and he was quite overwhelmed. As for me, I had a generous glow that was cheap at the price of a church carpet. I had received less gratification and less gratitude when I presented the new silver communion set to St Barnabas.

I had a great many things to think about in those days. I made out a list of questions and possible answers, but I seemed only to be working around in a circle. I always ended where I began. The list was something like this:

Who had entered the house the night before the murder?

Thomas claimed it was Mr Bailey, whom he had seen on the footpath, and who owned the pearl cuff link.

Why did Arnold Armstrong come back after he had left the house the night he was killed?

No answer. Was it on the mission Louise had mentioned?

Who admitted him?

Gertrude said she had locked the east entry. There was no key on the dead man or in the door. He must have been admitted from within, by someone who belonged there, or who had already arrived in the house.

Who had been locked in the clothes chute?

Someone unfamiliar with the house, obviously. Only two people were missing from the household, Rosie and Gertrude. Rosie had been at the lodge with Louise. Therefore—but was it Gertrude? Might it not have been the mysterious intruder again?

Who had accosted Rosie on the drive?

Again perhaps the nightly visitor. It seemed more likely someone who suspected a secret at the lodge. Was Louise under surveillance?

Who had passed Louise on the circular staircase?

Could it have been Thomas? The key to the east entry made this a possibility. But why was he there, if it was indeed he?

Who had made the hole in the trunk-room wall?

It was not merely vandalism. It had been done quietly and with deliberate purpose. If I had only known how to read the purpose of that gaping aperture, what I might have been saved in anxiety and mental strain!

Why had Louise left her people and come home to hide at the lodge?

There was no answer as yet to this, or to the next questions.

Why did both she and Doctor Walker warn us away from the house?

Who was Lucien Wallace?

What did Thomas see in the shadows the night he died?

What was the meaning of the subtle change in Gertrude?

Was Jack Bailey an accomplice or a victim in the looting of the Traders' Bank?

What all-powerful reason made Louise determine to marry Doctor Walker?

The examiners were still working on the books of the Traders' Bank, and it was probable that several weeks would elapse before everything was cleared up. The firm of expert accountants who had examined the books some two months before testified that every bond, every piece of valuable paper, was there at that time. It had been shortly after their examination that the president, who had been in bad health, had gone to California. Jack Bailey was still ill at the Knickerbocker, and in this as in other ways Gertrude's conduct puzzled me. She seemed indifferent, refused to discuss matters pertaining to the bank, and never to my knowledge either wrote to him or went to see him. Gradually I came to the conclusion that Gertrude, with the rest of the world, believed her lover guilty and although I believed it myself, for that matter, I was irritated by her indifference. Girls in my day did not meekly accept the public's verdict as to the man they loved.

But presently something occurred that made me think that under Gertrude's surface calm there was a seething flood of suppressed excitement.

Tuesday morning the detective made a careful search of the grounds, but he found nothing. In the afternoon he disappeared, and it was late that night when he came home. He said he would have to go back to the city the following day, and arranged with Halsey and Alex to guard the house.

Liddy came to me on Wednesday morning with her black silk apron held up like a bag, and her eyes big with virtuous wrath. It was the day of Thomas's funeral in the village, and Alex and I were in the conservatory cutting flowers for the old man's casket. Liddy is never so happy as when she is making herself wretched, and now her mouth drooped while her eyes were triumphant.

"I always said there were plenty of things going on here right under our noses that we couldn't see," she said, holding out her apron.

"I don't see with my nose," I remarked. "What have you got there?" Liddy pushed aside a half dozen geranium pots, and in the space thus cleared she dumped the contents of her apron, a handful of tiny bits of paper. Alex had stepped back but I saw him watching her curiously.

"Wait a moment, Liddy," I said, "You have been going through the library paper basket again!"

Liddy was arranging her bits of paper with the skill of long practice and paid no attention.

"Did it ever occur to you," I went on, putting my hand over the scraps, "that when people tear up their correspondence it is for the express purpose of keeping it from being read?"

"If they wasn't ashamed of it they wouldn't take so much trouble, Miss Rachel," Liddy said oracularly. "More than that, with things happening every day, I consider it my duty. If you don't read and act on this, I shall give it to that Jamieson, and I'll venture he'll not go back to the city today."

That decided me. If the scraps had anything to do with the mystery, ordinary conventions had no value. So Liddy arranged the scraps, like working out a puzzle picture, and she did it with much the same eagerness. When it was finished she stepped aside while I read it.

"Wednesday night, nine o'clock. Bridge," I read aloud. Then, aware of Alex's stare, I turned on Liddy.

"Someone is to play bridge tonight at nine o'clock," I said. "Is that your business, or mine?"

Liddy was aggrieved. She was about to reply when I scooped up the pieces and left the conservatory.

"Now then," I said, when we got outside, "will you tell me why you choose to take Alex into your confidence? He's no fool. Do you suppose he thinks anyone in this house is going to play bridge tonight at nine o'clock, by appointment? I suppose you have shown it in the kitchen, and instead of my being able to slip down to the bridge tonight quietly and see who is there, the whole household will be going in a procession."

"Nobody knows it," Liddy said humbly. "I found it in the basket in Miss Gertrude's dressing room. Look at the back of the sheet." I turned over some of the scraps, and, sure enough, it was a blank deposit slip from the Traders' Bank. So Gertrude was going to meet Jack Bailey that night by the bridge! And I had thought he was ill! It hardly seemed like the action of an innocent man, this avoidance of daylight and of his fiance's people. I decided to make certain by going to the bridge that night.

After luncheon Jamieson suggested that I go with him to Richfield, and I consented.

"I am inclined to place more faith in Doctor Stewart's story," he said, "since I found that scrap in old Thomas's pocket. It bears out the statement that the woman with the child and the woman who quarreled with young Armstrong are the same. It looks as if Thomas had stumbled onto some affair that was more or less discreditable to the dead man, and out of loyalty to the family had kept it to himself. Then, you see, your story about the woman at the cardroom window begins to mean something. It is the nearest approach to anything tangible that we have had yet."

Warner took us to Richfield in the car. It was about twenty-five miles by railroad, but by taking a series of atrociously rough short cuts we got there very quickly. It was a pretty little town on the river, and back on the hill I could see the Mortons' big country house, where Halsey and Gertrude had been staying until the night of the murder.

Elm Street was almost the only street and number fourteen was easily found. It was a small white house, dilapidated without having gained anything picturesque, with a bay window and a porch only a foot or so above the bit of lawn. There was a baby carriage in the path, and from a swing at the side came the sound of conflict. Three small children were disputing vociferously, and a faded young woman with a kindly face was trying to hush the clamor. When she saw us she untied her gingham apron and came around to the porch.

"Good afternoon," I said. Jamieson lifted his hat, without speaking. "I came to inquire about a child named Lucien Wallace."

"I'm glad you've come," she said. "In spite of the other children I think the little fellow is lonely. We thought perhaps his mother would be here today."

Jamieson stepped forward.

"You are Mrs Tate?" I wondered how the detective knew.

"Yes, sir."

"Mrs Tate, we want to make some inquiries. Perhaps in the house–"

"Come right in," she said hospitably. And soon we were in the little shabby parlor, exactly like a thousand of its type. Mrs Tate sat uneasy, her hands folded in her lap.

"How long has Lucien been here?" Mr Jamieson asked.

"Since a week ago last Friday. His mother paid one week's board in advance; the other has not been paid."

"Was he ill when he came?"

"No, sir, not what you'd call sick. He was getting better of typhoid, she said, and he's picking up fine."

"Will you tell me his mother's name and address?"

"That's the trouble," the young woman said, frowning. "She gave her name as Mrs Wallace, and she said she had no address. She was looking for a boardinghouse in town. She said she worked in a department store and couldn't take care of the child properly, and he needed fresh air and milk. I had three children of my own, and one more didn't make much difference in the work. But I wish she would pay this week's board."

"Did she say what store it was?"

"No, sir, but all the boy's clothes came from King's. They're far too good for the country."

There was a chorus of shouts and shrill yells from the front door, followed by the loud stamping of children's feet and a throaty "whoa, whoa!" Into the room came a tandem team of two chubby youngsters, a boy and a girl, harnessed with a clothesline and driven by a laughing boy of about seven in tan overalls. The small driver caught my attention at once. He was a beautiful child, and although he showed traces of recent severe illness his skin had now the clear transparency of health.

"Whoa, Flinders," he shouted. "You're goin' to smash the wagon." Jamieson coaxed him over by holding out a lead pencil, striped blue and yellow.

"Now then," he said, when the boy had taken the lead pencil and was testing its usefulness on the detective's cuff. "I'll bet you don't know what your name is!"

"I do," said the boy. "Lucien Wallace."

"Great! And what's your mother's name?"

"Mother, of course. What's your mother's name?" And he pointed to me! I am going to stop wearing black. It doubles a woman's age.

"And where did you live before you came here?" Jamieson was polite enough not to smile.

"Grossmutter," he said. And I saw Jamieson's eyebrows go up.

"German," he commented. "Well, young man, you don't seem to know much about yourself."

"I've tried it all week," Mrs Tate broke in. "The boy knows a word or two of German, but he doesn't know where he lived or anything about himself."

Jamieson wrote something on a card and gave it to her.

"Mrs Tate," he said, "I want you to do something. Here is some money for the telephone call. The instant the boy's mother appears here call up that number and ask for the person whose name is there. You can run across to the drugstore on an errand and do it quietly. Just say, 'The lady has come.'"

"The lady has come," repeated Mrs Tate. "Very well, sir, and I hope it will be soon. The milk bill alone is almost double what it was."

"How much is the child's board?" I asked.

"Seven dollars a week, including his washing."

"Very well," I said. "Now, Mrs Tate, I'm going to pay last week's board and a week in advance. If the mother comes, she is to know nothing of this visit. Absolutely not a word. And in return for your silence you may use this extra money for something for your own children."

Her tired, faded face lighted up and I saw her glance at the little Tates' small feet. Shoes, I divined, the feet of the genteel poor being almost as expensive as their stomachs.

As we went back Jamieson made only one remark. I think he was laboring under the weight of a great disappointment.

"Is King's a children's outfitting place?" he asked.

"Not especially. It's a general department store."

He was silent after that, but he went to the telephone as soon as we got home and called up King and Company, in the city. After a time he got the general manager, and they talked for some time. When Mr Jamieson hung up the receiver he turned to me.

"The plot thickens," he said with his ready smile. "There are four women named Wallace at King's, none of them married, and none over twenty. I think I shall go up to the city tonight. I want to go to the Children's Hospital. But before I go, Miss Innes, I wish you would be more frank with me than you have been yet. I want you to show me the revolver you picked up in the tulip bed."

So he had known all along!

"It was a revolver, Mr Jamieson," I admitted, cornered at last, "but I can't show it to you. It is not in my possession."

22

At dinner that night Jamieson suggested sending a man out in his place for a couple of days, but Halsey was certain there would be nothing more, and felt that he and Alex could manage the situation. The detective went back to town early in the evening and by nine o'clock Halsey, who had been playing golf, as a man does anything to take his mind away from trouble, was sleeping soundly on the big davenport in the living room.

I sat and knitted, pretending not to notice when Gertrude got up and wandered out into the starlight. As soon as I was satisfied that she had gone, however, I went out cautiously. I had no intention of eavesdropping, but I wanted to be certain that it was Jack Bailey she was meeting. Too many things had occurred in which Gertrude was or appeared to be involved to allow anything to be left in question.

I went slowly across the lawn, skirted the hedge to a break not far from the lodge, and found myself on the open road. Perhaps a hundred feet to the left the path led across the valley to the Country Club, and only a little way off was the footbridge over Casanova Creek. But just as I was about to turn down the path I heard steps coming toward me, and I shrank into the bushes. It was Gertrude, going back quickly toward the house.

I was surprised. I waited until she had had time to get almost to the house before I started. And then I stepped back again into the shadows. The reason why Gertrude had not kept her tryst was evident. Leaning on the parapet of the bridge in the moonlight and smoking a pipe was Alex, the gardener. I could have throttled Liddy for her carelessness in reading the torn note where he could hear. And I could cheerfully have choked Alex to death for his interference.

But there was no help for it. I turned and followed Gertrude slowly back to the house.

The frequent invasions of the house had effectually prevented any relaxation after dusk, We had redoubled our
vigilance as to bolts and window locks, but as Jamieson had
suggested we allowed the door at the east entry to remain
as before, locked by the Yale lock only. To provide only
one possible entrance for the invader, and to keep a con-
stant guard in the dark at the foot of the circular staircase,
seemed to be the only method.

In the absence of the detective Alex and Halsey arranged
to change off, Halsey to be on duty from ten to two and
Alex from two until six. Each man was armed, and as an
additional precaution the one off duty slept in a room near
the head of the circular staircase and kept his door open,
to be ready for emergency.

These arrangements were carefully kept from the servants, who were only commencing to sleep at night and
who retired one and all with barred doors and lamps that
burned until morning.

The house was quiet again Wednesday night. It was almost a week since Louise had encountered someone on the
stairs, and it was four days since the discovery of the hole
in the trunk-room wall. Arnold Armstrong and his father
rested side by side in the Casanova churchyard, and at the
Zion African Church on the hill a new mound marked the
last resting place of poor Thomas.

Louise was with her mother in town, and beyond a polite
note of thanks to me we had heard nothing from her. Doctor Walker had taken up his practice again, and we saw him
now and then flying along the road, always at top speed.
The murder of Arnold Armstrong was still unsolved, and I
remained firm in the position I had taken– to stay at Sunnyside until the thing was at least partly cleared up.

Yet for all its quiet it was on Wednesday night that perhaps the boldest attempt was made to enter the house. On
Thursday afternoon the laundress sent word she would like
to speak to me, and I saw her in my private sitting room, a
small room beyond the dressing room.

MaryAnne was embarrassed. She had rolled down her sleeves and tied a white apron around her waist, and she stood making folds in it with fingers that were red and shiny from soapsuds.

"Well, Mary," I said encouragingly, "what's the matter? Don't dare to tell me the soap is out."

"No, ma'am, Miss Innes." She had a nervous habit of looking first at my one eye and then at the other, her own optics shifting ceaselessly, right eye, left eye, right eye, until I found myself doing the same thing. "No, ma'am. I was askin' did you want the ladder left up the clothes chute?"

"The what?" I screeched, and was sorry the next minute. Seeing her suspicions were verified, MaryAnne had gone white, and stood with her eyes shifting more wildly than ever.

"There's a ladder up the clothes chute, Miss Innes," she said. "It's up that tight I can't move it, and I didn't like to ask for help until I spoke to you."

It was useless to dissemble; MaryAnne knew now as well as I did that the ladder had no business to be there. I did the best I could, however. I put her on the defensive at once.

"Then you didn't lock the laundry last night?"

"I locked it tight, and put the key in the kitchen on its nail."

"Very well, then you forgot a window."

MaryAnne hesitated.

"Yes'm," she said at last. "I thought I locked them all, but there was one open this morning."

I went out of the room and down the hall, followed by MaryAnne. The door into the clothes chute was securely bolted, and when I opened it I saw the evidence of the woman's story. A pruning ladder had been brought from where it had lain against the stable and now stood upright in the clothes shaft, its end resting against the wall between the first and second floors.

I turned to MaryAnne.

"This is due to your carelessness," I said. "If we had all been murdered in our beds it would have been your fault." She shivered. "Now, not a word of this through the house, and send Alex to me."

The effect on Alex was to make him apoplectic with rage, and with it all I fancied there was an element of satisfaction As I look back so many things are plain to me that I wonder I could not see at the time. It is all known now, and yet the whole thing was so remarkable that perhaps my stupidity was excusable.

Alex leaned down the chute and examined the ladder carefully.

"It's caught," he said with a grim smile. "The fools, to have left a warning like that! The only trouble is, Miss Innes, they won't be apt to come back for a while."

"I shouldn't regard that in the light of a calamity," I replied dryly. Until late that evening Halsey and Alex worked at the chute. They got down the ladder at last and put a new bolt on the door. As for myself, I sat and wondered if I had a deadly enemy, intent on my destruction.

I was growing more and more alarmed. Liddy had given up all pretense at bravery and slept regularly in my dressing room on the couch, with a prayer book and a game knife from the kitchen under her pillow, thus preparing for both the natural and the supernatural. And that was the way things stood that Thursday night, when I myself took a hand in the struggle.

23

About nine o'clock that night Liddy came into the living room and reported that one of the housemaids declared she had seen two men slip around the corner of the stable. Gertrude had been sitting staring in front of her, jumping at every sound. Now she turned on Liddy pettishly.

"Good heavens, Liddy," she said, "you're a bundle of nerves. What if Eliza did see some men around the stable? It may have been Warner and Alex."

"Warner is in the kitchen, miss," Liddy said, with dignity. "And if you had come through what I have you would be a bundle of nerves, too. Miss Rachel, I'd be thankful if you'd give me my month's wages tomorrow. I'll be going to my sister's."

"Very well," I said, to her evident amazement. "I will make out the check. Warner can take you down to the noon train."

Liddy's face was really funny.

"You'll have a nice time at your sister's," I went on. "Five children, hasn't she?"

"That's it," Liddy said, suddenly bursting into tears. "Send me away after all these years, and your new bathrobe only half done, and nobody knowin' how to fix the water for your bath."

"It's time I learned to prepare my own bath." I was knitting complacently. But Gertrude got up and put her arms around Liddy's shaking shoulders.

"You are two big babies," she said soothingly. "Neither one of you could get along for an hour without the other. So stop quarreling and be good. Liddy, go right up and lay out Aunty's night things. She is going to bed early."

After Liddy had gone I began to think about the men at the stable, and I grew more and more anxious. Halsey was aimlessly knocking the billiard balls around in the billiard room, and I called to him.

"Halsey," I said when he sauntered in, "is there a policeman in Casanova?"

"Constable," he said laconically. "Veteran of the war, one arm. In office to conciliate the Legion crowd. Why?"

"Because I'm uneasy tonight." And I told him what Liddy had said. "Is there anyone you can think of who could be relied on to watch the outside of the house tonight?"

"We might get Sam Bohannon from the club," he said thoughtfully. "It wouldn't be a bad scheme. He's a smart darky, and with his mouth shut and his shirt front covered you couldn't see him a yard off in the dark."

Halsey conferred with Alex, and the result in an hour was Sam. His instructions were simple. There had been numerous attempts to break into the house. It was the intention, not to drive intruders away, but to capture them. If Sam saw anything suspicious outside he was to tap at the east entry, where Alex and Halsey were to alternate in keeping watch through the night.

It was with a comfortable feeling of security that I went to bed that night. The door between Gertrude's rooms and mine had been opened, and, with the doors into the hall bolted, we were safe enough. Although Liddy persisted in her belief that doors would prove no obstacles to our disturbers.

As before, Halsey watched the east entry from ten until two. He had an eye to comfort and he kept vigil in a heavy oak chair, very large and deep. We went upstairs rather early, and through the open door Gertrude and I kept up a running fire of conversation. Liddy was brushing my hair and Gertrude was doing her own, with a long free sweep of her strong young arms.

"Did you know Mrs Armstrong and Louise are in the village?" she called.

"No," I replied, startled. "How did you hear it?"

"I met the oldest Stewart girl today, the doctor's daughter, and she told me they hadn't gone back to town after the funeral. They went directly to that little yellow house next to Doctor Walker's and are apparently settled there. They took the house furnished for the summer."

"Why, it's a bandbox," I said. "I can't imagine Fanny Armstrong in such a place."

"It's true, just the same. Ella Stewart says Mrs Armstrong has aged terribly and looks as if she is hardly able to walk."

I lay and thought over some of these things until midnight. The electric lights went out then, blinking once or twice in warning before they died entirely and we were embarked on the darkness of another night.

Apparently only a few minutes had elapsed, during which my eyes were becoming accustomed to the darkness, when I noticed that the windows were reflecting a faint pinkish light. Liddy noticed it at the same time and I heard her jump up. At that moment Sam's deep voice boomed from somewhere just below.

"Fire!" he yelled. "The stable's on fire!"

I could see him on the drive, and a moment later Halsey joined him. Alex was awake and running down the stairs, and in five minutes from the time the fire was discovered three of the maids were sitting on their trunks in the drive, although excepting a few sparks there was no fire nearer than a hundred yards.

Gertrude seldom loses her presence of mind, and she had gone to the telephone. But by the time the Casanova volunteer fire department came toiling up the hill the stable was a furnace, with the car safe but blistered in the road. Some gasoline cans exploded just as the volunteer department got to work, which shook their nerves as well as the burning building.

The stable, being on a hill, was a torch to attract the population from every direction. Rumor had it that Sunnyside was burning, and it was amazing how many people threw something over their night clothes and rushed to the excitement. I take it Casanova has few fires and Sunnyside was furnishing the people, in one way and another, the greatest excitements they had had for years.

The stable was off the west wing, and I hardly know how I came to think of the circular staircase and the unguarded door at its foot. Liddy was putting my clothes into sheets preparatory to tossing them out the window when I found her, and I could hardly persuade her to stop.

"I want you to come with me, Liddy," I said. "Bring a candle and a couple of blankets."

She lagged behind considerably when she saw me making for the east wing, and at the top of the staircase she balked.

"I am not going down," she said firmly.

"There is no one guarding the door there," I explained. "Who knows? This may be a scheme to draw everybody away from this end of the house and let someone in here."

The instant I had said it I was convinced I had hit on the explanation, and that perhaps it was already too late. It seemed to me as I listened that I heard stealthy footsteps on the east porch, but there was so much shouting outside that it was impossible to tell. Liddy was on the point of retreat.

"Very well," I said. "Then I shall go down alone. Run back to Mr Halsey's room and get his revolver. But don't shoot down the stairs if you hear a noise. Remember I'll be down there. And hurry."

I put the candle on the floor at the top of the staircase and took off my bedroom slippers. Then I crept down the stairs, going very slowly and listening with all my ears. I was keyed to such a pitch that I felt no fear. Like the condemned who sleep and eat the night before execution, I was no longer able to suffer apprehension. I was past that. Just at the foot of the stairs I stubbed my toe against Halsey's big chair, and had to stand on one foot in a soundless agony until the pain subsided to a dull ache. And then I knew I was right. Someone had put a key into the lock, and was turning it. For some reason it refused to work, and the key was withdrawn. There was a muttering of voices outside, and I had only a second. Another trial and the door would open. The candle above made a faint gleam down the well-like staircase, and at that moment with only a second to spare I thought of a plan.

The heavy oak chair almost filled the space between the newel post and the door. With a crash I turned it on its side and wedged it against the door, its legs against the stairs. I could hear a faint scream from Liddy at the crash, and then she came down the stairs on a run, with the revolver held straight out in front of her.

"Thank God," she said, in a shaking voice. "I thought it was you."

I pointed to the door, and she understood.

"Call Mr Halsey or Alex, out the windows at the other end of the house," I whispered. "Run. Tell them not to wait for anything."

She went up the stairs at that, two at a time. Evidently she collided with the candle, for it went out and I was left in darkness.

I was really astonishingly cool. I remember stepping over the chair and gluing my ear to the door, and I shall never forget feeling it give an inch or two there in the darkness, under a steady pressure from without. But the chair held, although I could hear an ominous cracking of one of the legs. Then without the slightest warning the cardroom window broke with a crash. I had my finger on the trigger of the revolver, and as I jumped it went off, right through the door. Someone outside swore roundly, and for the first time I could hear what was said.

"I'm getting the hell out of here," someone was saying.

"Did it get you?"

"Only a scratch."

Evidently they had abandoned the door and were moving toward the broken window. There was some argument I could not hear. Then as I looked into the cardroom a small man put his leg over the sill and stepped cautiously inside.

I fired again, and something that was glass or china crashed to the ground. But I had not hit him. In the darkness he was moving steadily toward me, and I thought he had a gun in his hand.

It was time for retreat and I knew it. I don't recall running up the circular staircase. I must have, however, for I found Gertrude standing there looking ready to faint. Certainly I cut a peculiar figure, in my bare feet and dressing gown, with a gun in my hand. But I had no time to talk. There was the sound of footsteps in the lower hall, and someone came running up the stairs in the dark.

I had gone berserk, I think. I leaned over the stair rail and fired again. And Halsey below yelled at me.

"What are you doing up there?" he yelped. "You missed me by an inch."

"They're in the house," I managed to say. "In the card-room."

After that I disgraced myself by fainting for the first time in my life. When I came around Liddy was rubbing my temples with hair tonic and the search was in full blast.

The men were gone. The stable burned to the ground that night, while the crowd shrieked at every falling rafter and the volunteer fire department sprayed it with a garden hose. And in the house Alex and Halsey searched every corner of the lower floor, finding no one.

The truth of my story was shown by the broken window and the overturned chair. That the man I had seen had got upstairs was almost impossible. He had not used the main staircase, there was no way to the upper floor in the east wing, and Liddy had been at the window in the west wing where the servants' stair went up. But we did not go to bed at all. Sam Bohannon and Warner helped in the search, and not a closet escaped scrutiny. Even the cellars were given a thorough overhauling without result. The door in the east entry had a hole through it where my bullet had gone, and there were a few drops of blood there. The hole slanted downward and the bullet was embedded in the porch.

"Somebody will walk lame," Halsey said, when he had marked the course of the bullet. "It's too low to have hit anything but a leg or foot."

From that time on I watched every person I met for a limp, and to this day the man who halts in his walk is an object of suspicion to me. But Casanova had no lame men. The nearest approach to it was an old fellow who tended the safety gates at the railroad, and he, I learned on inquiry, had an artificial leg. Our man had gone, and the large and expensive stable at Sunnyside was a heap of smoking rafters and charred boards. Warner swore the fire was incendiary, and in view of the attempt to enter the house there seemed to be no doubt of it.

24

If Halsey had only taken me fully into his confidence throughout the whole affair, it would have been much simpler. If he had been altogether frank about Jack Bailey, and if the day after the fire he had told me what he suspected, there would have been no further harrowing period for all of us. But young people refuse to profit by the experience Cf their elders, and sometimes the elders are the ones to suffer.

I was much used up the day after the fire, and Gertrude insisted on my going out for some fresh air. The car was temporarily out of commission, and she finally got a trap from the Casanova livery man. But just as we turned from the drive into the road we passed a woman. She had put down a small valise and stood inspecting the house and grounds minutely. I should hardly have noticed her had it not been for the fact that she had been horribly disfigured by what looked like burns.

"Ugh!" Gertrude said, when we had passed. "What a face! I shall dream of it tonight. Get up, Flinders."

"Flinders?" I asked. "Is that the horse's name?"

"It is." She flicked the horse's stubby mane with the whip. It was a long time since she had driven a horse and she was enjoying it. "He didn't look like a livery horse, and the liveryman said he had bought him from the Armstrongs when they purchased a couple of cars and did away with their stable. Nice Flinders, good old boy!"

Flinders was certainly not a common name for a horse, and yet the youngster at Richfield had named his prancing, curly-haired little horse Flinders. It set me thinking.

At my request Halsey had already sent word of the fire to the agent from whom we had secured the house. Also, he had called Jamieson by telephone, and somewhat guardedly had told him of the previous night's events. Jamieson had promised to come out that night, and tv bring another man with him. I did not consider it necessary to notify Mrs Armstrong, in the village. She certainly knew of the fire, and in view of my refusal to give up the house an interview would probably have been unpleasant enough. But as we passed Doctor Walker's white-and-green house I thought of something.

"Stop here, Gertrude," I said. "I am going to get out."

"To see Louise?" she asked.

"No, I want to ask this young Walker something."

She was curious, I knew, but I did not wait to explain. I went up the walk to the house, where a brass sign at the side announced the office, and went in. The reception room was empty, but from the consulting room beyond came the sound of two voices, not very amicable.

"It's an outrageous figure," someone was storming. Then the doctor's quiet tone, evidently not arguing, merely stating something. But I had no time to listen to some person probably disputing his bill, so I coughed. The voices ceased at once. A door closed somewhere, and the doctor entered from the hail of the house. He looked sufficiently surprised at seeing me.

"Good afternoon, doctor," I said formally. "I shall not keep you from your patient. I wish merely to ask you a question."

"Won't you sit down?"

"It won't be necessary. Doctor, has anyone come to you, either early this morning or today, to have you treat a bullet wound?"

"Nothing so startling has happened to me," he said, smiling. "A bullet wound! Things must be lively at Sunnyside."

"I didn't say it was at Sunnyside. But as it happens it was. If any such case comes to you will it be too much trouble for you to let me know?"

"I shall be only too happy," he said. "I understand you have had a fire up there too. A fire and a shooting in one night is rather lively for a quiet place like that."

"It's as quiet as a boiler room," I replied, as I turned to go.

"And you are still going to stay?"

"Until I am burned out," I responded. Then on my way down the steps I turned around suddenly.

"Doctor," I asked at a venture, "have you ever heard of a child named Lucien Wallace?"

Clever as he was his face changed and stiffened. He was on his guard again in a moment.

"Lucien Wallace?" he repeated. "No, I think not. There are plenty of Wallaces around, but I don't know any Lucien."

I was as certain as possible that he did. People do not lie readily to me, and this man lied beyond a doubt. But there was nothing to be gained now. His defenses were up and I left, half irritated and wholly baffled.

Our reception was entirely different at Doctor Stewart's. Taken into the bosom of the family at once, Flinders tied outside and nibbling the grass at the roadside, Gertrude and I drank some homemade elderberry wine and told briefly of the fire. Of the more serious part of the night's experience, of course, we said nothing. But when at last we had left the family on the porch and the doctor was untying our steed I asked him the same question I had put to Doctor Walker.

"Shot!" he said. "Bless my soul, no. Why, what have you been doing up at the big house, Miss Innes?"

"Someone tried to enter the house during the fire, and was shot and slightly injured," I said hastily. "Please don't mention it. We want to make as little of it as possible."

There was one other possibility, and we tried that. At Casanova station I saw the stationmaster, and asked him if any trains left Casanova between one o'clock and daylight. There was none until six A.M. The next question, however, required more diplomacy.

"Did you notice on the six-o'clock train any person, any man, who limped a little?" I asked. "Please try to remember: we are trying to trace a man who was seen loitering around Sunnyside last night before the fire."

He was all attention in a moment.

"I was up there myself at the fire," he said volubly. "I'm a member of the volunteer company. First big fire we've had Since the summerhouse burned over to the club golf links. My wife was sayin' the other day, 'Dave, you might as well 'a' saved the money you spent on that there helmet and shirt.' And here last night they came in handy. Blew that siren so hard I hadn't time scarcely to get 'em on."

"And did you see a man who limped?" Gertrude put in as he stopped for breath.

"Not at the train, ma'am," he said. "No such person got on here today. But I'll tell you where I did see a man that limped. I didn't wait till the fire company left. There's a fast freight goes through at four forty-five and I had to get down to the station. I seen there wasn't much more to do anyhow at the fire–we'd got the flames under control–" Gertrude looked at me and smiled– "so I started down the hill. There was folks here and there goin' home, and along by the path to the Country Club I seen two men. One was a short fellow. He was sitting on a big rock, his back to me, and he had something white in his hand, as if he was tying up his foot. After I'd gone on a piece I looked back, and he was hobbling on and–excuse me, miss–he was swearing something sickening."

"Did they go toward the club?" Gertrude asked suddenly, leaning forward.

"No, miss. I think they came into the village. I didn't get a look at their faces, but I know every chick and child in the place and everybody knows me. When they didn't shout at me–in my uniform, you know–I took it they were strangers."

So all we had for our afternoon's work was this: someone had been shot by the bullet that went through the door, he had not left the village by train, and he had not called in a physician. Also, Doctor Walker knew who Lucien Wallace was, and his very denial made me confident that in that one direction at least we were on the right track.

The thought that the detective would be there that night was the most cheering thing of all, and I think even Gertrude was glad of it. Driving home that afternoon I saw her in the clear sunlight for the first time in several days, and I was startled to see how thin she looked. She was colorless too, and all her bright animation was gone.

"Gertrude," I said, "I have been a very selfish old woman. You are going to leave this miserable house tonight. Annie Morton is going to Scotland next week, and you are going with her."

To my surprise she flushed painfully.

"I don't want to go, Aunt Ray," she said. "Don't make me leave now."

"You're losing your health and your good looks," I said decidedly. "You should have a change."

"I shan't stir a foot." She was equally decided. Then, more lightly: "You and Liddy need me to arbitrate between you every day in the week."

Perhaps I was growing suspicious of everyone, but it seemed to me that Gertrude's gaiety was forced and artificial. I watched her covertly during the rest of the drive, and I did not like the two spots of crimson in her pale cheeks. But I said nothing more about sending her to Scotland. I knew she would not go.

25

That day was destined to be an eventful one, for when I entered the house and found Eliza the cook ensconced in the upper hail on a chair, with MaryAnne doing her best to stifle her with household ammonia and Liddy rubbing her wrists–whatever good that is supposed to do–I knew that the ghost had been walking again, this time in daylight.

Eliza was in a frenzy of fear. She clutched at my sleeves when I went close to her and refused to let go until she had told her story. Coming just after the fire, the household was demoralized, and it was no surprise to me to find Alex and the undergardener struggling down the stairs with a heavy trunk between them.

"I didn't want to do it, Miss Innes," Alex said. "But she was so excited I was afraid she would do as she said, drag it down herself and scratch the staircase."

I was hying to get my hat off and to keep the women quiet at the same time. "Now, Eliza, when you have washed your face and stopped bawling," I said, "come into my sitting room and tell me what has happened."

Liddy put away my things without speaking. The very set of her shoulders expressed disapproval.

"Well," I said, when the silence became uncomfortable, "things seem to be warming up."

Silence from Liddy, and a long sigh.

"If Eliza goes, I don't know where to look for another cook." More silence.

"Rosie is probably a good cook." Sniff.

"Liddy," I said at last, "don't dare to deny that you are having the time of your life. You positively gloat in this excitement. You never looked better. It's my opinion all this running around and getting jolted out of a rut has stirred up that torpid liver of yours."

"It's not myself I'm thinking about," she said, goaded into speech. "Maybe my liver was torpid and maybe it wasn't. But I know this. I've got some feelings left, and to see you standing at the foot of that staircase shootin' through the door–I'll never be the same woman again."

"Well, I'm glad of that. Anything for a change," I said coldly. And in came Eliza, flanked by Rosie and MaryAnne.

Her story, broken with sobs and corrections from the other two, was this: At two o'clock (two-fifteen, Rosie insisted) she had gone upstairs to get a picture from her room to show MaryAnne. (A picture of a lady, MaryAnne interposed.) She went up the servants' staircase and along the corridor to her room, which lay between the trunk room and the unfinished ballroom. She heard a sound as she went down the corridor, like someone moving furniture, but she was not nervous. She thought it might be men examining the house after the fire the night before, but she looked in the trunk room and saw nobody. She went into her room quietly. The noise had ceased, and everything was quiet. Then she sat down on the side of her bed, and, feeling faint–she was subject to spells–("I told you that when I came, didn't I, Rosie?" "Yes'm, indeed she did!")–she put her head down on her pillow and– "Took a nap. All right!" I said. "Go on."

"When I came to, Miss Inner, sure as I'm sittin' here I thought I'd die. Somethin' hit me on the face and I set up, sudden-like. And then I seen the plaster drop, droppin' from a little hole in the wall. And the first thing I knew an iron bar that long" (fully two yards by her measure) "shot through that hole and tumbled on the bed. If I'd been still sleeping" ("Fainting," corrected Rosie) "I'd 'a' been hit on the head and killed!"

"I wisht you'd heard her scream," put in MaryAnne. "And her face as white as a pillow slip when she tumbled down the stairs."

"No doubt there is some natural explanation for it,

Eliza," I said. "You may have dreamed it, for one thing. But if it is true, the metal rod and the hole in the wall will show it."

Eliza looked a little bit sheepish.

"The hole's there all right, Miss Innes," she said. "But the bar was gone when MaryAnne and Rosie went up to pack my trunk."

"That wasn't all." Liddy's voice came funereally from a corner. "Eliza said that from the hole in the wall a burning eye looked down at her!"

"The wall must be at least six inches thick," I said with asperity. "Unless the person who drilled the hole carried an eye on the ends of a stick Eliza couldn't possibly have seen it."

But the fact remained, and a visit to Eliza's room proved it. I might jeer all I wished. Someone had drilled a hole in the unfinished wall of the ballroom passing between the bricks of the partition, and meeting the unresisting plaster of Eliza's room had sent the rod flying onto her bed. I had gone upstairs alone, and I confess the thing puzzled me. In two or three places in the wall small apertures had been made, none of them of any depth. But not the least mysterious thing was the disappearance of the iron implement that had been used.

I remembered a story I read once about an impish dwarf that lived in the spaces between the double walls of an ancient castle. I wondered vaguely if my original idea of a secret entrance to a hidden chamber could be right after all, and if we were housing some erratic guest who played pranks on us in the dark, and destroyed the walls so that he might listen, hidden safely away, to our amazed investigations.

MaryAnne and Eliza left that afternoon, but Rosie decided to stay. It was about five o'clock when the taxi came from the station to get them, and, to my amazement it had an occupant. Matthew Geist, the driver, asked for me and explained his errand with pride.

"I've brought you a cook, Miss Innes," he said. "When the message came to come up for two girls and their trunks I supposed there was something doing, and as this here woman had been looking for work in the village I thought I'd bring her along."

Already I had acquired the true suburbanite ability to take servants on faith. I no longer demanded written and unimpeachable references. I, Rachel Innes, have learned not to mind if the cook sits down comfortably in my sitting room when she is taking the orders for the day, and to be grateful if the silver is not cleaned with scouring soap. So that day I merely told Liddy to send the new applicant in. When she came, however, I could hardly restrain a gasp of surprise. It was the woman with the scarred face.

She stood somewhat awkwardly just inside the door, but she had an air of self-confidence that was inspiring. Yes, she could cook. She was not a fancy cook, but she could make good soups and desserts if there was anyone to take charge of the salads. And so in the end I took her. As Halsey said when we told him, it didn't matter much about the cook's face if only it was clean.

I have spoken of Halsey's restlessness. On that day it seemed to be more than ever a resistless impulse that kept him out until after luncheon. I think he hoped constantly that he might meet Louise driving over the hills in her small coupe. Possibly he did meet her occasionally, but from his continued gloom I felt sure the situation between them was unchanged.

Part of the afternoon I believe he read. Gertrude and I were out, as I have said, and at dinner we both noticed that something had occurred to distract him. He was disagreeable, which is unlike him, nervous and looking at his watch every five minutes, and he ate almost nothing. He asked twice during the meal on what train Jamieson and the other detective were coming, and had long periods of abstraction during which he dug his fork into my damask cloth and did not hear when he was spoken to. He refused dessert and left the table early, excusing himself on the ground that he wanted to see Alex.

Alex, however, was not to be found. It was after eight when Halsey ordered the car, and started down the hill at a pace which even for him was unusually reckless. Shortly after, Alex reported that he was ready to go over the house, preparatory to closing it for the night. Sam Bohannon came at a quarter before nine, and began his patrol of the grounds, and with the arrival of the two detectives to look forward to I was not especially apprehensive.

At half past nine I heard the sound of a car driven furiously up the drive. It came to a stop in front of the house, and immediately after there were hurried steps on the veranda. Our nerves were not what they should have been, and Gertrude, always apprehensive lately, was at the door almost instantly. A moment later Louise had burst into the room and stood there bareheaded and breathing hard.

"Where is Halsey?" she demanded. Above her plain black frock her eyes looked big and somber, and the rapid drive had brought no color to her face. I got up and drew forward a chair.

"He hasn't come back," I said quietly. "Sit down, child. You're not strong enough for this kind of thing."

I don't think she even heard me.

"He hasn't come back?" she asked, looking from me to Gertrude. "Do you know where he went? Where can I find him?"

"For heaven's sake, Louise," Gertrude burst out, "tell us what is wrong. Halsey's not here. He's gone to the station for Mr Jamieson. What has happened?"

"To the station, Gertrude? You are sure?"

"Yes," I said. "Listen. There's the whistle of the train now."

She relaxed a little at our matter-of-fact tone, and allowed herself to drop into a chair.

"Perhaps I was wrong," she said heavily. "He will be here in a few moments, if everything is all right."

We sat there, the three of us, without attempt at conversation. Both Gertrude and I recognized the futility of asking Louise any questions. Quite obviously she did not intend to talk. I know all our ears were strained for the first throb of the motor as it turned into the drive and commenced the climb to the house. But ten minutes passed, fifteen, twenty. I saw Louise's hands grow rigid as they clutched the arms of her chair. I watched Gertrude's bright color slowly ebbing away, and around my own heart I seemed to feel the grasp of a giant hand.

Twenty-five minutes, and then a sound. But it was not the chug of the motor, it was the unmistakable rattle of the Casanova taxi. Gertrude drew aside the curtain and peered into the darkness.

"It's the taxi, I am sure," she said, evidently relieved. "Something has gone wrong with the car, and no wonder, the way Halsey went down the hill."

It seemed a long time before the creaking vehicle came to a stop at the door. Louise rose and stood watching, her hand at her throat. And then Gertrude opened the door, admitting Jamieson and a stocky, middle-aged man. Halsey was not with them. When the door had closed and Louise realized that Halsey had not come her expression changed. From tense watchfulness to relief, and now again to absolute despair, her face was an open page.

"Halsey?" I asked unceremoniously, ignoring the stranger. "Didn't he meet you?"

"No." Jamieson looked slightly surprised. "I rather expected the car, but we got up all right."

"You didn't see him at all?" Louise demanded breathlessly.

Jamieson knew her at once, although he had not seen her before. She had kept to her rooms until the morning she left.

"No, Miss Armstrong," he said. "I saw nothing of him. What's wrong?"

"Then we have to find him," she asserted. "Every instant is precious. Mr Jamieson, I have reason for believing that he is in danger, but I don't know what it is. Only he must be found."

The stocky man had said nothing. Now he went quickly toward the door.

"I'll catch the taxi if I can and hold it," he said. "Is the gentleman down in the town?"

"Mr Jamieson," Louise said impulsively, "I can use the taxi. Take my coupe–it's outside and it's fast–and drive like mad. Try to find Halsey's car. It ought to be easy to trace. Only don't lose a moment."

The new detective had gone and a moment later Jamieson drove rapidly down the drive. Louise stood looking after them. When she turned around she faced a Gertrude who stood indignant, almost tragic, in the ball.

"You know what danger Halsey is in, Louise," she said accusingly. "I believe you know this whole horrible thing, this mystery we're struggling with. If anything happens to Halsey I'll never forgive you."

Louise only raised her hands despairingly and dropped them again. "I care as much as you do. Maybe more," she said despairingly. "I tried to warn him, but he wouldn't listen."

"Now listen, both of you," I said, as briskly as I could. "We are making a lot of trouble out of something perhaps very small. Halsey was probably late. He's always late. Any moment we may hear the car coming up the road."

But it did not come. After a half hour of suspense Louise went out quietly and did not come back. I hardly knew she was gone until I heard the station taxi moving off. And at eleven o'clock the telephone rang. It was Jamieson.

"I have found your car, Miss Innes," he said. "It has collided with a freight car on the siding above the station. No, Mr Innes was not there, but we shall probably find him. Better send Warner for the car."

But they did not find him. At four o'clock the next morning we were still waiting for news, while Alex watched the house and Sam the grounds. At daylight I dropped into exhausted sleep. Halsey had not come back, and there was no word from the two detectives.

26

Nothing that had gone before had been as bad as this. The murder and Thomas's sudden death we had been able to view in a detached sort of way. But with Halsey's disappearance everything was altered. Our little circle, intact until now, was broken. We were no longer onlookers who saw a battle passing around them. We were the center of action. Of course, there was no time then to voice such an idea. My mind seemed able to hold only one thought, that Halsey had been wickedly dealt with and that every minute lost might be fatal.

Jamieson came back about eight o'clock the next morning. He was covered with mud, and his hat was gone. Altogether we were a sad-looking trio which gathered around a breakfast no one could eat. Over a cup of black coffee the detective told us that he had learned of Halsey's movements the night before. Up to a certain point the car had made it easy enough to follow him. And I gathered that Burns, the other detective, had followed a similar car for miles at dawn, only to find it was carrying a family with several children.

"He left here about ten minutes after eight," Jamieson said. "He went alone, and at eight-twenty he stopped at Doctor Walker's. I went to the doctor's about midnight, but he had been called out on a case and had not come back by four o'clock. From the doctor's it seems Mr Innes walked across the lawn to the cottage Mrs Armstrong and her daughter have taken. Mrs Armstrong had gone to bed, and he said perhaps a dozen words to Miss Louise. She will not say what they were, but the girl evidently suspects what has occurred. That is, she suspects foul play but she doesn't know of what sort. Then apparently he started directly for the station. He was going very fast; the flagman at the Carol

Street crossing says he saw the car pass and recognized it. Along somewhere in the dark stretch between Carol Street and the depot the car evidently swerved suddenly–perhaps someone in the road–and went full into the side of a freight train. We found it there, badly smashed."

"And Halsey?" My lips were stiff.

"No sign of him, Miss Innes. Not even any indication that he had been hurt. In a way it's curious. If he was in the car when it hit–"

Gertrude shuddered.

"We examined every inch of track. The freight had gone, but there was no sign of trouble."

"But surely he can't be gone!" I cried. "Aren't there traces in the mud? Anything?"

"There is no mud, only dust. There hasn't been any rain lately. And the footpath there is of cinders. Miss Innes, I am inclined to think that he has met some sort of trouble. I don't think he's been murdered." I shrank from the word. "Burns is back in the country, on a clue we got from the night clerk at the drugstore. There will be two more men here by noon, and word has gone out over the teletype. If he's around we'll find him."

"What about the creek?" Gertrude asked with stiff lips. "If he was knocked unconscious, they might nave–"

She did not finish, but Jamieson knew what she meant.

"The creek is shallow now. If it were swollen with rain it would be different. There's hardly any water in it. Now, Miss Innes," he said, turning to me, "I must ask you some questions. Had Mr Innes any possible reason for going away like this without warning?"

"None whatever, so far as I know."

"He went away once before," he persisted. "And you were as sure then."

"He did not leave the car jammed into the side of a freight car before."

"No, but he left it for repairs in a garage a long distance from here. Do you know if he had any personal enemies? Anyone who might wish him out of the way?"

"Not that I know of, unless–no, I cannot think of any."

"Was he in the habit of carrying money?"

"He never carried it far. No, he never had more than enough for current expenses."

He got up and began to pace the room. It was an un-wonted concession to the occasion.

"Then I think we get at it by elimination. The chances are against flight. If he was hurt, we find no sign of it. It looks almost like a kidnapping. This young Doctor Walker, have you any idea why Mr Innes should have gone there last night?"

"I can't understand it," Gertrude said thoughtfully. "I don't think he knew Doctor Walker at all. Anyhow their relations could hardly have been even friendly, under the circumstances."

Jamieson pricked up his ears, and little by little he drew from us the unfortunate story of Halsey's love affair, and the fact that Louise was going to marry the doctor.

He listened attentively.

"There are some interesting developments here," he said thoughtfully. "The woman who claims to be the mother of Lucien Wallace has not come back. Your nephew has apparently been spirited away. There is an organized attempt being made to enter this house. In fact it has been entered. Witness the incident with the cook yesterday. And I have a new piece of information." He looked carefully away from Gertrude. "Mr John Bailey is not at his Knickerbocker apartments, and I don't know where he is. It's a Chinese puzzle. Nothing fits together, unless Mr Bailey and your nephew have again–"

And once again Gertrude surprised me. "They are not in any plot," she said hotly. "I know where Mr Bailey is. My brother is not with him."

The detective turned and looked at her keenly.

"Miss Gertrude," he said, "if you and Louise Armstrong would only tell me everything you know and surmise about this business, I should be able to do a great many things. I believe I could find your brother, and I might be able to– well, to do some other things." But Gertrude's face did not change.

"Nothing I know could help you to find Halsey," she said stubbornly. "I know as little of his disappearance as you do, and I can only say this: I don't trust Doctor Walker. I think he hated Halsey, and he would get rid of him if he could."

"Perhaps you are right. In fact, I had some such theory myself. But Doctor Walker went out late last night to a serious case in Summitville, and he's still there. Burns traced him. We have made guarded inquiry at the Greenwood Club, and through the village. There is absolutely nothing to go on but this. On the embankment above the railroad, at the point where we found the car, is a small house. An old woman and a daughter who is very lame live there. They say that they distinctly heard the shock when the car hit the freight, and they went to the bottom of their garden and looked over. The car was there. They could see the lights, and they thought someone had been injured. It was very dark, but they could make out two figures, standing together. The women were curious, and leaving the fence they went back and by a roundabout path down to the road. When they got there the car was still standing, the headlights broken and the front of it badly crushed, but there was no one to be seen."

He went away soon after, and to Gertrude and me was left the woman's part, to watch and wait. By luncheon nothing had been found, and I was about frantic. I went upstairs to Halsey's room finally, from sheer inability to sit across from Gertrude any longer and meet her terror-filled eyes.

Liddy was in my dressing room, suspiciously red-eyed, and trying to put a right sleeve in a left armhole of a new blouse for me. I was too much shaken to scold.

"What name did that woman in the kitchen give?" she demanded, viciously ripping out the offending sleeve.

"Bliss. Mattie Bliss," I replied.

"Bliss. M.B. Well, that's not what she has on her suitcase. It is marked N.F.C."

The new cook and her initials troubled me not at all. I put on my hat and sent for what the Casanova garage called a limousine. Having once made up my mind to a course of action I am not one to turn back. Warner drove me. He was plainly disgusted, and he drove the wreck as he would my own car, with the result that I was on the verge of catastrophe all the time I was out.

But Warner also had something on his mind, and after we had turned into the road he voiced it.

"Miss Innes," he said over his shoulder, "I overheard a part of a talk yesterday that I didn't understand. It wasn't my business to understand it, for that matter. But I've been thinking all day that I'd better tell you. Yesterday afternoon while you and Miss Gertrude were out, I had got the car in some sort of shape again after the fire, and I went to the library to call Mr Innes to see it. I went into the living room, where Miss Liddy said he was, and halfway cross to the library I heard him talking to someone. He seemed to be walking up and down and he was in a rage, I can tell you."

"What did he say?"

"The first thing I heard was–excuse me, Miss Innes, but it's what he said. 'The damned rascal,' he said, 'I'll see him in'–well, in hell was what he said, 'in hell first.' Then somebody else spoke up. It was a woman. She said, 'I warned them, but they thought I would be afraid.'"

"A woman? Did you wait to see who it was?"

"I wasn't spying, Miss Innes," Warner said with dignity. "But the next thing caught my attention. She said, 'I knew there was something wrong from the start. A man isn't well one day and dead the next without some reason.' I thought she was speaking of Thomas."

"And you don't know who it was!" I protested. "Warner, you had the key to everything in your hands and didn't use it."

However, there was nothing to be done. I resolved to make an inquiry when I got home, and in the meantime my present errand absorbed me. This was nothing less than to see Louise Armstrong and to attempt to drag from her what she knew, or suspected, of Halsey's disappearance. But here, as in every direction I turned, I was baffled.

A neat maid answered the bell, but she stood squarely in the doorway and it was impossible to preserve one's dignity and pass her.

"Miss Armstrong is very sick and unable to see anyone," she said. I did not believe her. She was a poor liar.

"And Mrs Armstrong, is she also ill?"

"She's with Miss Louise and can't be disturbed."

"Tell her it's Miss Innes, and that it is a matter of the greatest importance."

"It wouldn't be any good, Miss Innes. My orders are positive."

At that moment a heavy step sounded on the stairs. Past the maid's white-trapped shoulder I could see a familiar thatch of gray hair, and in a moment I was face to face with Doctor Stewart. He was very grave, and his customary geniality was tinged with restraint.

"You are the very woman I want to see," he said promptly. "Send away your car and let me drive you home. What's this about your nephew?"

"He has disappeared, doctor. Not only that, but there is every evidence that he has been either abducted or–" I could not finish. The doctor helped me into his shabby car in silence. Until we had gone a little distance he did not speak. Then he turned and looked at me.

"Now tell me about it," he said.

He heard me through without speaking, but his air of gravity did not change.

"So you think Louise knows something?" he said when I had finished. "I don't. In fact, I'm sure of it. The best evidence of it is this: she asked me if he had been heard from, or if anything had been learned. She won't allow Walker in the room, and she made me promise to see you and tell you not to give up the search for him. Find him, and find him soon. He's alive. That's the message."

"Well," I said, "if she knows all that she knows more. She's a very cruel and ungrateful girl."

"She is a very sick girl," he said gravely. "Neither you nor I can judge her until we know everything. But both she and her mother are ghosts of their former selves. Under all this, these two sudden deaths, this bank robbery, the invasions at Sunnyside and Halsey's disappearance, there is some mystery that, mark my words, will come out someday. And when it does, we shall find Louise a victim. Her mother too, perhaps."

I had not noticed where we were going, but now I saw we were beside the railroad and from a knot of men standing near the track I divined that it was here the car had been found. But the siding was empty. Except for a few bits of splintered wood on the ground there was no sign of the accident.

"Where is the freight car that was rammed?" the doctor asked a bystander.

"It was taken away at daylight, when the train was moved."

There was nothing to be gained. He pointed out the house on the embankment where the old lady and her daughter had heard the crash and seen two figures beside the car. Then we drove slowly home. I had the doctor put me down at the gate and I walked to the house, past the lodge where we had found Louise and, later, poor Thomas; up the drive where I had seen a man watching the lodge and where, later, Rosie had been frightened; past the east entrance, where so short a time before the most obstinate effort had been made to enter the house, and where, that night two weeks ago, Liddy and I had seen the strange woman. Not far from the west wing lay the blackened ruins of the stables. I felt like a ruin myself as I paused on the broad veranda before I entered the house.

Two more detectives had arrived in my absence, and it was a relief to turn over to them the responsibility of the house and grounds. Jamieson, they said, had arranged for more to assist in the search for Halsey, and the country was being scoured in all directions.

The household staff was again depleted that afternoon. Liddy was waiting to tell me that the new cook had gone, bag and baggage, without waiting to be paid. No one had admitted the visitor Warner had heard in the library, unless possibly the missing cook with the scarred face. Again I was working in a circle.

27

The next four days, from Saturday to the following Tuesday, we lived or existed in a state of the most dreadful suspense. We ate only when Liddy brought in a tray, and then very little. The papers of course had got hold of the story, and we were besieged by newspapermen. From all over the country false clues came pouring in and raised hopes that crumbled again to nothing. Every morgue within a hundred miles, every hospital, had been visited without result.

Jamieson personally took charge of the organized search and every evening, no matter where he happened to be, he called us by long-distance telephone. It was the same formula. "Nothing today. A new clue to work on. Better luck tomorrow." And heartsick we would put down the receiver and sit back again to our vigil.

The inaction was deadly. Liddy cried all day and, because she knew I objected to tears, sniffed audibly around the corner.

"For heaven's sake, smile!" I snapped at her. And her ghastly attempt at a grin, with her swollen nose and red eyes, made me hysterical. I laughed and cried together and pretty soon, like the two old fools we were, we were sitting together weeping into the same handkerchief.

Things were happening of course all the time, but they made little or no impression. The Emergency Hospital called up Doctor Stewart and reported that Mrs Watson was in a critical condition. I understood also that legal steps were being taken to terminate my lease at Sunnyside. Louise was out of danger but very ill, and a trained nurse guarded her like a gorgon. There was a rumor in the village, brought up by Liddy from the butcher's, that a wedding had already taken place between Louise and Doctor Walker, and this roused me for the first time to action.

On Tuesday then I sent for the car from the garage in the village and prepared to go out. As I waited at the porte-cochere I saw the undergardener, an inoffensive grayish-haired man, trimming borders near the house. The day detective was watching him, sitting on what had been the carriage block. When he saw me he got up.

"Miss Innes," he said, taking off his hat, "do you know where Alex the gardener is?"

"Why, no. Isn't he here?" I asked.

"He's been gone since yesterday afternoon. Have you employed him long?"

"Only a couple of weeks."

"Is he efficient? A capable man?"

"I hardly know," I said vaguely. "The place looks all right, and I know very little about such things. I know much more about boxes of roses than bushes of them."

"This man," pointing to the assistant, "says Alex isn't a gardener. That he doesn't know anything about plants."

"That's very strange," I said, thinking hard. "He came to me from the Brays, who are in Europe."

"Exactly." The detective smiled. "Every man who cuts grass isn't a gardener, Miss Innes, and just now it is our policy to believe every person around here a rascal until he proves to be the other thing."

Warner came up with the car then, and the conversation stopped. As he helped me in, however, the detective said something further.

"Not a word or sign to Alex, if he comes back," he said cautiously. I went first to Doctor Walker's. I was tired of beating about the bush, and I felt that the key to Halsey's disappearance was here at Casanova, in spite of Jamieson's theories.

The doctor was in. He came at once to the door of his consulting room, and there was no mask of cordiality in his manner.

"Please come in," he said curtly.

"I shall stay here, I think, doctor." I did not like his face or his manner. There was a subtle change in both. He had thrown off the air of friendliness, and I thought too that he looked anxious and haggard.

"Doctor Walker," I said, "I have come to you to ask some questions, I hope you will answer them. As you know, my nephew has not yet been found."

"So I understand," he said stiffly.

"I believe if you would you could help us, and that leads to one of my questions. Will you tell me what was the nature of the conversation you held with him the night he was attacked and carried off?"

"Attacked! Carried off!" he said, with pretended surprise. "Really, Miss Innes, don't you think you exaggerate? I understand this is not the first time Mr Innes has—disappeared."

"You're quibbling, doctor. This is a matter of life and death. Will you answer my question?"

"Certainly. He said his nerves were bad, and I gave him a prescription for them. I am violating professional ethics when I tell you even as much as that."

I could not tell him he lied. I think I looked it. But I hazarded a random shot.

"I thought perhaps," I said, watching him narrowly, "that it might be about Nina Carrington."

For a moment I thought he was going to strike me. He grew livid, and a small crooked blood vessel in his temple swelled and throbbed. Then he forced a short laugh.

"Who is Nina Carrington?" he asked.

"I am about to discover that," I replied, and he was quiet at once. It was not difficult to realize that he feared Nina Carrington a good deal more than he did the devil. As a result our leave-taking was brief. In fact we merely stared at each other over the waiting-room table, with its litter of year-old magazines. Then I turned and went out.

"To Richfield," I told Warner, and on the way I thought and thought hard.

"Nina Carrington, Nina Carrington," the roar and rush of the wheels seemed to sing the words. "Nina Carrington, N.C." and then I knew, knew as surely as if I had seen the whole thing. There had been an N.C. on the suitcase belonging to the woman with the scarred face. How simple it all seemed. Mattie Bliss had been Nina Carrington. It was she Warner had heard in the library. It was something she had told Halsey that had taken him frantically to Doctor Walker's office, and from there perhaps to his death. If we could find the woman we might find what had become of Halsey.

We were almost at Richfield now, so I kept on. My mind was not on my errand there now. It was back with Halsey on that memorable night. What was it he had said to Louise that had sent her up to Sunnyside, half wild with fear of him? I made up my mind, as the car drew up before the Tate cottage, that I would see Louise if I had to break into the house with a gun.

Almost exactly the same scene as before greeted my eyes at the cottage: Mrs Tate, the baby carriage in the path, the children at the swing, all were the same.

She came forward to meet me, and I noticed that some of the anxious lines had gone out of her face. She looked young, almost pretty.

"I am glad you've come back," she said. "I think I will have to be honest and give you back your money."

"Why?" I asked. "Has the mother come?"

"No, but someone came and paid the boy's board for a month. She talked to him for a long time, but when I asked him afterward he didn't know her name."

"A young woman?"

"Not very young. About forty, I suppose. She was small and fair-haired, just a little bit gray, and very sad. She was in deep mourning, and I think when she came she expected to go at once. But the child, Lucien, interested her. She talked to him for a long time, and she looked much happier when she left."

"You are sure this was not the real mother?"

"Oh mercy, no! Why, she didn't know which of the three was Lucien. I thought perhaps she was a friend of yours, but of course I didn't ask."

"She was not scarred in the face?" I asked at a venture.

"No, indeed. A skin like a baby's. But perhaps you'll know the initials. She gave Lucien a handkerchief and forgot it. It was very fine, black-bordered, and it had three hand-worked letters in the corner–F.B.A."

"No," I said with truth enough, "she is not a friend of mine." F.B.A. was Fanny Armstrong, without a chance of doubt!

With another warning to Mrs Tate as to silence we started back to Sunnyside. So Fanny Armstrong knew of Lucien Wallace, and was sufficiently interested to visit him and pay for his support. Who was the child's mother and where was she? Who was Nina Carrington? Did either of them know where Halsey was, or what had happened to him?

On the way home we passed the little cemetery where Thomas had been laid to rest. I wondered if Thomas could have helped us to find Halsey, had he lived. Farther along was the more imposing burial ground, where Arnold Armstrong and his father lay in the shadow of a tall granite shaft. Of the three, I think Thomas was the only one sincerely mourned.

28

The bitterness toward the dead president of the Traders' Bank seemed to grow with time. Never popular, his memory was execrated by people who had lost nothing, but who were filled with disgust by constantly hearing new stories of the man's grasping avarice. The Traders' had been a favorite bank for small tradespeople, and in its savings department it had solicited even the smallest deposits. People who had thought to be self-supporting to the last found themselves confronting the poorhouse, their few hundred dollar savings wiped away. All bank failures have this element, however, and the directors were trying to promise twenty per cent on deposits.

But like everything else those days the bank failure was almost forgotten by Gertrude and myself. We did not mention Jack Bailey. I had found nothing to change my impression of his guilt, and Gertrude knew how I felt. As for the murder of the bank president's son, I was of two minds. One day I thought Gertrude knew or at least suspected that Jack had done it; the next I feared that it had been Gertrude herself, that night alone on the circular staircase. And then the mother of Lucien Wallace would obtrude herself, and an almost equally good case might be made against her. There were times of course when I was disposed to throw all those suspicions aside and fix definitely on the unknown, whoever that might be.

I had my greatest disappointment when it came to tracing Nina Carrington. The woman had gone without leaving a trace. Scarred as she was it should have been easy to follow her, but she was not to be found. A description to one of the detectives on my arrival home had started the ball rolling. But by night she had not been found. I told Gertrude then about the telegram to Louise when she had been ill before, about my visit to Doctor Walker, and my

Suspicions that Mattie Bliss and Nina Carrington were the same. She thought, as I did, that there was little doubt of it. I said nothing to her, however, of the detective's suspicions about Alex. Little things that I had not noticed at the time now came back to me. I had an uncomfortable feeling that perhaps Alex was a spy, and that by taking him into the house I had played into the enemy's hand. But at eight o'clock that night Alex himself appeared, and with him a strange and repulsive individual. They made a queer pair, for Alex was almost as disreputable as the tramp, and he had a badly swollen eye.

Gertrude had been sitting listlessly waiting for the evening message from Jamieson, but when the singular pair came in as they did, without ceremony, she jumped up and stood staring. Winters, the detective who watched the house at night, followed them and kept his eyes sharply on Alex's prisoner. For that was the situation as it developed.

He was a tall lanky individual, ragged and dirty, and just now he looked both terrified and embarrassed. Alex was too much engrossed to be either, and to this day I don't think I ever asked him why he went off without permission the day before.

"Miss Innes," Alex began abruptly, "this man can tell us something very important about the disappearance of Mr Innes. I found him trying to sell this watch."

He took a watch from his pocket and put it on the table. It was Halsey's watch. I had given it to him on his twenty-first birthday, and I was dumb with apprehension.

"He says he had a pair of cuff links also, but he sold them–"

"Fer a dollar'n half," put in the disreputable individual hoarsely, with an eye on the detective.

"He's not dead?" I implored. The tramp cleared his throat.

"No'm," he said huskily. "He was used up pretty bad, but he weren't dead. He was comin' to hisself when I–" He stopped and looked at the detective. "I didn't steal it, Mr

Winters," he whined. "I found it in the road, honest to God I did."

Mr Winters paid no attention to him. He was watching Alex.

"I'd better tell what he told me," Alex broke in. "It will be quicker. When Mr Jamieson calls up we can start him right. Mr Winters, I found this man trying to sell that watch on Fifth Street. He offered it to me for three dollars."

"How did you know the watch?" Winters snapped at him.

"I'd seen it before. As a matter of fact I used it at night when I was watching at the foot of the staircase." The detective was satisfied. "When he offered the watch to me I knew it, and I pretended I was going to buy it. We went into an alley and I got the watch." The tramp shivered. It was plain how Alex had secured the watch. "Then I got the story from this fellow; He claims to have seen the whole affair. He says he was in an empty freight car, in the car the automobile struck."

The tramp broke in here and told his story, with frequent interpretations by Alex and Mr Winters. He used a strange argot, in which familiar words took unfamiliar meanings, but it was gradually made clear to us.

On the night in question the tramp had been "pounding his ear," as he put it, in an empty boxcar along the siding at Casanova. The train was going west, and due to leave at dawn. The tramp and the "brakey" were friendly, and things going well. About ten o'clock, perhaps earlier, a terrific crash against the side of the car roused him. He tried to open the door but could not move it. He got out on the other side, and as he did so he heard someone groan.

The habits of a lifetime made him cautious. He slipped onto the bumper of a car and peered through. An automobile had struck the car, and was badly smashed. The taillight was burning, but the headlights were out. Two men were stooping over someone who lay on the ground. Then the taller of the two started on a dogtrot along the train looking for an empty. He found one four cars away and ran back again. The two lifted the unconscious man into the empty boxcar, and getting in themselves stayed for three or four minutes. When they came out, after closing the sliding door, they cut up over the railroad embankment toward the town. One, the short one, seemed to limp.

The tramp was wary. He waited for ten minutes or so. Some women came down a path to the road and inspected the automobile. When they had gone, he crawled into the car in question and closed the door again. Then he lighted a match. The figure of a man, unconscious, gagged, and with his hands tied, lay at the far end. The tramp lost no time. He went through his pockets, found a little money and the cuff links, and took them. Then he loosened the gag–it had been cruelly tight–and went his way, again closing the door of the boxcar. Outside on the road he found the watch. He got on the fast freight east some time after and rode into the city. He had sold the cuff links, but on offering the watch to Alex he had been "copped."

The story with its cold recital of brutality was done. I hardly knew if I was more anxious or less. That it was Halsey there could be no doubt. How badly he was hurt, how far he had been carried, were the questions that demanded immediate answer. But it was the first real information we had had. At least my boy had not been murdered outright. But instead of vague terrors there was now the real fear that he might be lying in some strange hospital receiving the casual attention commonly given to charity cases. Even this, had we known it, would have been paradise to the terrible truth. I wake yet and feel myself cold and trembling with the horror of Halsey's situation for three days after his disappearance.

Winters and Alex disposed of the tramp with a warning. It was evident he had told us all he knew. We had occasion, within a day or two, to be doubly thankful that we had given him his freedom. When Jamieson telephoned that night we had news for him, but he told me what I had not realized before, that it would not be possible to find Halsey at once even with this clue. The cars by this time, three days, might be scattered over the Union. But he said to keep on hoping, that it was the best news we had had. And in the meantime, consumed with anxiety as we were, things were happening at the house in rapid succession.

We had one peaceful day, then Liddy took sick in the night. I went in when I heard her groaning and found her with a hot-water bottle to her face and her right cheek swollen until it was glassy.

"Toothache?" I asked, not too gently. "You deserve it. A woman of your age, who would rather go around with an exposed nerve in her head than have the tooth pulled! It would be over in a moment."

"So would hanging," Liddy protested, from behind the hot-water bottle.

I was hunting around for cotton and laudanum.

"You have a tooth just like it yourself, Miss Rachel," she whimpered. "And I'm sure Doctor Boyle's been trying to take it out for years."

There was no laudanum and Liddy made a terrible fuss when I proposed carbolic acid, just because I had put too much on the cotton once and burned her mouth. I'm sure it never did her any permanent harm. Indeed, the doctor said afterward that living on a liquid diet had been a splendid rest for her stomach. But she would have none of the acid and she kept me awake groaning, so at last I got up and went to Gertrude's door. To my surprise, it was locked.

I went around by the hall and into her bedroom that way. The bed was turned down, and her dressing gown and pajamas lay ready in the little room next, but Gertrude was not there. She had not undressed.

I don't know what terrible thoughts came to me in the minute I stood there. Through the door I could hear Liddy grumbling, with a squeal now and then when the pain stabbed harder. Then automatically I got the medicine and went back to her.

It was fully a half hour before Liddy's groans subsided. At intervals I went to the door into the hall and looked out, but I saw and heard nothing suspicious. Finally when Liddy had dropped into a doze I even ventured as far as the head of the circular staircase, but there floated up to me only the even breathing of Winters, the night detective, sleeping just inside the entry. And then far off I heard the rapping noise that had lured Louise down the staircase that other night, two weeks before. It was over my head, and very faint, three or four short muffled taps, a pause and then again, stealthily repeated.

The sound of Winters's breathing was comforting. With the thought that there was help within call something kept me from waking him. I did not move for a moment. Ridiculous things Liddy had said about a ghost–I am not at all superstitious, except perhaps in the middle of the night with everything dark–things like that came back to me. Almost beside me was the clothes chute. I could feel it, but I could see nothing. As I stood listening intently I heard a sound near me. It was vague, indefinite. Then it ceased. There was an uneasy movement and a grunt from the foot of the circular staircase, and silence again. I stood perfectly still, hardly daring to breathe.

Then I knew I had been right. Someone was stealthily passing the head of the staircase and coming toward me in the dark. I leaped against the wall for support, for my knees were giving away. The steps were close now, and suddenly I thought of Gertrude. Of course it was Gertrude. I put out one hand in front of me but I touched nothing. My voice almost refused me, but I managed to gasp out, "Gertrude!"

"Good God!" a man's voice exclaimed just beside me. And then I collapsed. I felt myself going, felt someone catch me, and a horrible blackness, then nothing.

When I came to it was dawn. I was lying on the bed in Louise's room, with a cherub on the ceiling staring down at me, and there was a blanket from my own bed thrown over me. I felt weak and dizzy, but I managed to get up and totter to the door. At the foot of the circular stair-case Winters was still asleep. Hardly able to stand I crept back to my room. The door into Gertrude's room was no longer locked. She was sleeping like a tired child. And in my dressing room Liddy hugged a cold hot-water bottle and mumbled in her sleep.

"There's some things you can't hold with handcuffs," she was muttering thickly.

29

For the first time in twenty years I kept my bed that day. Liddy was alarmed to the point of hysteria and sent for Doctor Stewart just after breakfast. Gertrude spent the morning with me, reading something, I forget what. I was too busy with my thoughts to listen. I had said nothing to the two detectives. If Jamieson had been there, I would have told him everything, but I could not go to these strange men and tell them my niece had been missing in the middle of the night, that she had not gone to bed at all, or that while I was searching for her through the house I had met a stranger who when I fainted had carried me into a room and left me there, to get better or not as it might happen.

The whole situation was incredible. Had the issues been less vital it would have been absurd. Here we were, guarded day and night by private detectives with an extra man to watch the grounds, and yet we might as well have lived in a Japanese paper house for all the protection we had.

And there was something else. The man I had met in the darkness had been even more startled than I, and about his voice when he muttered his muffled exclamation there was something vaguely familiar. All that morning while Gertrude read aloud and Liddy watched for the doctor, I was puzzling over that voice, without result.

And there were other things too. I wondered what Gertrude's absence from her room had to do with it all, or if it had any connection.

I tried to think that she had heard the rapping noises before I did and gone to investigate, but I'm afraid I was a moral coward that day.

I could not ask her.

Perhaps the diversion was good for me. It took my mind from Halsey, and the story we had heard the night before. But the day was a long vigil, with every ring of the telephone full of possibilities. Doctor Walker came up, sometime just after luncheon, and asked for me.

"Go down and see him," I instructed Gertrude. "Tell him I'm out. For mercy's sake don't say I'm sick. Find out what he wants, and from this time on instruct the servants that he is not to be admitted. I loathe the man."

Gertrude came back very soon, her face rather flushed.

"He came to ask us again to get out," she said, picking up her book with a jerk. "He says Louise wants to come here, now that she is recovering."

"And what did you say?"

"I said we were very sorry we couldn't leave, but we would be delighted to have Louise come up here with us. He looked daggers at me. And he wanted to know if we would recommend Eliza as a cook. He has brought a patient, a man, out from town, and is increasing his establishment. That's the way he put it."

"I wish him joy of Eliza," I said tartly. "Did he ask for Halsey?"

"Yes. I told him we were on the track, and that it was only a question of time. He said he was glad, although he didn't appear to be, but he said not to be too sanguine."

"Do you know what I believe?" I asked. "I believe, as firmly as I believe anything, that Doctor Walker knows something about Halsey, and that he could put his finger on him if he wanted to."

There were several things that day that bewildered me. About three o'clock Jamieson telephoned from the Casanova station and Warner went down to meet him. I got up and dressed hastily, and the detective was shown up to my sitting room.

"No news?" I asked, as he entered. He tried to look encouraging, without success. I noticed that he looked tired and dusty, and although he was ordinarily impeccable in his appearance it was clear he was at least two days from a razor.

"It won't be long now, Miss Innes," he said. "I have come out here on a peculiar errand, but I'll tell you about it later. First, I want to ask some questions. Did anyone come out here yesterday to repair the telephone and examine the wires on the roof?"

"Yes," I said promptly; "but it was not the telephone. He said the wiring might have caused the fire at the stable. I went up with him myself, but he only looked around. He didn't do anything."

"Good for you!" he applauded. "Don't allow anyone in the house that you don't trust, and don't trust anybody. Not everybody is an electrician who wears rubber gloves."

He refused to explain further, but he got a slip of paper out of his pocketbook and opened it carefully.

"Listen," he said. "You heard this before and scoffed. In the light of recent developments I want you to read it again. You are a clever woman, Miss Innes. Just as surely as I sit here there's something in this house that is wanted very badly by a number of people. The lines are closing up, Miss Innes."

The paper was the one he had found among Arnold Armstrong's effects, and I read it again:

"........ by altering the plans for .... rooms may be possible. The best way, in my opinion, would be to .... the plan for .... in one of the ..... rooms .... chimney."

"I think I understand," I said slowly. "Someone is searching for a secret room, and he is trying in every possible way to get into the house. He's been in the house, for that matter. The hole in the wall upstairs–"

"Why do you say 'he'?" he inquired with interest.

"I've seen one of them."

But he made no comment on that. He got up, shaking down his trouser legs as he did so, and confronted me with a grave face.

"Miss Innes," he said, "I don't think there's any doubt that at least some of the money from the Traders' Bank is concealed in this house. I believe young Walker knows it, that he came back from California to get it, and when he failed to put Mrs Armstrong and Louise back here he has consistently tried to break in. He's succeeded twice."

"Three times," I corrected him, and told him about my experience the night before. "But it wasn't Walker last night. He has someone working with him. It wasn't he who caught me when I fainted. I'd know his voice anywhere."

He lit a cigarette and paced the floor before he spoke again.

"There's something else that puzzles me," he said, stopping before me. "Who and what is the woman Nina Carrington? If she came here as Mattie Bliss, what did she tell Halsey that sent him racing to Doctor Walker's and then to see Miss Armstrong? If we could find that woman we might have the whole thing."

"Mr Jamieson, did you ever think that Paul Armstrong might not have died a natural death?"

He gave me a curious glance.

"We're checking on that with the Coast now," he said. But there was no time for more. Gertrude came in, announcing a man below to see him.

"I want you present at this interview, Miss Innes," he said. "May Riggs come up? He has left Doctor Walker and he has something he wants to tell us."

Riggs came into the room diffidently, but Jamieson put him at his ease. He kept a careful eye on me, however, and slid into a chair by the door when he was asked to sit down.

"Now, Riggs," began Jamieson briskly, "you are to say what you have to say before this lady. She is Miss Innes and is certainly interested."

"You promised you'd keep it quiet, Mr Jamieson." Riggs plainly did not trust me. There was nothing friendly in the glance he turned on me.

"Yes, yes. You will be protected. But first of all, did you bring what you promised?"

Riggs produced a roll of papers from under his coat and handed them over. Jamieson examined them with lively satisfaction and passed them to me. "The blueprints of Sunnyside," he said. "What did I tell you? Now, Riggs, we're ready."

"I'd never have come to you, Mr Jamieson," he began, "if it hadn't been for Miss Armstrong. When Mr Innes was spirited away like, and Miss Louise got sick because of it, I thought things had gone far enough. I'd done some things for the doctor before that wouldn't bear looking into, but I turned a bit squeamish."

"Did you help with my nephew's kidnapping?" I asked, leaning forward.

"No, ma'am. I didn't ever know of it until the next day, when it came out in the Casanova *Weekly Ledger*. But I know who did it all right. I'd better start at the beginning.

"When Doctor Walker went away to California with the Armstrong family there was talk in the town that when he came back he would be married to Miss Armstrong, and we all expected it. First thing I knew I got a letter from him, in the West. He seemed to be excited, and he said Miss Armstrong had taken a sudden notion to go home. He sent me some money, and I was to watch for her to see if she went to Sunnyside, and wherever she was not to lose sight of her until he got back here. I traced her to the lodge, and I guess I scared you on the drive one night, Miss Innes."

"You scared Rosie worse," I observed dryly.

Riggs grinned sheepishly.

"I only wanted to make sure Miss Louise was there. Rosie started to run, and I tried to stop her and tell her some sort of story to account for my being there. But she wouldn't wait."

"And the broken china in the basket?"

"Well, broken china's death to rubber tires," he said. "I hadn't any complaint against you people here, and your car was a good one."

So Rosie's highwayman was explained.

"Well, I telegraphed the doctor where Miss Louise was and I kept an eye on her. Just a day or so before they came home with the body I got another letter, telling me to watch for a woman whose face had bad scars from a burn. Her name was Carrington, and the doctor made things pretty strong. If I found any such woman loafing around I was not to lose sight of her for a minute until he got back.

"Well, I would have had my hands full, but the other woman didn't show up for a good while, and when she did the doctor was home."

"Riggs," I asked abruptly, "did you get into this house a day or two after I took it, at night?"

"I did not, Miss Innes. I've never been in this house before. Well, the Carrington woman didn't show up until the night Mr Halsey disappeared. Then she came to the office late and the doctor was out. She waited around, walking the floor and acting pretty excited. When the doctor didn't come back she was in an awful way. She wanted me to hunt him, and when he didn't appear she called him names and said he couldn't fool her. There was murder being done, and she would see him swing for it.

"She struck me as being an ugly customer, and when she left about eleven o'clock and went across to the Armstrong house in the village I wasn't far behind her. She walked all around the house first, looking up at the windows. Then she rang the bell, and the minute the door was opened she was through it and into the hail."

"How long did she stay?"

"That's the queer part of it," Riggs said, looking puzzled. "She didn't come out that night at all. I went to bed at daylight and that was the last I heard of her until the next day, when I saw her on a truck at the station, covered with a sheet. She'd been struck by the express and you'd hardly have known her. She was dead, of course. The station agent said she was crossing the track to take the up-train to town when the express struck her."

I was profoundly shocked. The death itself was horrible enough. But also we had apparently reached another dead end. Even Jamieson looked stunned.

"So that's that," I said. "We're back where we started."

Riggs, however, spoke up eagerly.

"It's not as bad as that," he said. "The Carrington woman came from the town in California where Mr Armstrong died, and she knew something. I lived with Doctor Walker seven years, and I know him well. There are few things he is afraid of, but he was afraid of her. I think he killed Mr Armstrong out there himself. That's what I think. What else he did I don't know, but he fired me and pretty nearly strangled me for telling Mr Jamieson here about Mr Innes's having been in his office the night he disappeared, and about my hearing them quarreling."

Jamieson turned to me.

"What was it Warner heard the Carrington woman say to your nephew in the library, Miss Innes?" he inquired.

"She said 'I knew there was something wrong from the start. A man isn't well one day and dead the next without some reason.'"

So the Carrington woman had known or suspected something, and now she was dead. Like the two Armstrong men, and my poor Thomas. And Halsey was still God only knew where.

30

It was on Wednesday that Riggs told us the story of his connection with some of the situations which had been previ-
ously unexplained. Halsey had been gone since the Friday
night before, and with the passage of each day I felt that his
chances were lessening. I knew well enough that he might
be carried thousands of miles in the box car, locked in perhaps without water or food. I had read of cases where bod-
ies had been found locked in cars on isolated sidings in the
West, and my spirits went down with every hour.

His recovery was destined to be almost as sudden as his
disappearance, and was due directly to the tramp Alex had
brought to Sunnyside. It seems the man was grateful for
his release, and when he learned something of Halsey's
whereabouts from another member of his fraternity he was
prompt in letting us know.

On Wednesday evening Jamieson, who had been down
at the Armstrong house trying to see Louise and failing,
was met near the gate at Sunnyside by an individual as repulsive and unkempt as the one Alex had captured. The
man knew the detective, and he gave him a piece of dirty
paper, on which were scrawled the words—"Innes at City
Hospital, Johnsville." The tramp who brought the paper
pretended to know nothing except that the paper had been
passed along from a "friend" in Johnsville, who seemed to
know the information would be valuable to us.

Again the long-distance telephone came into requisition.
Jamieson called the hospital, while we crowded around
him. And when there was no longer any doubt that it was
Halsey, and that he would probably recover, we all laughed
and cried together. I am sure I kissed Liddy, and I have had
terrible moments since when I seem to remember kissing
Jamieson too, in the excitement.

Anyhow by eleven o'clock that night Gertrude was on her way to Johnsville, three hundred and eighty miles away, and accompanied by Rosie. The domestic force was now down to MaryAnne and Liddy, with the undergardener's wife coming every day to help out. Fortunately Warner and the detectives were keeping bachelor hall in the lodge. Out of deference to Liddy they washed their dishes once a day, and they concocted queer messes according to their several abilities. They had one triumph which they ate regularly for breakfast, and which formed a sort of odorous aura about them the rest of the day. It was bacon and onions, fried together. They were almost pathetically grateful, however, I noticed, for an occasional broiled tenderloin steak.

It was not until Gertrude and Rosie had gone and Sunnyside had settled down for the night, with Winters at the foot of the staircase, that Jamieson broached a subject he had evidently planned before he came.

"Miss Innes," he said, stopping me as I was about to go to my room upstairs, "how are your nerves tonight?"

"I have nor.e," I said, almost gaily. "With Halsey found, my troubles have gone."

"I mean," he persisted, "do you feel as though you could go through with something rather unusual?"

"The most unusual thing I can think of would be a peaceful night. But if anything is going to happen don't dare to let me miss it."

"Something is going to happen," he said. "And you're the only woman I can think of that I can take along." He looked at his watch. "Don't ask me any questions, Miss Innes. Put on heavy shoes and some old dark clothes, and make up your mind not to be surprised at anything."

Liddy was sleeping the sleep of the just when I went upstairs, and I hunted out my things cautiously. The detective was waiting in the ball, and I was astonished to see Doctor Stewart with him. They were talking confidentially together, but when I came down they stopped. There were a few preparations to be made, the locks to be gone over,

Winters to be instructed as to renewed vigilance, and then after extinguishing the hall light we crept in the darkness through the front door and into the night.

I asked no questions. I felt that they were doing me honor in making me one of the party, and I would show them I could be as silent as they. We went across the fields, passing through the woods that reached almost to the ruins of the stable, going over stiles now and then, and sometimes climbing over fences, Only once somebody spoke, and then it was an emphatic bit of profanity from Doctor Stewart when he ran into a barbed-wire fence.

We were joined at the end of five minutes by another man, who fell into step with the doctor silently. He carried something over his shoulder which I could not make out. In this way we walked for perhaps twenty minutes. I had lost all sense of direction: I merely stumbled along in silence, allowing Jamieson to guide me this way or that as the path demanded. I hardly know what I expected. Once when through a miscalculation I jumped a little short over a ditch and landed above my shoe tops in the water and ooze I remember wondering if this was really I, and if I had ever tasted life until that summer. I walked along with the water sloshing in my shoes, and I was actually cheerful. I remember whispering to Jamieson that I had never seen the stars so lovely, and that it was a mistake, when the Lord had made the night so beautiful, to sleep through it!

The doctor was not happy, however. He kept muttering about doing unlawful things and what would happen to him when the thing came out. If it ever did. And I remember Jamieson replying that what might happen to Doctor Stewart was nothing to what the department would do to him unless he could prove his case.

We were all puffing somewhat when we finally came to a halt. I confess that just then even Sunnyside seemed a cheerful spot. We had paused at the edge of a level cleared place, bordered all around with primly trimmed evergreen trees. Between them I caught a glimpse of starlight shining down on rows of white headstones, and an occasional more imposing monument or towering shaft. In spite of myself I drew my breath in sharply. We were on the edge of the Casanova churchyard.

I saw now both the man who had joined the party and the implements he carried. It was Alex, armed with two long-handled spades. After the first shock of surprise, I flatter myself if I was not cool I was at least quiet. We went in single file between the rows of headstones, and although when I found myself last I had an instinctive desire to keep looking back over my shoulder, I found when the first uneasiness is past that a cemetery at night is much the same as any other country place, filled with vague shadows and unexpected noises. Once, indeed

–but Mr Jamieson said it was an owl and I tried to believe him.

In the shadow of the Armstrong granite shaft we stopped. I think the doctor wanted to send me back.

"It's no place for a woman," I heard him protesting angrily. But

Jamieson said something about witnesses, and the doctor came over and felt my pulse.

"Anyhow, I don't believe you're any worse off here than you would be in that nightmare of a house," he said finally, and put his coat on the steps of the shaft for me to sit on.

There is an air of finality about a grave. One watches the earth thrown in, with the feeling that this is the end. Whatever has gone before, whatever is to come in eternity, that particular temple of the soul has been given back to the elements from which it came. So there is a sense of desecration, of a reversal of the everlasting fitness of things, in resurrecting a body from its mother earth. Nevertheless, I sat quietly by and watched Alex and Jamieson steaming over their work, without a single qualm except the fear of detection.

The doctor kept a keen lookout, but no one appeared. Once in a while he came over to me, and gave me a reassuring pat on the shoulder.

"I never expected to come to this," he said once. "There's one thing sure, I'll not be suspected of complicity. A doctor is generally supposed to be handier at burying folks than at digging them up."

Then the uncanny moment came when Alex and Jamieson tossed the spades on the grass, and I confess I hid my face. There was a longish period of strain I know, while the heavy coffin was being raised, and I felt my composure going. For fear I would shriek I tried to think of something else, of what time Gertrude would reach Halsey, or of anything but the grisly reality that lay just beyond me on the grass.

Then I heard a low exclamation from the detective and I felt the pressure of the doctor's fingers on my arm.

"Now, Miss Innes," he said gently. "If you will come over–"

I held on to him frantically, and somehow I got there and looked down. The lid of the casket had been raised and a silver plate on it proved we had made no mistake. But the face that showed in the light of the lantern was a face I had never seen before. The man who lay before us was not Paul Armstrong.

31

What with the excitement of the discovery, the walk home under the stars in wet shoes and draggled skirts, and getting upstairs and undressed without rousing Liddy, I was completely used up. What to do with my shoes was the greatest puzzle of all, there being no place in the house safe from Liddy, until I decided to slip upstairs the next morning and drop them into the hole the "ghost" had made in the trunk-room wall.

I went to bed after I reached this decision, but only to a light sleep in which I lived over again the events of the night. Again I saw the group around the silent figure on the grass, and again as had happened at the grave I heard Alex's voice, tense and triumphant: "Now we've got them," he said. Only, in my nervous condition he seemed to say it over and over, until I finally took a sleeping tablet to shut out his voice.

I wakened early in spite of my fatigue, and lay there thinking. Who was Alex? I no longer believed he was a gardener. Who was the man whose body we had resurrected? And where was Paul Armstrong? Probably living safe in some extraditionless country on the fortune he had stolen. Did Louise and her mother know of the shameful and wicked deception? What had Thomas known, and Mrs Watson? And who was Nina Carrington?

This last question, it seemed to me, was answered. In some way the woman had learned of the substitution, and had tried to use her knowledge for blackmail. Nina Carrington's own story had died with her, but however it happened it was clear that she had carried her knowledge to Halsey the afternoon Gertrude and I were looking for clues to the man I had shot on the east veranda.

Halsey had probably been half crazed by what he heard, since it was evident Louise was marrying Doctor Walker to keep the shameful secret for her mother's sake. Always reckless, he had gone at once to

Doctor Walker and denounced him. There had been a scene, and he left on his way to the station to meet and notify Jamieson of what he had learned. The doctor was active mentally and physically. Accompanied perhaps by Riggs, who had shown himself not overscrupulous until he quarreled with his employer, he had gone to the railroad embankment. But what had happened after that I did not know. It seemed likely that he had knocked Halsey unconscious so that the car hit the freight. Or with Halsey out cold he had himself directed the car and jumped before it struck.

I still think my reconstruction good, if not entirely correct.

There was a telegram that morning from Gertrude.

"Halsey conscious and improving. No fracture. Home as soon as possible.

Gertrude."

With Halsey found and getting better, and with at last something to work on, I began that day, Thursday, with fresh courage. As Jamieson had said, the lines were closing up. That I was to be caught and almost finished in the closing was happily unknown to us all.

It was late when I got up. I lay in my bed, looking around the four walls of the room and trying to imagine behind what one of them a secret chamber might lie. Certainly in daylight Sunnyside deserved its name. Never was a house more cheery and open, less sinister in general appearance. There was not a corner apparently that was not clear and above board, and yet I believed firmly that somewhere behind its handsomely papered walls there lay a hidden space, with all the possibilities it would involve.

I did not believe that a reputable architect would supply such a hiding spot and then keep quiet about it, in view of the enormous publicity the press had given us. And that morning I called the only contractor in Casanova. He had done no work in the house himself, he said. But something had been done a year or so before. The workmen had come by truck from the city. That was all he knew, but it was enough.

I made a mental note to have the house measured during the day to discover any discrepancy between the outer and inner walls, and I tried to recall again the exact wording of the paper Jamieson had found.

The slip had said "chimney." It was the only clue, and a house as large as Sunnyside was full of them. There was an open fireplace in my dressing room, but none in the bedroom, and as I lay there looking around I thought of something that made me sit up suddenly. The trunk room just over my head had an open fireplace and a brick chimney, and yet there was nothing of the kind in my room. I got out of bed and examined the opposite wall closely. There was apparently no flue, and I knew there was none in the hail just beneath. The house was heated by steam, as I have said before. In the living room was a huge open fireplace, but it was on the other side.

Why did the trunk room have both a radiator and an open fireplace? Architects were not usually erratic. It was not fifteen minutes before I was upstairs, armed with a tape measure in lieu of a foot rule, eager to justify Jamieson's opinion of my intelligence, and firmly resolved not to tell him of my suspicion until I had more than theory to go on. The hole in the trunk-room wall still yawned there, between the chimney and the outer wall. I examined it again, with no new result. The space between the brick wall and the plaster and lath one, however, now had a new significance. The hole showed only one side of the chimney, and I determined to investigate what lay in the space on the other side of the mantel.

I worked feverishly. Liddy had gone to the village to market, it being her firm belief that the store people sent short measure unless she watched the scales, and that since the failure of the Traders' Bank we must watch the corners, and I knew that what I wanted to do must be done before she came back. I had no tools, but after rummaging around I found a pair of garden scissors and a hatchet, and thus armed I set to work. The plaster came out easily, but the lathing was more obstinate. It gave under my blows, only to spring back into place again, and the necessity for caution made it doubly hard.

I had a blister on my palm when at last the hatchet went through and fell with what sounded like the report of a gun to my overstrained nerves. I sat on a trunk, waiting to hear Liddy fly up the stairs, with the household behind her like the tail of a comet. But nothing happened, and with a growing feeling of uneasiness I set to work enlarging the opening.

The result was absolutely nil. When I could hold a lighted candle in the opening I saw precisely what I had seen on the other side of the chimney, a space between the true wall and the false one, possibly seven feet long and about three feet wide. It was in no sense of the word a secret chamber, and it was evident it had not been disturbed since the house was built, It was a supreme disappointment.

It had been Jamieson's idea that the hidden room, if there was one, would be found somewhere near the circular staircase. In fact I knew that he had once investigated the entire length of the clothes chute, hanging to a rope, with this in view. I was reluctantly about to concede that he had been right when my eyes fell on the mantel and fireplace. The latter had evidently never been used. It was closed with a metal fire front, and only when the front refused to move, and investigation showed that it was not intended to be moved, did my spirits revive.

I hurried into the next room. Yes, sure enough there was a similar mantel and fireplace there, similarly closed. In both rooms the chimney flue extended well out from the wall. I measured with the tape line, my hands trembling so that I could scarcely hold it. They extended two feet and a half into each room, which, with the three feet of space between the two partitions, made eight feet to be accounted for. Eight feet in one direction and almost seven in the other–what a chimney it was!

But I had only located the hidden room. I was not in it, and no amount of pressing on the carving of the wooden mantels, no search of the floors for loose boards, none of the customary methods availed at all. That there was a means of entrance, and probably a simple one, I could be certain. But what? What would I find if I did get in? Was the detective right, and were the bonds and money from the Traders' Bank there? Or was our whole theory wrong? Would not Paul Armstrong have taken his booty with him when he went West? Even if he had not, if Doctor Walker was in the secret he would have known how to enter the chimney room. Then who had dug the other hole in the false partition?

I determined to keep my discovery to myself until I could make another attempt to get into the room, and was able to face Jamieson that morning with what I hope was my usual calm. He himself, however, showed a certain eagerness and suppressed excitement.

I gathered that the body had been restored to its grave and that he like myself was still playing a waiting game. Which was a mistake on my part at least.

32

Liddy discovered the fresh break in the trunk-room while we were at luncheon, and ran shrieking down the stairs. She maintained that as she entered unseen hands had been digging at the plaster, that they had stopped when she went in, and that she had felt a gust of cold damp air. In support of her story she carried in my wet and muddy shoes, which I had unluckily forgotten to hide, and held them out to the detective and myself.

"What did I tell you?" she said dramatically. "Look at 'em. They're yours, Miss Rachel, and covered with mud and soaked to the tops. I tell you, you can scoff all you like! Something's been wearing your shoes. As sure as you sit there, there's the smell of the graveyard on them. How do we know they weren't tramping through the Casanova graveyard last night, and sitting on the graves!"

Jamieson almost choked to death. "I wouldn't be at all surprised if they were doing that very thing, Liddy," he said, when he got his breath. "They certainly look like it."

I think he already had a plan on which he was working, and which was meant to be a coup. But things went so fast there was no time to carry it into effect. The first thing that occurred was a message from the Emergency Hospital that Mrs Watson was dying and had asked for me. I did not care much about going. There may be a sort of melancholy pleasure to be had out of a funeral, with its pomp and ritual, but I shrank from a deathbed. However, Liddy got out the black things I keep for such dismal occasions, and I went. I left Jamieson and another detective going over every inch of the circular staircase, pounding, probing and measuring. I was inwardly elated to think of the surprise I was going to give them that night, and as it turned out I did surprise them, almost into collapse.

I drove from the train to the Emergency Hospital, and was at once taken to a ward. There, in a gray-walled room in a high iron bed lay

Mrs Watson. She was very weak, and she only opened her eyes and looked at me when I sat down beside her. I was conscience-stricken. We had been so engrossed that I had left this poor creature to die without even a word of sympathy.

The nurse gave her a stimulant, and in a little while she was able to talk. But so broken and half coherent was her story that I shall tell it in my own way. In an hour from the time I entered the hospital I had heard a sad and pitiful narrative, and had seen a woman slip into the unconsciousness that is only a step from death.

Briefly, the housekeeper's story was this:

She was almost forty years old, and had been the sister-mother of a large family of children. One by one they had died, and been buried beside their parents in a little town in the Middle West. There was only one sister left, the baby, Lucy. On her the older girl had lavished all the love of an impulsive and emotional nature. When Anne, the elder, was thirty-two and Lucy was nineteen, a young man had come to the town. He was going east after spending the summer at a celebrated ranch in Wyoming, one of those places where wealthy men send worthless and dissipated sons for a season of temperance, fresh air and riding. The sisters of course knew nothing of this, and the young man's ardor carried them away. In a word, seven years before Lucy Haswell had married a young man whose name was given as Aubrey Wallace.

Anne Haswell had married a carpenter in her native town, and was a widow. For three months everything went fairly well. Aubrey took his bride to Chicago, where they lived at a hotel. Perhaps the very unsophistication that had charmed him in Valley Mill jarred on him in the city. He had been far from a model husband, even for the three months, and when he disappeared Anne was almost thankful. It was different with the young wife, however. She drooped and fretted, and on the birth of her baby boy she had died. Anne took the child, and named him Lucien.

Anne had had no children of her own, and on Lucien she had lavished all her aborted maternal instinct. On one thing she was determined, however. That was that Aubrey Wallace should educate his boy. It was a part of her devotion to the child that she should be ambitious for him. He must have every opportunity. And so she came east. She drifted around, doing plain sewing and keeping a home somewhere always for the boy. Finally, she realized that her only training had been domestic, and she put the boy in an Episcopalian home and secured the position of housekeeper to the Armstrongs.

There she found Lucien's father, this time under his own name. It was Arnold Armstrong.

I gathered that there was no particular enmity at that time in Anne's mind. She told him of the boy, and threatened exposure if he did not provide for him. And for a time at least he did so. Then he realized that Lucien was the ruling passion in this lonely woman's life. He found out where the child was hidden, and threatened to take him away. Anne was frantic. The positions became reversed. Where Arnold had given money for Lucien's support, as time went on he forced money from Anne Watson instead until she was always penniless. The lower Arnold sank in the scale, the heavier his demands became. With the rupture between him and his family things were worse, and Anne took the child from the home and hid him in a farmhouse near Casanova, on the Claysburg road. There she went sometimes to see the boy, and there he had taken fever. The people were Germans, and he called the farmer's wife Grossmutter. He had grown into a beautiful boy, and he was all Anne had to live for.

The Armstrongs left for California, and Arnold's persecutions began anew. He was furious over the child's disappearance and she was afraid he would do her some hurt.

She left the big house and went down to the lodge. When I had rented Sunnyside, however, she had thought the persecutions would stop. She had applied for the position of housekeeper, and secured it.

That had been on Saturday, and that night Louise arrived unexpectedly from the West. Thomas sent for Mrs Watson and then went for Arnold Armstrong at the Greenwood Club. Anne had been fond of Louise. Apparently she reminded her of Lucy. She did not know what the trouble was, but Louise had been in a state of terrible excitement. Mrs Watson tried to hide from Arnold when he appeared, but he did not stay long. He had quarreled with Louise and left the lodge in an ugly mood.

Watching from a window she saw him go up to Sunnyside and apparently be admitted there. But he stayed only a few minutes and then departed.

In the meantime she and Thomas had got Louise quiet, and a little before three she herself started up to the house. Thomas had a key to the east entry, and he gave it to her.

On the way across the lawn she was confronted by Arnold, who for some reason was determined to get into the house again. He had a golf stick in his hand, which he had picked up somewhere, and on her refusal to admit him he had struck her with it. One hand had been badly cut, and it was that, poisoning having set in, which caused her present condition. She broke away in a frenzy of rage and fear, and got into the house while Gertrude and Jack Bailey were at the front door. She went upstairs, hardly knowing what she was doing. Gertrude's door was open, and Halsey's revolver lay there on the bed. She picked it up and ran part way down the circular staircase, where she could hear Arnold fumbling at the lock outside. She slipped down quietly and opened the door, and he was inside before she had got back to the stairs. It was quite dark, but she could see his white shirt bosom. From the fourth step she fired. As he fell, she heard Gertrude in the billiard room scream, and she was fairly trapped. When the alarm

was raised she had had no time to get upstairs. She hid outside in the grounds until everyone was down on the lower
floor. Then she slipped upstairs and threw the revolver out
of an upper window, going down again in time to admit the
men from the Greenwood Club.

If Thomas had suspected her, he had never told. When
she found the hand Arnold had injured was growing worse
she gave the address of Lucien at Richfield to the old man,
and almost a hundred dollars. The money was for Lucien's
board until she recovered. Now she had sent for me to ask
me if I would try to interest the Armstrongs in the child.
When she found herself growing worse she had written to
Mrs Armstrong, telling her nothing but that Arnold's legiti-
mate child was at Richfield, and imploring her to recognize
him. She was dying, she said, the boy was an Armstrong,
and entitled to his father's share of the estate. The papers
were in her trunk at Sunnyside, with letters from the dead
man which would prove what she said. She was going. She
would not be judged by earthly laws, and somewhere else
perhaps Lucy would plead for her. It was she who had crept
down the circular staircase the night Jamieson had heard
someone there. When he followed her, she had fled madly
through the first door she came to. She had fallen down
the clothes chute, and been saved by the basket of sheets
underneath. I could have cried with relief. It had not been
Gertrude, after all!

That was the story. Sad and tragic though it was, the very
telling of it seemed to relieve the dying woman. She did
not know that Thomas was dead, and I did not tell her. I
promised to look after little Lucien, and sat with her until the intervals of consciousness grew shorter and finally
ceased altogether. She died that night.

33

As I drove rapidly back to the house from Casanova station in the taxi I saw the detective Burns loitering across the street from the Walker place. So Jamieson was already putting the screws on, lightly now but ready to give them a twist or two, I felt certain, very soon.

The house was quiet. Two steps of the circular staircase had been pried off without result, and beyond a second message from Gertrude, that Halsey insisted on coming home and they would arrive that night, there was nothing new. Jamieson, having failed to locate the secret room, had gone to the village. I learned afterward that he called at Doctor Walker's, under pretense of an attack of acute indigestion, and before he left had inquired about the evening trains to the city. He said he had wasted a lot of time on the case, and a good bit of the mystery was in my imagination! The doctor was under the impression that the house was guarded day and night. Well, give a place a reputation like that, and you don't need a guard at all–thus Jamieson. And sure enough, late in the afternoon the two detectives, accompanied by Jamieson himself, walked down the main street of Casanova and took a city-bound train.

That they got off at the next station and walked back again to Sunnyside at dusk was not known at the time. Personally I knew nothing of either move. I had other things to absorb me at that time.

Liddy brought me some tea while I rested after my trip, and on the tray was a small book from the Casanova library. It was called *The Unseen World* and had a cheerful cover on which a half dozen sheeted figures linked hands around a headstone.

At this point in my story, Halsey always says: "Trust a woman to add two and two together, and make six." To which I retort that if two and two plus x makes six, then to discover the unknown quantity is the simplest thing in the world. That a houseful of detectives missed it entirely was because they were busy trying to prove that two and two make four.

The depression due to my visit to the hospital left me at the prospect of seeing Halsey again that night. It was about five o'clock when Liddy left me for a nap before dinner, having put me into a gray-silk dressing gown and a pair of slippers. I listened to her retreating footsteps, and as soon as she was safely belowstairs I went up to the trunk room. The place had not been disturbed, and I proceeded once again to try to discover the entrance to the hidden room. The openings on either side, as I have said, showed nothing but perhaps three feet of brick wall. There was no sign of an entrance–no levers, no hinges, to give a hint. Either the mantel or the roof, I decided, and after a half hour at the mantel, productive of absolutely no result, I decided to try the roof.

I am not fond of a height. The few occasions on which I have climbed a stepladder have always left me dizzy and weak in the knees. The top of the Washington Monument is as impossible to me as the elevation of the presidential chair. And yet I climbed out onto the Sunnyside roof without a second's hesitation. Like a dog on a scent, like my bearskin progenitor with his spear and his wild boar, to me now there was the lust of the chase, the frenzy of pursuit, the dust of battle. I got quite a little of the latter on me as I climbed from the unfinished ballroom out through a window to the roof of the east wing of the building, which was only two stories in height.

Once out there, access to the top of the main building was rendered easy–at least it looked easy–by a small vertical iron ladder, fastened to the wall outside of the ballroom and perhaps twelve feet high. The twelve feet looked short from below, but they were difficult to climb. I gathered my gown around me and succeeded finally in making the top of the ladder. Once there, however, I was completely out of breath. I sat down, my feet on the top rung, and put my hairpins in more securely, while the wind belied my dressing gown out like a sail. I had torn a great strip of the silk loose, and now I ruthlessly finished the destruction of the thing by jerking the strip free and tying it around my head.

From far below the smallest sounds came up with peculiar distinctness. I could hear the paper boy whistling down the drive, and I heard something else. I heard the thud of a stone, and a spit followed by a long and startled meiou from Beulah. I forgot my fear of a height, and advanced boldly almost to the edge of the roof.

It was half past six by that time, and growing dusk.

"You boy, down there!" I called.

The paper boy turned and looked around. Then seeing nobody he raised his eyes. It was a moment before he located me. When he did he stood for one moment as if paralyzed, then he gave a horrible yell and dropping his papers bolted across the lawn to the road without stopping to look around. Once he fell, and his impetus was so great that he turned an involuntary somersault. He was up and off again without any perceptible pause, and he leaped the hedge–which I am sure under ordinary stress would have been quite a feat for any man.

With Johnny Sweeny a cloud of dust down the road and the dinner hour approaching I hurried on with my investigations. Luckily the roof was flat, and I was able to go over every inch of it. But the result was disappointing; no trap door revealed itself, no window, nothing but a couple of pipes two inches across and standing perhaps eighteen inches high and three feet apart, with a cap to prevent rain from entering and raised to permit the passage of air. I picked up a pebble from the roof and dropped it down, listening with my ear at one of the pipes. I could hear it strike on something with a sharp, metallic sound, but it was impossible for me to tell how far it had gone.

I gave up finally and went down the ladder again, getting in through the ballroom window without being observed.

I went back at once to the trunk room, and sitting down on a box I gave my mind as consistently as I could to the problem before me. If the pipes in the roof were ventilators to the secret room, and there was no trap door above, the entrance was probably in one of the two rooms between which it lay. Unless indeed the room had been built with the house, and the opening then closed with a brick and mortar wall.

The mantel fascinated me. Made of wood and carved, the more I looked the more I wondered that I had not noticed before the absurdity of such a mantel in such a place. It was covered with scrolls and panels, and finally by the merest accident I pushed one of the panels to the side. It moved easily, revealing a small brass knob.

It is not necessary to detail the fluctuations of hope and despair, and not a little fear of what lay beyond, with which I twisted and turned the knob. It moved, but nothing seemed to happen, and then I discovered the trouble. I pushed the knob vigorously to one side, and the whole mantel swung loose from the wall almost a foot, revealing .a cavernous space beyond.

I took a long breath, closed the door from the trunk room into the hall–thank Heaven, I did not lock it–and pulling the mantel door wide open I stepped into the chimney room. I had time to get a hazy view of a small portable safe, a common wooden table and a chair, then the mantel door swung to and clicked behind me. I stood quite still for a moment in the darkness, unable to comprehend what had happened. Then I turned and beat furiously at the door with my fists. It was closed and locked again, and my fingers in the darkness slid over a smooth wooden surface without a sign of a knob.

I was furiously angry, at myself, at the mantel-door, at everything. I was not afraid of suffocating. Before the thought had come to me I had already seen a gleam of light from the two small ventilating pipes in the roof. But they supplied air and nothing else. The room itself was shrouded in blackness.

I sat down in the stiff-backed chair and tried to remember how many days one could live without food and water. When that grew monotonous and rather painful I got up and, according to the time-honored rule of people shut in unknown and ink-black prisons, I felt my way around. It was small enough, goodness knows. I felt nothing but a splintery surface of wood, and in endeavoring to get back to the chair something struck me full in the face and fell with the noise of a thousand explosions to the ground. When I had gathered up my nerves again I found it had been the bulb of a swinging electric light, and that had it not been for the accident I might have starved to death in an illuminated sepulcher.

I must have dozed off. I am sure I did not faint. I was never more composed in my life. I remember planning, if I was not discovered, who would have my things. I knew Liddy would want my heliotrope foulard, and she's a fright in lavender. Once or twice I heard mice in the partitions, and so I sat on the table with my feet on the chair. I imagined I could hear the search going on through the house, and once someone came into the trunk room. I could distinctly hear footsteps.

"In the chimney! In the chimney!" I called with all my might, and was rewarded by a piercing shriek from Liddy and the slam of the trunk-room door.

I felt easier after that, although the room was oppressively hot and enervating. I had no doubt the search for me would now come in the right direction, and after a little I got down to the chair and dropped into a doze.

How long I slept I do not know. It must have been several hours, for I had been tired from a busy day, and I wakened stiff from my awkward position. I could not remember where I was for a few minutes, and my head felt heavy and congested. Gradually I roused to my surroundings, and to the fact that in spite of the ventilators the air was bad and growing worse. I was breathing long, gasping respirations, and my face was damp and clammy. I must have been there a long time, and the searchers were probably hunting outside the house, dredging the creek or beating the woodland. I knew that another hour or two would find me unconscious, and with my inability to cry out would go my only chance of rescue. It was the combination of bad air and heat probably, for some inadequate ventilation was coming through the pipes. I tried to retain my consciousness by walking the length of the room and back, over and over, but I had not the strength to keep it up, so I sat down on the chair again, my back against the wall.

The house was very still. Once my straining ears seemed to catch a footfall beneath me, possibly in my own room. I groped for the chair from the table, and pounded with it frantically on the floor. But nothing happened. I realized bitterly that if the sound was heard at all no doubt it was classed with the other rappings which had so alarmed us recently.

It was impossible to judge the flight of time. I measured five minutes by counting my pulse, allowing seventy-two beats to the minute. But it took eternities, and toward the last I found it hard to count. My head was confused.

And then I heard sounds from below me, in the house. There was a peculiar throbbing, vibrating noise which I felt rather than heard, much like the pulsing beat of fire engines in the city. For one awful moment I thought the house was on fire, and every drop of blood in my body gathered around my heart. Then I knew. It was the engine of the car, and Halsey had come back. Hope sprang up afresh. Halsey's clear head and Gertrude's intuition might do what Liddy's hysteria and three detectives had failed to discover.

After a time I thought I had been right. There was certainly something going on down below. Doors were slamming, people were hurrying through the halls, and certain high notes of excited voices penetrated to me shrilly. I hoped they were coming closer, but after a time the sounds died away below and I was left once more to the silence and heat, to the weight of the darkness, to the oppression of walls that seemed to close in on me and stifle me.

The first warning I had was a stealthy fumbling at the lock of the mantel-door. With my mouth open to scream I stopped. Perhaps the situation had rendered me acute, perhaps it was instinctive. Whatever it was I sat without moving, while someone outside in absolute stillness ran his fingers over the carving of the mantel and found the panel.

Now the sounds below redoubled. From the clatter and jarring I knew that several people were running up the stairs, and as the sounds approached I could even hear what they said.

"Watch the staircases!" Jamieson was shouting. "Damnation, there's no light here!" And then a second later: "All together now. One– two–three–"

The door into the trunk room had evidently been locked from the inside. At the second that it gave, opening against the wall with a crash and evidently tumbling somebody into the room, the stealthy fingers beyond the mantel-door gave the knob the proper impetus, and the door swung open and closed again. Only–and Liddy always screams and puts her fingers in her ears at this point–only now I was not alone in the chimney room. There was someone else in the darkness, someone who breathed hard and was so close I could have touched him with my hand.

I was in a paralysis of terror. Outside there were excited voices and incredulous oaths. The trunks were being jerked around in a frantic search, the windows were thrown open, only to show a sheer drop of forty feet. And the man in the room with me leaned against the mantel-door and listened. His pursuers were plainly baffled, and I heard him draw a long breath and turn to grope his way through the blackness. Then he touched my hand, cold, clammy, death-like.

A hand in an empty room! He drew in his breath, the sharp intaking of horror that fills lungs suddenly collapsed. Beyond jerking his hand away instantly he made no movement. I think absolute terror had him by the throat, for he stepped back without turning, retreating foot by foot from the Dread in the corner, and I do not think he breathed.

Then with the relief of space between us I screamed, ear-splittingly, madly, and they heard me outside.

"In the chimney!" I shrieked. "Behind the mantel! The mantel!"

With an oath the figure hurled itself across the room at me, and I screamed again. In his blind fury he had missed me, and I heard him strike the wall. That one time I escaped him, and now I was across the room and had got the chair. He stood for a second, listening, then he made another rush and I struck out with my weapon. I think it stunned him, for I had a second's respite when I could hear him breathing, and someone shouted outside:

"We can't get in. How does it open?"

But the man in the room had changed his tactics. I knew he was creeping on me, inch by inch, and I could not tell from where. And then he caught me. He held his hand over my mouth, and I bit him. I was helpless, strangling, and someone was trying to break in the mantel from the wall at the side. It began to yield somewhere, for a thin wedge of yellowish light was reflected on the opposite wall. When he saw that my assailant dropped me with a curse. Then the opposite wall swung open noiselessly, closed again without a sound, and I was alone. The intruder was gone.

"In the next room!" I called wildly. "The next room!" But the sound of blows on the mantel drowned my voice. By the time I had made them understand a couple of minutes had elapsed. The pursuit was taken up then by all except Alex, who was determined to liberate me. When I stepped out into the trunk room, a free woman again, I could hear the chase far below.

I must say, for all Alex's anxiety to set me free, he paid little enough attention to my plight. He jumped through the opening into the secret room, and picked up the portable safe.

"I am going to put this in Mr Halsey's room, Miss Innes," he said, "and I'll send one of the detectives to guard it."

I hardly heard him. I wanted to laugh and cry in the same breath, to crawl into bed and have a cup of tea and scold Liddy and do any of the thousand natural things that I had never expected to do again. And the air! The touch of the cool night air on my face!

As Alex and I reached the second floor Jamieson met us. He was grave and quiet, and he nodded comprehendingly when he saw the safe.

"Will you come with me for a moment, Miss Innes?" he asked soberly, and on my assenting he led the way to the east wing. There were lights moving around below, and some of the maids were standing gaping down. They screamed when they saw me, and drew back to let me pass. There was a sort of hush over the scene. Alex behind me muttered something I could not hear, and brushed past me without ceremony. Then I realized that a man was lying doubled up at the foot of the staircase, and that Alex was stooping over him.

As I came slowly down, Winters stepped back and Alex straightened himself, looking at me across the body with impenetrable eyes. In his hand he held a shaggy gray wig, and before me on the floor lay the man whose headstone stood in Casanova churchyard–Paul Armstrong.

Winters told the story in a dozen words. In his headlong flight down the circular staircase with Winters just behind, Armstrong had pitched forward violently, struck his head against the door to the east veranda, and broken his neck. He had died as Winters reached him. As the detective finished I saw Halsey, pale and shaken, in the cardroom doorway, and for the first time that night I lost my self-control. I put my arms around my boy, and for a moment he had to support me. But a second later over Halsey's shoulder I saw something that turned my emotion into other channels. For behind him in the shadowy cardroom were Gertrude and Alex, the gardener, and– there is no use mincing matters–he was kissing her!

I was unable to speak. Twice I opened my mouth, then I turned Halsey around and pointed. They were quite un-conscious of us. Her head was on his shoulder, his face against her hair. As it happened, it was Jamieson who broke up the tableau.

He stepped over to Alex and touched him on the arm.

"And now," he said quietly, "how long are you and I to play our little comedy, Mr Bailey?"

34

Of Doctor Walker's sensational escape that night to South America, of the recovery of over a million dollars in cash and securities in the safe from the chimney room, the papers have kept the public well informed. Of my share in discovering the secret chamber they have been singularly silent. The inner history has never been told. Lieutenant Jamieson got all kinds of credit, and some of it he deserved. But if Jack Bailey as Alex had not traced Halsey and insisted on the disinterring of Paul Armstrong's casket, if he had not suspected the truth from the start, where would the detective have been?

When Halsey learned the truth he insisted on going the next morning, weak as he was, to Louise; and by night she was at Sunnyside under Gertrude's particular care, while her mother had gone to Barbara Fitzhugh's.

What Halsey said to Mrs Armstrong I never knew, but that he was considerate and chivalrous I feel confident. It was Halsey's way always with women.

He and Louise had no conversation together until that night. Gertrude and Alex–I mean Jack–had gone for a walk, although it was nine o'clock and anybody but a pair of young geese would have known the night air was chilly, and that it is next to impossible to get rid of a summer cold.

At half after nine, growing weary of my own company, I went downstairs to find the young people. At the door of the living room I paused. Gertrude and Jack had returned and were there, sitting together on a divan, with only one lamp lighted. They did not see or hear me, and I beat a hasty retreat to the library. But here again I was driven back. Louise was sitting in a deep chair, looking the happiest I had ever seen her, with Halsey on the arm of the chair holding both her hands.

It was no place for an elderly spinster. I retired to my upstairs sitting room and got out Sally Klinefelter's lavender slippers. Ah, well, the foster motherhood would soon have to be put away in camphor again.

The next day, by degrees, I got the whole story.

Paul Armstrong had a besetting evil, the love of money. Common enough, but he loved money not for what it would buy but for its own sake. An examination of the books showed no irregularities in the past year since John had been cashier, but before that, in the time of Anderson, the old cashier who had died, much strange juggling had been done with the records. The railroad in New Mexico had apparently drained the banker's private fortune, and he determined to retrieve it by one stroke. This was nothing less than the looting of the bank's securities, turning them into money and making his escape.

But the law has long arms. Paul Armstrong had evidently studied the situation carefully. Just as they say that the only good Indian is a dead Indian, so the only safe defaulter is a dead defaulter. He decided to die, to all appearances, and thus when the hue and cry subsided be able to enjoy his money almost anywhere he wished.

The first necessity was an accomplice. The connivance of Doctor Walker was suggested by his love for Louise. The man was unscrupulous, and with the girl as a bait Paul Armstrong soon had him fast. The plan was apparently the acme of simplicity; a small town in the West, an attack of heart disease, a body from a medical college dissecting room shipped in a trunk to Doctor Walker by a colleague in San Francisco, and palmed off for the supposed dead banker. What was simpler?

The woman, Nina Carrington, was the cog that slipped. What she only suspected, what she really knew, we never learned. Early in life she had evidently been badly burned in a fire, and so scarred that marriage was improbable. When and how her suspicions were aroused in California we never learned, but it was obviously her hope that by blackmailing Doctor Walker she could secure funds or indefinite support. In any case she made his situation desperate. To pay the woman to keep quiet would be confession. He denied the whole thing, and she went to Halsey.

It was this that had taken Halsey to the doctor the night be disappeared. He accused the doctor of the deception and threatened him with police action at once. I believe too that he saw Louise that night and demanded to know her part in the plot. However that may be, during the interval he was in the Armstrong house either Walker or

Paul Armstrong–still lame where I had shot him–had concealed himself in the back of his car. Near the railroad track he had been struck over the head and after he had been removed the car was driven head on into the freight train.

In whatever manner it was done, for three days Halsey lay in the boxcar tied hand and foot, suffering tortures of thirst, delirious at times, and discovered by a tramp at Johnsville only in time to save his life.

As to Paul Armstrong, at the last moment his plans had been frustrated. Sunnyside, with its hoard in the chimney room, had been rented without his knowledge! Attempts to dislodge me having failed, he was driven to breaking into his own house. The ladder in the chute, the burning of the stable and the entrance through the cardroom window, all were in the course of a desperate attempt to get into the chimney room.

Louise and her mother had from the first been the great stumbling blocks. The plan had been to send Louise away until it was too late for her to interfere, but she came back to the hotel where they were living in California just at the wrong time. There was a terrible scene. The girl was told that something of the kind was necessary; that the bank was about to close and her stepfather would either avoid arrest and disgrace in this way or kill himself. Fanny Armstrong was a weakling, but Louise was more difficult to manage. She had no love for her stepfather, but her devotion to her mother was entire and self-sacrificing. Forced into acqui-escence by her mother's appeals and overwhelmed by the situation, the girl finally consented and escaped.

From somewhere in Colorado she sent an anonymous telegram to Jack Bailey at the Traders' Bank. Trapped as she was, she did not want to see an innocent man arrested. The telegram, received on Thursday, had sent the cashier to the bank that night in a frenzy.

Louise arrived at Sunnyside and found the house rented. Not knowing what to do she sent for Arnold at the Green-wood Club, and told him a little, not all. She told him that there was something wrong, that the bank was about to close, and that his father was responsible. Of the conspir-acy she said nothing. To her surprise Arnold already knew, through Bailey that night, that things were not right. More-over, he suspected what Louise did not, that the money was hidden at Sunnyside. He had a scrap of paper that indi-cated a concealed room somewhere.

His cupidity was aroused at once. Eager to get Halsey and Jack

Bailey out of the house, he went up to the east entry, and in the billiard room gave Bailey what he had refused earlier in the evening, the address of Paul Armstrong in Califor-nia and a telegram which had been forwarded to the club for Bailey from Doctor Walker. It was in response to one Bailey had sent, and it said that Paul Armstrong was very ill.

Bailey was almost desperate. He decided to go West and see Armstrong, and to force him to admit the facts. But the catastrophe at the bank occurred sooner than he had expected. On the moment of starting West, at Andrews station where Jamieson had located the car, he read that the bank had closed and going back to town surrendered himself.

Bailey had known Paul Armstrong intimately. He did not believe the money was gone. It was hardly possible in the interval since the securities had been taken. Where was it? From some chance remark let fall some months earlier by Arnold Armstrong when he had been drinking, he felt sure there was a hidden room at Sunnyside, and tried to see the architect of the building. But, like the contractor, if he knew of such a room he refused any information.

It was at that time Halsey came forward with his plan. I had seen Bailey only once and that casually. He suggested that Jack make certain alterations in his appearance, shaving off his small mustache and changing the way he wore his hair, and buying some cheap clothing. In this disguise he could probably find some work on the property, and look it over whenever he got a chance.

"I told him you were half blind," Halsey said. "Half deaf too. I'm afraid you were rather a shock to him."

"Then it was reciprocal," I retorted. "He had me scared out of my wits."

For of course it had been Jack Bailey, alias Alex, who had been our ghost. Not only had he alarmed Louise–and himself, he admitted–on the circular staircase, but he had dug the hole in the trunk-room wall, and later sent Eliza into hysterics. The note Liddy had found in Gertrude's scrapbasket was from him, and it was he who had shocked me into fainting by the clothes chute and, with Gertrude's help, had carried me to Louise's room. Gertrude, I learned, had watched all night beside me, in an extremity of anxiety.

That old Thomas had seen his master and thought he had seen his ghost, there could be no doubt. Of that story of Thomas's, about seeing Jack Bailey in the footpath between the club and Sunnyside the night Liddy and I heard the noise on the circular staircase, that too was right. On the night before Arnold Armstrong was murdered Bailey had made his first attempt to search for the secret room. He secured Arnold's keys from his room at the club and got into the house, armed with a golf stick for sounding the walls. He ran against the hamper at the head of the stairs, caught his cuff link in it and dropped the golf stick with a crash. He was glad enough to get away without an alarm being raised, and he took the late train to town.

The oddest thing to me was that Jamieson had known for some time that Alex was Jack Bailey. But the face of the pseudo gardener was very queer indeed when that night in the cardroom the detective turned to him and said:

"How long are you and I going to play our little comedy, Mr Bailey?"

Well, it is all over now. Paul Armstrong rests in Casanova churchyard, and this time there is no mistake. I went to the funeral, because I wanted to be sure he was really buried. And I looked at the step of the shaft where I had sat that night and wondered if it was all real. Sunnyside is for sale, but I shall not buy it. Little Lucien Armstrong is living with his step-grandmother, and she is recovering gradually from troubles which had extended over the entire period of her second marriage. Anne Watson lies not far from the man she killed, and who as surely caused her death. And Thomas, the fourth victim of the conspiracy, is buried on the hill. With Nina Carrington's, five lives were sacrificed in the course of this grim conspiracy.

There will be two weddings before long, and Liddy has asked for my heliotrope to wear to the church. I knew she would. She has wanted it for three years, and she was quite ugly the time I spilled coffee on it. Otherwise we are very quiet, just the two of us. Liddy still clings to her ghost theory, and points to my wet and muddy shoes in the trunk room as proof. I am grayer than I was, I admit, but I haven't felt so well in a dozen years. Sometimes when I am bored I ring for Liddy, and we talk things over. When Warner married Rosie, Liddy sniffed and said what I took for faithfulness in Rosie had been nothing but mawkishness. I have not yet outlived Liddy's contempt because I gave them silver knives and forks as a wedding gift.

So we sit and talk, and sometimes Liddy threatens to leave and often I discharge her, but we stay together somehow. I am talking of renting a house next year, and Liddy says to be sure there is no ghost. To be perfectly frank, I never really lived until that summer. Time has passed since I began this story. My neighbors are packing up for another summer. Liddy is having the awnings put up, and the window boxes filled. But Liddy or no Liddy, I shall advertise tomorrow for a house in the country, and I don't care if it has a Circular Staircase.